SARAH BENNETT has been reading for ~~~~~~~~~~ can member. Raised in a family of bookworm~~~~~~~~~e affair with books of all genres has culminated in the ultimate Happy Ever After: getting to write her own stories to share with others.

Born and raised in a military family, she is happily married to her own Officer (who is sometimes even A Gentleman). Home is wherever he lays his hat, and life has taught them both that the best family is the one you create from friends as well as relatives.

When not reading or writing, Sarah is a devotee of afternoon naps and sailing the high seas, but only on vessels large enough to accommodate a casino and a choice of restaurants.

You can connect with her via twitter @Sarahlou_writes or on Facebook www.facebook.com/SarahBennettAuthor

D0522354

Sunshine Over Bluebell Castle

SARAH BENNETT

HQ
An imprint of HarperCollins*Publishers* Ltd
1 London Bridge Street
London SE1 9GF

This edition 2019

First published in Great Britain by
HQ, an imprint of HarperCollins*Publishers* Ltd 2019

ISBN: 978-0-00-833100-9

Printed and bound in Great Britain by
CPI Group (UK) Ltd, Croydon, CR0 4YY

For Charlotte –
thank you for believing in me when I don't
always believe in myself

Chapter 1

After a fruitless afternoon fighting with the overgrown tangle of thorns all but blocking the entrance to the maze which formed the centrepiece of the long neglected formal gardens of Bluebell Castle, Igraine Ludworth – Iggy to everyone but her formidable great-aunt, Morgana – was ready for nothing more than a quiet cry in a hot shower. Like the labours of Sisyphus, trying to make sense of the mess so many years of neglect had wrought to the gardens was starting to feel like a pointless exercise. It would take months of hard work, a bucketload of money, and a team full of assistants; the first she could manage, the other two ... well a girl could dream.

Shoving at the frizzy, sweaty dark snarl of a fringe haphazardly shortened with a pair of secateurs in a foolish act of frustration the previous week, Iggy had just reached the end of the pathway leading to the enormous gravel driveway in front of the castle when she heard the sound of a vehicle crunching over the stones. Frustrations and her dire need for a shower forgotten, Iggy hurried as fast as her wellies would carry her towards the battered Land Rover pulling up on the other side of the enormous circular fountain and flower bed occupying pride of place in the centre of the drive.

'You're back, you're back! How was it?' Iggy asked her brother Arthur and his girlfriend as they clambered out of the vehicle. As the new baronet, Arthur had been invited to the local primary school to give out the prizes at their speech day, and he'd taken his girlfriend along for moral support.

Though the eldest of triplets, Igraine had been passed over in the line of succession of their family's lands and title to Arthur, the middle child, as she had the misfortune of being the wrong sex. Had it not been for the blatant sexism etched in every word of the entailment of the Ludworth Baronetcy, it might have been Iggy presenting the prizes instead of Arthur.

There weren't many times she was grateful for the words 'Firstborn, legitimate male offspring', but from the harassed look upon her brother's face, now might be one of them.

'They all wanted to take a selfie with me, like I was some kind of celebrity,' he said, shaking his head in bemusement at the idea.

'Well, you are the king of the castle, so to speak,' she teased as she followed them up the stairs. The grin he shot her told her he knew she was only joking. Arthur might hold the title, but Bluebell Castle, as the locals had so quaintly nicknamed their ancestral home, was as much hers as it was Arthur's, and their other brother Tristan's, too.

As she and Tristan had told Arthur in more than one showdown when he tried to shield them from the worst of their current financial woes – they'd succeed or fail together. Nine months in the same womb, followed by nigh on thirty years of unshakeable loyalty between them could not be swept away by something as stupid as which one of them got to stick the word Baronet in front of their name.

As part of their plans to secure the family finances, Iggy had recently taken on the mammoth challenge of putting their overgrown grounds to rights so they could open up the estate to the public.

Reminded once more of how she'd spent her day, Iggy eased

herself from the group hug. 'I need a shower, I've been battling with the brambles all day.'

'Well, I didn't like to say anything ...' Arthur wrinkled his nose, eyes alight with mischief.

As Iggy took a playful swing towards his head, she found her arm captured by Lucie. 'Goodness, look at the state of you, you're scratched to bits! I'll go and find Mrs W and see if she's got some antiseptic cream.'

Mrs Walters – known affectionately by all as Mrs W – was the castle's super-efficient housekeeper who, together with Maxwell the butler and Betsy the cook, kept things running. Though staff numbers had been cut to the bone over recent years, the three of them maintained a standard Iggy found frankly breathtaking.

With a laugh, Iggy gently extracted her arm and smoothed the sleeve of her top down over the mess on her arm. 'I've got a medicine cabinet full of stuff like that. A few scratches come with the territory. Besides—' she gave the pair of them an arch look '—I'm sure you've got better things to be doing than worrying about me.'

'Indeed we do!' Arthur swept a giggling Lucie up into his arms. 'Miss Kennington here still owes me several more apologies for running out on me.' The pair's courtship had been something of a rocky road, and it was only a few weeks since they'd resolved everything between them.

'I said I was sorry, but I'm happy to do so again,' Lucie murmured, in the kind of tone reserved for whispered intimacies.

And that was definitely Iggy's cue to depart. 'I'll leave you two to it.'

After hurrying up the front steps of the castle, Iggy shoved open one half of the enormous studded wooden door, only to find herself besieged by a cacophony of licking tongues and wagging tails as the castle's pack of unruly dogs charged up to greet her. 'All right, all right, you'd think I'd been gone for a month instead of a few hours,' she said, trying to calm them with pats to their heads and affectionate ear rubs. 'God, you're soppy bunch.'

She'd just managed to toe off her filthy wellies and shoo the dogs clear of the door and halfway back towards the jumble of cushions and beds which occupied the space directly before the huge fireplace dominating the back wall of the great hall, when Nimrod, one of a pair of greyhounds let out a huge bark of welcome and swerved around her outstretched hand. Bella, the other greyhound, let out a keening yap and flew after him. The pretty brindle dog adored Lucie almost as much as Arthur did. Knowing she had no chance of holding the rest of the pack at bay now Arthur's presence had been announced, Iggy stepped out of the way to let them charge pell-mell back across the hall to greet their beloved master, and the new mistress of the castle.

Taking care not to slip on the tiled floor in her thick woollen socks, Iggy made her way to the curving staircase and began to climb, her knees aching in protest after a day spent bending and crouching in the gardens. She had no plans for the evening – like most other evenings in recent memory – so perhaps she would forgo her planned shower and indulge in a soak in the claw-foot tub which dominated her bathroom. While she was alone she could catch up on the latest gossip about her favourite celebrity, the rock star of the gardening world – Will Talbot. Though she wouldn't be caught dead admitting it, her fascination with him went beyond his amazing skills with plants and his innovative design skills. With his close-cropped hair and a wicked scar slicing across one cheek, Will was the most attractive man Iggy had ever seen.

Tristan had been reading one of the tabloids at breakfast that morning and she'd found herself staring at her secret crush as he scowled out from the front page. She'd waited until everyone had gone before filching the paper and hiding it up in her room for later study.

Yes, a hot bath and a bit of gossip was just what the doctor ordered, she decided.

Lost in thought, she didn't notice Arthur was calling for her until he all but yelled her name. Turning as she reached the wide balcony at the head of the stairs, she couldn't help but smile at the sight of her brother on his knees surrounded by a mass of wriggling dogs, Lucie was curled up beside him, Bella ensconced firmly in her lap. Leaning on the balcony railing, Iggy called down, 'What's all the yelling about?'

'I only said your name five times, cloth-ears,' Arthur replied, the good-natured grin on his face turning into a startled laugh when Nimrod took advantage of his distraction to swipe a lick under his chin. 'I wanted to have a chat with you,' he continued. 'Can you come and join me in my study before dinner? Say about half seven?'

Wondering what could be so important he would interrupt his and Lucie's first-night-home celebrations for, Iggy frowned, before nodding in agreement. 'There's nothing wrong, is there?'

'Not at all,' her brother assured her, but didn't elaborate further.

She stared down at him for a few more moments as though she might have developed a previously unknown mind-reading ability in the two weeks he'd been down in London, but he remained as opaque as ever. Knowing Arthur as she did, there was no point in pushing him to reveal something before he was ready to talk about it. Might as well bash her head against the thick stone of the castle walls. With a shrug and a wave, she continued along the maze of corridors until she reached her bedroom in the wing traditionally occupied by the family.

*

Feeling loose and relaxed after a blissful hour in the bath, Iggy tried not to wince as she applied some antiseptic cream to the wicked-looking scratch stretching across most of the underside of her left forearm. Ignoring the soreness, she pressed her finger carefully along the length of the shallow wound, double-checking there was no remnant of the thorn which had abraded her skin.

A nasty infection had put her out of action for almost a week the previous year when a thorn tip had become stuck beneath the thumbnail of her dominant right hand. Doing anything had been excruciating, and the enforced period of rest while the antibiotics the doctor had prescribed did their job had driven her to distraction. Lesson learnt, she was scrupulous about wearing thick leather gloves whilst working in the garden, and in checking and cleaning any of the myriad little injuries she incurred.

With her damp hair secured on top of her head in a scruffy knot, she dressed in a pair of slim-leg black trousers and a loose olive-green silk T-shirt her aunt Morgana had given her for her birthday, claiming the colour enhanced Iggy's hazel eyes, or some such nonsense. She'd never been a clotheshorse and couldn't understand the fascination some of her friends at college had had with dressing in the latest fashion. Then again, they'd had their mothers around to whisk them off on shopping trips. Perhaps if she'd had a similar maternal bond, things might have been different. Eyeing herself in the mirror, Iggy let out a snort of derision. If there was a maternal bone anywhere in Helena Ludworth-Mills-Wexford-Jones's body, Iggy had never found it.

Having abandoned her husband and children before the triplets' third birthday, Iggy's mother had flitted in and out of her life at irregular intervals. They'd last heard from her on New Year's Eve when Helena had called to berate Arthur for cutting off her allowance. She'd had three subsequent husbands to support her, but she somehow expected their father to continue to fund her from beyond the grave. Arthur had stuck to his guns – surprising Iggy as he'd never quite seemed to give up on their mother in the same way she and Tristan had – and told her there was no more money to be had. It was to be hoped that might be the end of it and she'd finally leave them in peace, but Iggy somehow doubted it. In twenty-six years, Helena had never done anything of benefit for her children, so why would she start now?

Iggy reached for the handle on the closed door of Arthur's study, then paused. She'd almost caught him and Lucie *in flagrante* when they'd been trying to keep their relationship a secret. Given the soppy way they'd been looking at each other earlier, it might be best to approach with some caution. Raising her hand, she rapped her knuckles on the aged oak, entering only once Arthur bade her to do so.

As she approached the empty chair on this side of her brother's desk, it occurred to Iggy that Arthur had finally shed the discomfort he'd had over assuming their father's mantle. At first, he'd seemed at pains to keep the room exactly as it had been, but though the changes made had been subtle, the study *felt* like it belonged to him now. The heavy marble bust of their grandfather had been moved from the corner of the desk to a less prominent position on one of the bookshelves. In its place sat a docking station for Arthur's phone with a set of speakers attached. Raucous laughter emanated from them, no doubt from one of the many sporting podcasts her brothers were great fans of.

A large, rumpled blanket softened the classical lines of a wingback chair by the window, a stack of the red ledgers the estate's record keepers had used for generations piled haphazardly on the floor beside it. Iggy knew they'd been sitting there since before Lucie had fled the estate and wondered what on earth her brother had said to Maxwell to prevent the butler from tidying them up. Their poor butler, a stickler for neatness, had been as devastated as any of them when they'd thought she'd left them forever, so perhaps it'd been him leaving the spot untouched like a little shrine.

'I had several meetings with the bank whilst I was in town.' Arthur said, drawing her attention away from the empty chair.

'About the painting?'

He nodded. 'Amongst other things. Although there's still a lot of work to do, with Lucie's assistance I was able to get an interim valuation assessment from Witherby's for it. Needless to say, our account manager was a lot more accommodating than when I was sorting out all the probate stuff.'

'I can imagine.' Iggy didn't try to keep the bitterness out of her voice. Where had the account manager been when their father had been investing in the dubious investment scheme which had brought them to the edge of ruin? Now they had a masterpiece from one of the most famous Pre-Raphaelite painters the country had ever produced, the staff at the bank must be salivating over the value of it.

'Quite.' Arthur lounged back in his chair, fingers steepled beneath his chin. 'Lucie's opened talks with a number of galleries about putting on a pre-auction exhibition here at the castle. A number of them are amenable to loaning out their Viggliorentos in return for a chance to study our painting before it hits the auction block. The bank like the idea as there's never been a definitive exhibition of his works before, and as well as being something to draw people through the gates, it'll help to cement the profile of the painting – and its price tag.'

'You're definitely going to sell it then?' It made sense, but she couldn't help but feel a pang of regret – though she quickly shook it off. Good fortune didn't smile often on the Ludworths, and it wasn't as though any of them had known the painting even existed until Lucie had followed the trail of breadcrumbs hidden in old Thomas's long-forgotten journals.

'I have to.' The guilt in Arthur's voice twisted her insides. The money from selling one item would help keep them afloat and allow them breathing space to put their longer-term plans for the castle into place.

Leaning forward, Iggy stretched her hand across the desk towards him. 'It's the right thing to do. Tristan will tell you the exact same thing.'

Arthur sighed. 'I know, but it's going to break Lucie's heart.' He closed his eyes for one long moment before sitting up straight and taking her hand. 'It can't be helped, and she'd leave me for good, I reckon, if I tried to hang onto the damn thing for her sake.'

Iggy gave his fingers a sympathetic squeeze before sitting back. 'So, is that what you wanted to tell me? That the pressure is off with the bank?'

'It's more than off, they're very much on board with our plans to secure the future of the castle and have extended me a decent line of credit.' Folding his arms, Arthur rested them against the desk, hazel eyes a match for hers twinkling. 'Tell me what you need.'

Taken aback by the question, Iggy frowned. 'In terms of what?'

'In terms of getting the gardens into shape. You're the one with the vision, so tell me what you need to bring it to life.'

Vision? Ha! At the moment it felt like there were so many ideas competing in her head, she was stumbling around in circles and getting precisely nowhere. Lucie had uncovered some of the original plans from when the gardens had been laid out in the eighteenth century. Rather than adding the clarity Iggy had hoped they would, they'd only added to her confusion as it had become clear to her that subsequent generations had altered many of the original set pieces. Trying to recreate the original plans on a shoestring would be next to impossible so she'd been straggling from one part of the garden to the next, tidying some bits but ignoring the later alterations because she might decide to dig them up later. She wasn't a designer, or a visionary – Tristan had got all the creative genes. 'I don't know where to start,' she confessed. It was a horribly deflating admission, but one she'd been hiding from for too long.

Surprise widened Arthur's hazel gaze. 'I thought you had it all in hand, you always act as though you've got everything under control.'

She screwed up her nose. 'When it comes to the land management stuff, I can do that standing on my head. I assumed sorting

9

out the gardens would be easy, but it's such a bloody mess and I'm terrified I'll change the wrong thing and ruin it. There's so much riding on it ...'

'Why the hell didn't you say something? You're not alone in this, Iggy, we succeed or fail together.' Arthur's admonishment stung all the more because it was the very same words she'd said to him not six months ago flying back in the other direction.

'God, you enjoyed that, didn't you?' She was laughing as she said it, rubbing her chest to acknowledge the accuracy of his verbal strike.

His grin was unrepentant. 'I did, rather.' He grew serious. 'Look, if you're worried about the money, don't be. When I felt overwhelmed with everything after Dad died, I found the only way to get through it was to finish a single task on the to-do list. Forget the big picture. Stop panicking about what you might or might not get wrong and tell me one thing right now that will make a real difference.'

He was probably expecting her to request a fancy piece of equipment, but there was really only one answer. Iggy might not have the vision to turn the gardens at Bluebell Castle from their current disaster zone to a visitor's paradise, but someone did. 'I need Will Talbot.'

Chapter 2

'You're on the wrong side again,' Melody Atkins hissed at Will Talbot as he reached down to help her out of the back of the white stretch limousine their talent agency had sent to collect them for yet another interminable evening out. Film premiere, nightclub opening, reality TV show party, after a while they all blurred into the same old bollocks. A scrum in front of the banks of paparazzi, warm alcohol and half-hearted attempts at conversation shouted over too-loud music. This was their third outing in four nights, and he'd lost track of what this evening's event was supposed to be celebrating. He'd been told to wear a tuxedo tonight, so probably a film premiere. Once the lights went down, he might even manage to fall asleep during the movie and catch up on some rest.

'Sorry.' Trying to rein his temper, Will stepped to the other side of the door and offered Melody his left arm. Melody hated the scar on the right side of his face, and had visibly shuddered in the past when she'd felt the puckered skin brush against her own. It was why she always insisted she stand on his left, why she'd made him practise the correct angle to pose at when they faced the banks of cameras outside these events.

At the first click of a camera shutter, her scowl of impatience shifted to a beaming smile that displayed her laser-whitened teeth. The brace she'd worn to straighten some non-existent imperfection had been removed a few days ago, leaving her free to dazzle the press pack with her brand new smile. Knowing the effort it'd taken her to get into the limo in the skintight gold sheath dress, Will braced his feet and gave her a good pull so she could propel herself upright without bending her legs too much.

'Hold on a minute.' Melody turned into him, lifting a hand brushing away a non-existent speck of dust from the satin lapel of his black dinner jacket. A solicitous gesture, the kind any girlfriend might make. Taking his cue, Will bent to kiss her cheek, making sure his left cheek touched hers. A barrage of camera flashes exploded, and he held himself in position a few extra moments as he waited for the shadows across his eyes from exposure to the harsh white light to fade.

Melody beamed up at him as though he held all the answers to her prayers. She might have started out on a reality show, but there was no sign these days of the sweet, pretty girl who'd won the nation's admiration and first prize in last season's series of *Bootcamp Babes*. Her naturally wavy blonde hair had been dyed a dazzling platinum almost as white as her shiny new smile and there was not so much as a hint of curl in the sleek curtain it had been ironed flat into. 'Ready?' he whispered, and when she nodded, he hooked his hand around her waist and steered her towards the waiting cameras.

When she'd signed with the same talent agency as him six months ago, Will had been happy to accept his manager's suggestion that he escort Melody to a couple of events until she found her feet. Having her on his arm had proved a welcome buffer against the scores of girls who tried to pick him up – not that Will was averse to the attentions of a pretty girl – especially after a couple had sold lurid stories to the papers about him.

Once they'd got chatting, Will had discovered for himself that the smart, funny person who'd been such a hit with the public was very much the real Melody. The outside might have changed, but that was all, and in a world where appearance was everything he couldn't blame her for submitting to the stylists' pressures to change up her look for something sexier.

In an effort to gain control of the narrative, they'd hatched a plan one night and decided to pose as a couple. Will could keep the trophy-hunters at bay, and at the same time offer some protection to Melody from the more persistent types who wanted a favour in return for promising to assist her career. They'd let their manager in on the secret, and he'd been over the moon with the plan. They got on well enough together – he just wished she didn't make such a big deal about the scar on his cheek.

The camera flashes were starting to give him a headache. In a practised gesture, Will turned his face as though pressing a kiss to Melody's temple. 'Enough, yeah?' he murmured, low enough for her ears only.

Leaning back a little more into him, Melody spoke through her unshifting grin with a skill that any ventriloquist would be proud of, 'A few moments more.'

Will flexed his fingers on her hip but didn't protest as he straightened up and resumed his supporting man pose. Melody had mentioned on the way there that she had a couple of auditions lined up, so he stood his ground and gave the cameras a moody glare. It was the kind of stuff they lapped up. According to the press, Melody was the girl next door who'd tamed Will's wild lad-about-town ways.

It was true, to some extent, but not in the way the press imagined. When he'd first got a taste of fame it had gone to Will's head somewhat, and the gossip columns had been full of pictures of him stumbling out of nightclubs. There was even one notorious shot of him snarling at a photographer who'd shoved a camera in his face and nearly blinded him. With his scar twisting his angry expression into something fierce and ugly, he'd looked like the archetypal thug they liked to infer he was. He'd been moaning about the press hassling him that night when he and Melody had hatched their plan.

'Stop giving them what they want, then,' she'd said, rolling her eyes at him as though it was the most obvious thing in the world.

'What *I* want is for them to leave me the hell alone,' he'd muttered into his vodka and coke.

'You're in the limelight now, so that's not going to happen. Not unless you become a hermit and stay home every night, and you can't afford that when you're building your brand.'

'You make it sound like I'm selling myself, but I'm just out to have a good time.'

The pitying look she'd given him had fairly withered him on the spot. It shouldn't be possible for a woman who barely reached his shoulder to look down on him, but she'd done a bloody good impression of it. 'You're an idiot, then.' With a quick move she'd switched their glasses around. 'Take a sip.'

When he did, he'd realised she was drinking straight coke. 'But you always act like the life and soul of the party.'

'Exactly,' she'd retorted. 'It's all an act. Nobody here cares about the real me. They want a certain image and so that's what I give them – but I do it on my terms, enough to catch their interest, but nothing scandalous.'

She was right. He was an idiot. 'And it's as easy as that, is it?'

'You know it's not. I can't do anything about it if some ex of mine decides to make a few quid by selling some holiday snaps, but I can manage my response to it.' Reaching for the glass she'd swapped, she took a big gulp of his vodka and coke. 'I won't say it doesn't hurt getting betrayed like that, but now I know not to trust anyone.'

'You're trusting me, though.'

She laughed. 'The way I see it, this is about mutual risk. What do either of us gain out of betraying the other over this arrangement? However we spin it, people will be mad because we're basically setting out to manipulate them.'

She had a point. 'So, how do we play this?'

They'd laid down a set of basic ground rules, and so far it'd worked to their mutual benefit. The press loved the idea of them together, and Will had got his act together regarding drinking in public. His reputation had improved, and people had started to pay more attention to his work and less to his personal escapades. The relentless merry-go-round was growing tiresome now, and Will had started to wonder about whether it was time for him to get off the publicity ride completely. He had a good stable of clients, and several of his projects had been featured in the weekend supplements. Their order book was full for the next twelve months, with enquiries coming in daily. The balance of those enquiries had also shifted from people attracted to his celebrity, to word-of-mouth recommendations from previous clients.

Melody placed her hand over his where it rested on her hip – their agreed signal to move on – and he turned her away from the bank of cameras to the small flight of steps leading into the Leicester Square cinema. Releasing her hip, he climbed the first couple before turning back to offer his hand. Cameras flashed once more, and he urged her up the stairs, keen to be out of the glare of the spotlight for a bit.

Once inside, he left Melody chatting to a television producer she'd worked with on *Bootcamp Babes* and edged his way through the packed crowd towards the bar. There were servers circulating with tray of drinks, but he preferred to know exactly what went into his glass these days. Having secured two sparkling mineral waters, he wove back to where he'd left Melody in time to hear her saying. 'Yes, Chris has mentioned the project to us, and it sounds like a lot of fun.'

The word 'us' had Will on immediate alert. If Melody was talking about what he thought she was, he'd wring her bloody neck. Handing her one of the glasses, he flashed her a look of warning behind the producer's back, adding a brief shake of his head for emphasis. Blithely ignoring him, Melody took a sip of her water before continuing. 'I think *Digging Deep* could be the perfect daytime show, a combination of *This Morning* and those garden makeover shows.'

Will downed half his drink as he counted silently to ten in an effort to hang onto his temper. Their manager had come up with a ridiculous idea for a combination gardening and chat show which Will and Melody would co-host. Whilst he showed some random celebrity or another how to make the most of their gardens, Melody would chat to them about their life and career. Although he could see the appeal of the show, Will had zero interest in expanding his current celebrity status any further. He already spent far less time than he wanted to with his hands in the dirt, it was just another distraction he didn't need right now.

The producer nodded along with every word. 'Right, right, that's exactly the positioning crying out for something new.' She glanced between the two of them. 'And you're such an attractive couple. The public can't seem to get enough of real-life partnerships on screen together.'

Curling his arm around Melody's waist, Will stared down into her eyes simultaneously hating and admiring the seeming love in her returning gaze. 'It's a shame I'm far too busy with my existing workload to consider taking on anything new right now, because I know Melody is just the kind of person to put others at their ease.' Turning away from the tightness in her expression, he cast a deprecating smile at the producer. 'Besides, I haven't exactly got the right kind of face for television.' He tilted his head, making sure the light would catch the thick scar across his cheek.

The producer's smile wavered for a second. 'I was under the impression you were fully on board with the project.'

Will shrugged. 'Like I said, it sounds like a lot of fun. Maybe we can revisit it further down the road, but I'm still establishing my business and that's my absolute priority for now.'

'Yes, of course. Well, it was lovely to catch up, Melody. Speak soon!' With a flurry of air kisses, the woman melted into the crowd.

Melody rounded on him the moment they were alone. 'What the hell was that?'

Leaning close, he brushed the side of his face she hated against her cheek. 'That was me refusing to be railroaded, darling. If you're going to break the rules of our deal, I'll push back.'

He felt her twitch against him before tilting her head back to meet his eyes. Through another brilliant smile she hissed. 'Fine. But remember that goes both ways.'

*

Those warning words were still ringing in his ears the next morning as Will scrambled around his flat, trying to field a phone call from his assistant, Anna, while he got himself ready for the day.

'But I thought they'd signed off the design a week ago?' His left hand clenched around his phone. This was not what he needed to hear when he was running on empty. The film premiere they'd attended had been for the latest instalment of a high-octane blockbuster crash and smash franchise, so his chances of catching a nap during the show had been nil. Melody had insisted on them going to the after-party, a punishment for him shutting down her conversation with the producer, he was sure. Not wanting to risk a public row with her, he'd gritted his teeth and gone along, but things were going to have to change. He was not a lapdog, and he would not be treated as one, especially when all these late nights left him feeling bad-tempered in the morning.

Trying to rub his forehead to ward off the headache he could already feel threatening to build, he almost whacked himself in the eye with the training shoe clutched in his right hand. 'Bollocks, hold on a minute,' he said into the phone.

Sinking down on the bottom step of the floating staircase that dominated the sleek, minimalist open plan-lower floor of his two-storey apartment, he flicked on the loud speaker on the phone before placing it beside him. He was already running late and as if falling into bed after 1 a.m. wasn't bad enough, he'd woken up on the hour, every hour, only to finally tumble into a deep sleep about forty minutes before his alarm went off.

To add insult to injury, one of the pods for his supposedly top-of-the-range coffee machine had burst, leaving him with a mug full of undrinkable brown sludge. And it had been the last pod in the box, of course. Exhausted and un-caffeinated was a dangerous combination first thing in the morning. He would have to make an emergency stop at a coffee shop on his way to his first appointment. 'Sorry, you were saying ...' He aimed the comment towards his phone, bending over to put on his trainers at the same time.

'They did. I had written confirmation from their PA that both Tony and Phillipa were thrilled with the design.' Anna, his genius assistant and all-round saver of his sanity, sighed, the sound the perfect counterpoint to the frustration bubbling inside him. 'Unfortunately, Phillipa showed the plans to her spiritual advisor who is concerned the positioning of the meditation area will generate negative energy.'

'Oh, for fu—'

'You already owe twenty quid to the swear jar,' Anna cut in. He could picture the neat rows of tally bars marching across the top of her jotter pad. Will had always had a foul mouth. Growing up on an inner-city council estate it'd been a part of the daily lexicon for the residents. His manager, Chris, claimed it was part of his edgy charm, and always seemed delighted when one of the tabloids featured a bleep clip on their website of Will telling one of their cameramen where to stick their equipment. When a meme of Will's swearing highlights had gone viral on social media, it had almost been enough for Will to vow he'd stop swearing on the spot. *Almost.*

He swallowed a sigh. Getting involved with Chris Maddison was just one of the many missteps Will had made in the whirlwind of the past couple of years since he'd gone from struggling landscaper to darling of the rich and famous thanks to an unexpected Best Show Garden award from the RHS at the Chelsea Flower Show.

Thankfully, he'd made one or two smart moves which went some way to negating the mistakes, most notably hiring Anna. He hadn't been on the lookout for an assistant, fearing bringing yet another person into his professional life would cede even more of the control that had been steadily slipping through his fingers like water. When she'd marched into the tiny, scruffy office in an unfashionable part of town (he'd refused to give it up even with his star firmly on the rise), C.V. in hand, it had been on the tip of his tongue to turn her away. Behind the mask of carefully applied make-up and the cheap high-street skirt suit she'd tried to dress up with a designer scarf, he'd caught a glimpse of desperation – a hint of the wild-eyed despair that said she knew she was wasting her time traipsing from business to business, but it was that or sit at home and cry.

It was a feeling he knew all too well after being turned away from every horticultural job he'd applied for after finishing college. Too inexperienced, too late the vacancy was already filled, too rough with his closely-shaven hair and the scar on his right cheek from an altercation with a bottle which had nearly cost him his eye and his liberty – though no one had ever come right out and said the last. They hadn't needed to; it had been written large in every disapproving glance.

Ready to give up on his dream, a despondent Will had trudged home to bemoan his fate to Mrs Tyler, his next-door neighbour and the reason why Will had become interested in gardening in the first place. She'd fed him a slab of homemade cake, listened to him whine for half an hour and then given him an envelope full of information about courses run by the Royal Horticultural Society – complete with details of their bursary scheme. Mrs Tyler had believed in him and given him the means to take charge of his own destiny, and Will had seized it with both hands.

Insanely busy and behind on several urgent commissions, Will had nevertheless found himself asking Anna to take a seat that day. Over a couple of mugs of black coffee – the milk in his fridge being several days past rancid – they'd chatted for an hour about anything and everything. Impressed by the force of her personality, Will had decided it was his turn to be someone else's Mrs Tyler. Anna had the brains and the drive to succeed, she just needed one person to give her a chance. His instincts had proven sound and Will had never once regretted offering her a job.

At the end of the first week, she'd plonked a large glass jar on his desk together with a sliding scale of fines depending on the severity of the swear word he used. Some employers might have been affronted at her brazenness, but she could just as easily have sued him for creating an unhealthy working environment. Besides, Anna had made such fantastic inroads into the chaos of his desk and diary he was happy to modify his language – or at least pay the price whenever he failed to do so.

'I know you've got your eye on that spa weekend,' Will said, his stress factor easing, which had no doubt been his assistant's intention when she'd interrupted him. Anna was free to spend the contents of the swear jar on whatever took her fancy, Will's only stipulation was that it should be on something frivolous rather than practical. Embracing the idea, Anna had so far enjoyed a hot air balloon experience, dinner at one of London's top Michelin-starred restaurants and a helicopter flight over the city. 'I'm just contributing to the cause.'

'And all donations are gratefully received. Now about the Cornwalls' roof terrace …'

Picking up his phone, Will headed towards the front door, pausing only to shoulder into the battered leather jacket he'd tossed over the back of the futon he hated with a passion. It had come with the rest of the furnishings as part of a package when he'd signed the lease for the apartment in one of the swanky new developments shooting up all over Battersea. Thankfully, the bed on the mezzanine upper floor was akin to sleeping on a cloud, and it wasn't like he ever had any guests staying who would need to sleep on the futon-cum-torture-device, so it could remain as an expensive coat rack until he got around to replacing it.

'Can't Nick sort it?' Even as he was saying the words, he knew it wasn't happening. Nick, an experienced landscaper almost twenty years Will's senior, was another one of his few good choices. Together with a small core team, Nick turned Will's designs into beautiful, living reality. *Lucky bastard.* Will was so busy building the brand and schmoozing the big clients, he couldn't remember the last time he'd had his hands in the soil.

It was churlish of him to be jealous of Nick, knowing how many people would bite their arm off for a chance to achieve Will's level of success, but on days like today he couldn't help but long for a simpler time when his days were spent digging and planting. But his skills with a spade weren't what the big clients were paying for. They wanted his name, his reputation, his presence. 'Forget I even said that. Can you contact Mrs—' he glanced at the diary on his phone '—Butler and postpone?'

'Already done.'

Will grinned as he patted his jacket pocket checking for his keys. Of course she'd already done it. 'You're a bloody superstar.'

'I know, and that's another 50p you owe me.'

'Shame on me.' Laughing, Will collected the rucksack he used to carry his work paraphernalia around, tugged his door closed behind him and pressed the call button for the lift. 'I'll call you back once I've finished at the Cornwalls'. Is it both of them?'

'Just Phillipa, I think. Tony had to go away for a new project, didn't he? I'm sure that's what all the rush was about in the first place.' Anna sighed, dreamily. 'Listen to me talking about Tony Cornwall like we're best mates or something.' Tony Cornwall was *the* darling of British theatre. Though he'd made successful forays into the world of film, drawing huge box office numbers for anything with his name attached to it, the stage was his first love. He'd helped make going to the theatre cool again.

'Yeah, you and Tony are like that.' Will crossed his fingers and held them up before realising the gesture was wasted as she couldn't see what he was doing.

Anna got the point, though, from the way she started laughing. 'Best mates, that's me and Tone. Talk to you in a bit.' She was still giggling as she rang off.

*

As he rode down from the twentieth floor, Will contemplated what he might say to alleviate his new clients. Young and old alike adored Tony, and from what Will could tell he seemed like a genuinely decent bloke. According to the numerous features written about him over the years, Tony and Phillipa had met and fallen in love whilst rehearsing for a Royal Shakespeare Company production of *Romeo and Juliet* in the mid-Eighties when they'd both been 21. Unlike those ill-fated young lovers, their story had a happy ending, as Tony was often quoted as saying.

Phillipa's star had also been on the rise until they'd decided to have a family and she'd stepped somewhat out of the limelight, choosing to stay at home from where she ran a hugely popular website dispensing advice and no-nonsense guidance on everything from child-rearing to fashion and healthy-eating. Her *Life is for Living* brand had branched out into a series of successful best-selling books and was always featuring in Top Ten lists in the media.

If he hadn't already been aware of the honour the golden couple were bestowing upon him when they'd selected Will to design a luxury outdoor space on the roof of their Hampstead home, his manager had driven the point home. *Sledgehammered* the point home. The moment he'd caught wind of their interest, Chris had insisted Will drop everything. He'd arranged an expensive meal out, pouring praise and champagne in equal measures until Will had been all but squirming with embarrassment over the fawning display. Tony, seeming to take it all in his stride, had cut through the nonsense and answered Will's questions with the easy charm that had made so much of the British public take him into their hearts.

A home consultation had followed – without Chris, much to Will's relief – and he'd thrown himself into designing a garden that would work for the multiple purposes the Cornwalls needed it to. With a combination of carefully positioned planters and eye-catching set pieces like an infinity-edged water feature, Will had divided the large area into a mixture of entertainment, family and contemplation spaces.

He'd been really pleased with it, could already picture in his mind's eye the family sitting around the rustic wooden table he'd selected for the dining area beneath a simple grid pagoda draped in fragrant strands of climbing honeysuckle, or Phillipa doing some morning yoga as the sun reflected off the still water of the infinity pool and the white rocks laid in spirals and swirls to create a zen space. *And negative energy, apparently.* With a snort of disgust and the hope he could keep from laughing, or losing his temper, Will exited into the underground garage and jogged towards his hybrid flatbed truck.

Chris had been appalled at his choice, telling Will he needed something sexy and sporty in line with the bad boy image his manager had cultivated for him in the press. But sexy and sporty was crap when it came to storage and Will had stuck to his guns. Wincing as he reversed out of his space, barely missing one of the many concrete pillars in the underground structure, Will considered the only thing one of the stupid sports cars Chris had pushed him towards might have had going for it was the ease of parking it.

He was just waiting for a gap in the traffic when his phone started ringing. Flicking the screen without taking his eyes off the queue of cars, he instantly regretted it when his manager's familiar voice boomed over the car speakers. 'Will, mate! How's it hanging this fine morning?'

Will cringed. Was there anything worse than a fifty-something bloke trying to be 'down wiv da kids' as Chris liked to put it. Double cringe. Spotting half a gap in front of a shiny, silver Mercedes, Will nudged his big truck into the traffic stream, reasoning that the owner of the Merc cared more about his lovely shiny bumpers than Will did. 'Morning, Chris. I'm a bit busy, actually, can I call you later?'

'Sure, sure! I get it, mate, no hassles from my end,' Chris started laughing as though he'd said something hilarious. 'But seriously, I've scored you a primo invite for this evening. You and Melody are attending the album launch for Clay Givens. He's making some noises about wanting her to appear in one of his videos.'

Unable to believe what he was hearing, Will lost concentration for a moment. The rear-end of a red hatchback loomed before him and he slammed on his brakes just in time. 'Christ!'

Clearly mistaking Will's exclamation of dismay for delight, Chris burbled on. 'I know, it's epic, right? Her profile is off the charts right now, "BB" is getting some fantastic repeat ratings now it's available on streaming services. Maybe we can get Clay to a guest on *Digging Deep*! What a coup that would be.'

'I've already told you I'm not doing that stupid bloody show!' Will yelled, but he was shouting at himself as Chris had already hung up. 'Shit!' he banged his hands in frustration on the steering wheel, startling himself when the horn blared loudly. The driver of the hatchback in front flicked him a rude hand gesture, assuming Will was honking at him. *Bloody hell*. Raising his hand in apology, Will was grateful when the sat nav directed him to turn off at the next junction. This day couldn't possibly get any worse …

Chapter 3

Phillipa Cornwall hadn't seemed that bothered about the plans for the roof terrace. They'd barely spent five minutes discussing her concerns with the design before she'd left him alone up there to fetch them both a drink. She'd returned with a pot of very strong Turkish coffee and two tiny cups, only to disappear shortly afterwards with a promise she'd be back. He was starting to feel like she was jerking his chain, that this whole thing was some kind of power play. When you were as famous as she was, perhaps it became second nature to assume everyone was at your beck and call. Whatever the reason, he was starting to resent her for wasting his time about something that could've been addressed via a couple of swapped emails.

He was about ready to gather his things and make his excuses when her familiar, breathy voice came from behind him. 'If you're finished with those designs, there's something else I'd like your assistance with.'

Jaw dropping was something he'd previously assumed was an acting exaggeration, and not something real people did until the moment he turned in his seat and saw her. Closing his eyes at the same time as he shut his gaping mouth, Will hoped perhaps he was hallucinating after the second very strong coffee he'd recently finished on a still empty stomach. He cracked open a lid and was once more greeted with the sight of his client posing against the doorway leading from the roof terrace back into the house. He might have been able to dismiss the flirty pose she'd adopted – hands clasping the frame behind her, back arched, one knee softly bent – if it wasn't for the fact the stylish navy dress she'd been wearing when she'd greeted him at the door not half an hour previously was now pooled at her feet, leaving her clad in nothing more than a tiny, sheer black nightgown thing. *Nope, not the coffee.*

Clamping his mouth tight against a litany of swear words that would earn Anna a full body massage at her dream spa weekend, Will urged his addled brain to think. When he was finally sure he could speak without cursing, he opened his lips. The sound he made was somewhere between a grunt and a sigh, the kind of noise he'd only ever heard a cartoon character make and he quickly shut his mouth again.

'I didn't think you'd be shy, *William,*' Phillipa stretched his name into a purr, which he supposed she thought was sexy, but only made him want to take a flying leap over the low parapet running around the edge of the roof terrace.

Not knowing what else to do, Will decided his only cause of action was to ignore it and try and stick to business. He bent to retrieve the sketchpad which had slipped from his fingers the moment she'd reappeared. 'I … I think I might have found a solution to the issue for the zen space. We can turn the angle of the pool by forty-five degrees, so the water runs from east to west. You'll be able to align your exercise mat in the same direction then, which I think was one of the main problems?' He offered her the sketchpad, making sure to keep his eyes fixed above her chin.

With a quirk of her lips, Phillipa took the pad from him and turned into the house. He almost sighed with relief, thinking he'd found a way to navigate free of the nightmare, until she paused to cast a knowing look over one shoulder. 'It's too bright outside to see this properly, come in and show me what you want to do.'

There was no mistaking the message behind those words, and as Will watched her slink inside with an exaggerated sway of her hips, he wondered how the hell he was going to extricate himself from this mess. It wasn't the first time a client had made a pass at him, though he had to hand Phillipa the prize for the most blatant seduction attempt to date.

Will blamed it on the ridiculous 'bad boy of gardening' image Chris had created for him. Eager, naïve, and somewhat blinded by his first taste of the spotlight, Will had allowed himself to be persuaded to play the part. It worked for chefs, after all, his manager had argued, so why not for a gardener? Embarrassing crap like this was the downside he hadn't banked upon when agreeing to it. Taking a deep breath, he followed in Phillipa's wake. If she persisted, he'd have to put her straight.

Somehow.

The contrast between the bright sunshine outside and the much darker interior left him disorientated for a moment. Pausing to let his eyes adjust, Will felt his heart sink as he saw the double doors leading to the master bedroom had been flung wide. Tony Cornwall had pointed it out on Will's previous visit, saying how as soon as he'd seen the fabulous views he'd refitted what had originally been staff quarters into a luxury suite. The door had remained closed so Will hadn't seen inside.

Right now, he wished he still hadn't. Perching on the edge of an enormous bed, Phillipa tossed his sketchpad down and patted a spot on the quilt next to her. Will didn't know what the term was for something larger than a super king, but this vast expanse of crisp white bedding could probably accommodate half a dozen people with room to spare. Even if she was sitting at the far edge of the bed, it will still be too close for comfort. The hounds of hell couldn't drag him over the threshold. 'Mrs Cornwall …'

'Call me Pippa. All my *very* good friends call me Pippa.' She patted the bed once more.

Keeping his feet firmly in place, Will crossed his arms over his chest. 'Mrs Cornwall.' He didn't like the way her confident smile wavered into an expression of confusion when he stressed her formal title once more, but it couldn't be helped. 'The sketches are pretty self-explanatory. Why don't you talk them over with your husband?' *Subtle, Will.* 'You can let my assistant know in due course.'

She seemed to crumple in upon herself, as though each word was sucking the confidence and vivacity out of her. How come doing the right and honourable thing could make him feel so awful? He checked his watch – not that he cared what the time was, he just needed an excuse to look away. 'I really should be going ...'

'Are you sure you can't stay?' She sounded less seductive and more desperate now, and although he felt sorry for her, he couldn't help a tinge of anger that she'd been the cause of her own embarrassment.

Fumbling for what else to say, he was saved by the bell – literally – when his phone starting ringing. He snatched it from his pocket, barely giving the unknown number a glance before he answered it. Even a marketing call would be a welcome reprieve. 'Will Talbot.'

'Mr Talbot? Iggy Ludworth, here. I'd like to discuss a job with you, if you're not busy.'

He didn't recognise the rather odd name, nor the forthright tones of the woman. His diary was blocked solid for the foreseeable future, and one half of Britain's golden couple was currently attempting to seduce him so no, he wasn't busy at all. Turning away from the scene before him, he lowered his voice in the hope Phillipa Cornwall wouldn't overhear him. 'It's not a great time, if I'm honest. Why don't you call my office and we can set up an appointment?'

'I've already spoken to your assistant; she was the one who gave me your number. Told me to give you a call straightaway, but perhaps I misunderstood her. I've sent through a few sample photographs as she suggested, but I'm under a bit of a time crunch so if you're too busy I'd rather you came out and said it straight.'

She had the clipped accents of a member of the upper class, and her forthright manner made him feel a bit like a stroppy teenager being scolded by a teacher. Patience already on a knife's edge, he was on the verge of telling her what she could do with her time crunch when a thought occurred to him. Why had Anna passed his private number on instead of dealing with it the way she did all the other enquiries that came into the business? Intrigued, he swallowed his snap of temper and asked, 'What's the job?'

A soft exhalation filled his ear. A sigh of ... relief? Perhaps Ms Iggy Ludworth wasn't quite as sure of herself as she sounded. And what the hell kind of name was Iggy, anyway? 'My brother owns an estate in Derbyshire and we're planning to open up to the public. I need your assistance to restore the formal gardens here at Ludworth Castle in time for the August bank holiday.'

Castle? Will gave a mental whistle. Upper class, indeed, he thought, picturing towering battlements looming over rolling acres of green. It'd be a hell of a challenge, too, something on a scale he'd never tackled before. Trying to contain the little buzz of excitement, he made a mental count of the months in his head. It was already the beginning of May ... He'd have to shuffle a few projects around, leave Nick and Anna to run things here and source a local work crew of his own. 'Sixteen months sounds doable, what's the budget?'

A throaty laugh echoed over the phone, so at odds with her frosty speaking voice. Deep, rich and wildly filthy, it shot straight to his groin. 'You've misunderstood me, Mr Talbot, I was referring to *this* bank holiday, not next year.'

The jolt of insta-lust withered in astonishment, and Will couldn't help his own shout of laughter. 'Is this a wind-up? You're taking the piss if you think I can pull something like that off in four months. I'm good, Ms Ludworth, but I'm not that bloody good. What you're suggesting isn't just ridiculous, it's fucking impossible! The planning alone would take more time than you have left.'

There was no humour in her next words. 'Oh, it can be done, Mr Talbot, and it will be done. I thought you might be up to the challenge, but apparently not. I thought you were more than your sordid reputation, but clearly I was wrong if you think it appropriate to swear at a potential client. I'm sorry I've wasted my time believing otherwise.'

The phone went dead, leaving Will gawping. *Wasted her time?* 'Has the whole world gone bloody crazy?' he muttered to himself.

A soft sniffle came from behind him. Forgetting snooty Ms Ludworth and her ludicrous expectations, Will spun on his heel. To his horror, tears were pouring down Phillipa's face, streaking her make-up and turning her already sheer nightdress even more see-through. Spotting a box of tissues on a dressing table across the room, he broke his cardinal rule of remaining on his side of the threshold to grab them. Not wanting to get too close to her, he proffered the box awkwardly from arm's length, taking a precautionary step backwards as soon as she took it.

'I'm sorry, I'm so sorry, God, you must think me such a stupid fool.' Phillipa began to sob in earnest, like her heart was breaking into pieces.

Embarrassment and guilt made him squirm. Instinct made him want to comfort her, but how could he when she was dressed like that? Wishing like hell he'd made a run for it when he'd the chance, he glanced towards the exit. His eyes alighted on a scrap of material poking around from behind the door. Reaching out he snagged the white towelling dressing gown with one hand. It was shorter than he would've preferred it to be, but at least it would cover everything that needed to be covered.

Moving gingerly towards the bed, he draped the robe around her shoulders and did his best to pull it around her without touching anything his hands had no business being anywhere near. Snatching at the material, Phillipa gripped it closed beneath her throat. The look she gave him, so full of shame and misery cut him off at the knees and he found himself sinking down beside her. 'It's all right. Please don't cry.' He patted her shoulder.

Before he could withdraw his hand, she turned and buried her face in his chest, leaving him no choice but to give her an awkward one-armed hug. 'You're a very attractive woman, Mrs Cornwall. It's just … you're married … and what with Tony being such a decent guy and everything, it just isn't right, you know?'

A bitter laugh broke through her tears. 'Oh, yes, Tony's *such* a decent guy. Isn't it marvellous the way he takes beautiful young actresses under his wing and offers them the benefit of his experience?'

Shocked to the core by what she was suggesting, Will pulled back to stare down at her. 'He's cheated on you?'

Shuddering, Phillipa swallowed back more tears and straightened up. 'Cheat*ing*,' she corrected. 'Present tense. He left yesterday with his latest paramour. Rehearsing for their new film, apparently.' She didn't need to make the gesture for him to hear the quotation marks around the word 'rehearsing'.

'I'm sorry, I thought you guys were rock solid.' Everything he'd ever seen or read about them implied a strong and happy relationship. Then again, everything she'd probably read about Will had made Phillipa think he'd be up for it. If the stuff in the papers about him was a combination of managed spin and made-up rubbish, wouldn't it be even more so for a couple infinitely more famous? 'So, this—' he gestured between the two of them '—was supposed to be a way to get your own back at him?'

She shrugged. 'What's good for the gander is good for the goose, and all that.' Using the crumpled tissue in her hand, she wiped at the streaks of mascara on her cheeks. 'I'm sorry, Will, you must think I'm ridiculous.'

'No!' Whatever anger he'd felt towards her for putting him in such a compromising position was redirected towards her cheating rat of a husband. Not all marriages were good, Christ knew his own parent's relationship had been a disaster, but at least they'd had the sense to call it a day. Taking her hand, he pressed a quick kiss to the back of it. 'I'm really sorry that you're hurting, Phillipa, but sleeping with me isn't the answer to your problems – ask any of my ex-girlfriends.'

She managed a watery chuckle, and Will felt his panic subside at last. Reaching out he brushed free a tendril of hair that had stuck to her cheek. Beneath the streaked make-up and the fine lines age had settled into her skin were hints of the beautiful woman she'd been in her heyday. Tony Cornwall was either mad, stupid or both. 'Shall we both take a deep breath and pretend the past half an hour never happened?'

Drawing her bottom lip between her teeth, she nodded. 'Thank you.'

And because he was British, there was only one thing left to say. 'Shall I make us a cup of tea?'

Half an hour later, looking much better after the tea, a sheepish-looking Phillipa escorted him to the front door. She'd washed her face and tied the dressing gown tight around her middle leaving her looking much smaller and more fragile than the woman who'd greeted him earlier. Pausing in the open doorway, Will tucked his hands in the front pockets of his jeans and gave her a smile. 'If you still want us to go ahead with the terrace, give Anna a call once you've decided on the alterations I've suggested. She'll make arrangements with you for when the installation team can start.'

'Thank you.' She hesitated for a moment then stretched up on tiptoe to pop a quick kiss on his cheek. 'You're a very good man, Will Talbot.'

He winked. 'That's our secret. Take care of yourself, Phillipa.'

*

As he made his way back towards his car parked several streets away thanks to some very stringent local parking restrictions,

32

Will couldn't help but feel thoroughly depressed. The Cornwalls had been married for longer than he'd been alive. Had they been unhappy with each other all that time? He shook his head at the idea of it. What a bloody waste.

Thankful to be free of such emotional entanglements, although even his pretend relationship with Melody was growing tiresome, he dug his phone out and browsed for messages. The first one was from Anna to say she'd cleared his calendar for the rest of the day in case things at the Cornwalls got complicated. He couldn't help but laugh. Complicated didn't even come close. Beneath that were a couple of sales offers from suppliers they used which he flicked without reading into a sub-folder for future reference.

The next message was from Iggy Ludworth and he was about to drop it into his trash folder when he spotted the thumbnail images attached. Curious, he clicked on the first one and stopped dead in his tracks, transfixed by the image of the top half of a statue poking out from a massive thicket of brambles. He moved onto the next photograph showing the remains of a walled garden, the red bricks of the short walls dividing the weed-strewn beds crumbling and broken. The third image was a distance shot over a collection of overgrown box hedges; the fourth a carpet of bluebells nodding beneath the boughs of an ancient oak. His heart pounded, excitement building inside him as he flicked his thumb to the next picture, then the next. The final few were too small to properly make out any detail, but they looked to be original design sketches, the paper on which they were drawn yellowed with age. As he rolled back up through the images the tips of his fingers began to itch. He could almost feel the rich, dark soil beneath them.

A belch of hot air hit him, followed by the acrid stench of diesel fumes from a delivery van stuck in the endless queue of traffic snaking along the street beside him. Wrinkling his nose, Will moved as far to the inside of the pavement as he could then continued towards his truck. When was the last time he'd breathed a lungful of air that didn't carry the taint of heavy traffic? Or looked up at a night's sky not stained orange from light pollution, for that matter?

He gave his phone one last wishful glance before unlocking his door and tossing it on the passenger seat along with his backpack. What was he doing daydreaming about fresh air and starry skies when he had a successful business right here that needed all his attention? Shaking his head, he slid into his seat. Running off to Derbyshire was a mad idea. As mad as the idea that it was possible to sort out the ruined gardens of Ludworth Castle in three short months.

And Will had sworn off doing mad things, hadn't he?

Chapter 4

Fuming after her brief, humiliating call with Will Talbot, Iggy marched from Arthur's office, determination in every stride. She would show that arrogant pig of man exactly what she was capable of. Couldn't be done? Ha! She'd bloody well show him otherwise. Her righteous march ended swiftly thanks to the sight of an unwelcome present deposited on the stone floor of the great hall by one of the dogs.

Looking from the small, brown pile in front of her to the unusually quiet array of pups and hounds sprawled before the fireplace, Iggy did her best not to laugh at the collection of innocent expressions staring back at her. 'This better be a one-off,' she admonished, as though they could understand what she was saying. 'Because I haven't got time for you lot to get sick.' The problem with having so many dogs was it was almost impossible to avoid them all getting ill if one of them caught a bug.

Keeping them under her watchful gaze in the hopes the guilty dog would give themselves away, she walked to the large wooden box next to the fireplace where they kept old newspapers and bits and pieces of dried kindling to help in lighting the fire. When she spotted the paper on the top of the pile, she couldn't help a self-satisfied grin from tweaking her mouth. It was the tabloid paper she'd dropped in there earlier – the one with Will Talbot scowling out from the front page which had put the stupid idea to call him in her head in the first place.

'Might as well be useful for something.' Snatching up the cover and the next few pages behind it, she returned to the offending spot in the middle of the hall and pressed Will's face into the still-soft poo as she scooped it up. She deposited the ball of paper in the empty bin in the small washroom near the door before washing her hands thoroughly. Collecting the bin when she'd finished, she headed back across the hall towards the servant's area to dispose of the parcel and to give Mrs W a head's up that the floor would need disinfecting.

*

Petty satisfaction proved a highly motivating tool, and Iggy pictured various soft parts of Will Talbot's anatomy as she hacked and slashed at the brambles crawling over the statue of Venus which stood in the basin of a long dead fountain opposite the entrance to the maze. By the time Tristan wandered out with a flask of tea and a couple of Betsy's homemade rock cakes tucked in his pocket, she was scratched to bits, but the worst of her anger had been exorcised and she'd uncovered most of the moss-stained marble figure.

'Blimey, you've made some progress this morning,' he observed, gaze sweeping over the piles of shorn brambles she'd raked off to one side.

'Not enough.' Pausing to shove her sweat-matted fringe back, Iggy did a couple of rotations and stretches to ease the ache in her back. Maybe Will had a point. It didn't matter how much effort she put in, there was no way things could be ready in time for the end of August. But she had to try. Blessed with what she called perseverance – and Arthur called bloody-minded pig-headedness – Iggy was never one to give up on a situation, often to her own detriment. Even when everyone else around her could read the writing on the wall, her instinct was to plough on, to stick to the plotted course and tough it out to the end.

Shaking off the wave of self-doubt, she squatted down beside her brother and accepted the plastic mug of tea he held out. The long-term future of her family was still at stake, and she was determined to do whatever she could to secure it. The estate farms were finally running well enough for her to be able to turn her attention to other projects. It had taken the best part of nine months of hard work since their father had passed on for her to convince their tenants she was up to the task of managing the estate, but she'd succeeded.

They were tough men and women – the land and necessity had bred them that way – and she didn't resent them for expecting her to prove her worth. Through the deprivations of a particularly harsh winter she'd worked side-by-side with them, rescuing stranded sheep high in the dales beyond the borders of the estate, fixing broken tractors and thawing frozen pipes.

Selling one painting, no matter how much it was worth, wasn't going to keep the castle running for the rest of her lifetime; it wasn't going to keep those farmers protected by a landlord who understood and respected their connection to the lands. Like Arthur and Tristan both, she wanted to ensure future generations didn't face the same heartache and insecurity they were currently coping with. Putting Bluebell Castle on the tourist map was an essential part of that, and they needed to open with a bang.

Tristan snagged the mug from her to wash down a mouthful of cake. 'Arthur told me about your plan to get Will Talbot involved with the garden renovations. I think it's a stroke of genius. His name's everywhere at the moment. If you could persuade him, or that gorgeous girlfriend of his to open the fete as well, it'd really draw the punters in.'

Stealing back the mug, Iggy drained the contents then held it out to him for a refill. 'It might've been a genius idea if he hadn't accused me of taking the piss.'

'Oh, Iggy, that's pants.' Tristan slung an arm around her shoulders and pulled her in for a quick hug. 'Wait? Did he actually say that?'

She nodded. 'That and a lot of other rude things. Ridiculous, effing impossible; can't be done; planning would take longer than I've got left to finish it.' She shrugged. 'There might have been more, but I hung up on him. Rude bastard.'

Her brother snorted. 'Bet he loved that.'

She brushed the crumbs from her rock cake off her jeans – a futile exercise given the dirt streaking them – and rose. 'What Will Talbot may or may not love is nothing to do with me.' When their eyes met, she read nothing but encouragement in her brother's gaze. Other people might have scolded her for being hot-headed and overreacting, but not Tris. He'd walk through fire for her, both he and Arthur would, and she'd do the same for them. 'Do you have time to look at the drawings with me this evening? I'm struggling a bit over what to do for the best.'

'Can't see the wood for the trees?'

She groaned at his terrible pun. 'Something like that.'

Having screwed the mug back onto the top of the flask, Tristan stood up beside her. ''Course I've got time. Bring them into the family room after dinner, and I'll take a look.' He tugged the end of a loose strand of hair that had escaped from her plait. 'Don't fret, Iggle-Piggle, we'll get it sorted out.'

'I hate it when you call me that,' she grumbled.

'I know, why else do you think I do it?' Flashing her an unrepentant grin, Tristan left her to it.

Iggy entered the family room with the various drawings Lucie had managed to dig up from the family archives secured in a roll under her arm. As usual, several of the dogs had commandeered the floor in front of the fireplace, even though it was too warm for the hearth to be lit. With a few gentle toe nudges, she managed to stir them, eliciting a chorus of grumbles and whines as they begrudgingly yielded the space to her.

She'd barely unrolled the first drawing before Arthur's greyhound, Nimrod, tried to walk over it. 'No!' Iggy grabbed the dog and pulled him into her lap before his claws could damage the delicate paper. With a hug to show him he wasn't in trouble, she shooed the dog away and rolled the drawing back up. 'This isn't going to work, is it?' she said to the milling dogs as she stood.

'Talking to yourself again?' It was Arthur, with Lucie on his heels.

'It's the only way I get any sense,' she retorted with a quick grin. 'I need to evict these hooligans.' She gestured towards the dogs. 'Give us hand, will you?'

Between the three of them, they managed to remove the dogs in short order. 'You'd think we were locking them out in the stables or something,' Lucie said, as she watched the dogs skulk across to the far end of the great hall where their enormous pile of cushions and blankets stretched out in front of the fireplace. Taking up most of one end of the hall, it dated back to the origins of the castle.

'They'll get over it,' Arthur said as the three of them returned to the family room. 'What are you up to?'

Resuming her spot on the floor, Iggy glanced up at him. 'Tristan is going to help me with a plan for the gardens.' She spread out a couple of the drawings then sat back on her heels.

Arthur hunkered down beside her. 'You said earlier about not knowing what to leave and what to change. Show me what you mean.'

'See, here?' She pointed at a complicated pattern of hedges and pathways. 'This was the original layout for the Lady's garden.' The most formal part of the grounds, it had once been the highlight of the gardens with its sculptured topiaries and regimented flower beds. Using her finger, she traced the central feature, a flowerbed surrounded by a ring of curlicue hedges. 'At some point this was removed and replaced with that ugly bronze fountain.'

'The one with the hideous dolphins, or whatever they're supposed to be?' Arthur laughed. 'You used to be terrified of them when we were kids.'

Iggy gave a shudder. Like something out of a nightmare, the oddly shaped creatures spewing water from grinning jaws full of razor-sharp teeth still freaked her out. Whoever had sculpted them had clearly never seen anything that actually lived in the ocean. 'I'd love to rip those horrible things out and get them melted down. I can follow this plan and reinstate that part of the garden, but it will take several years for the hedges to grow in properly, so it might end up looking a bit sparse and disappointing.'

'Can't you use mature plants?'

She shook her head. 'It'd be better in the long run to use smaller plants that can grow together and eventually merge into what looks like one seamless plant. Bigger ones won't create the same uniform effect.' She sighed. 'It would be easier to compromise by just removing the sculpture and turning the base of the fountain into a reflecting pool. I can add a few water lilies and aquatics.'

'I think you should go for recreating the original design,' Arthur said. 'No one is going to expect the gardens to be perfect, Iggy.'

'But we're asking people to spend their hard-earned money,' she argued. 'We need to put on a display for them.'

'And you will, but Rome wasn't built in a day. Don't you think people will be more interested in the story of how you've gone about the restoration? We could put up some display boards, either out in the gardens themselves, or as part of the indoor exhibitions Lucie and I are planning. Some before, during and after photos would be a great addition.'

It hadn't really occurred to her before, but it sounded promising. 'I suppose so, but I'm looking for ways to reduce the amount of work I have to do, not add to it.'

The door swung open to admit Tristan and their Uncle Lancelot. 'What's this? Have you started without me?' Tristan joined them on the carpet whilst Lancelot made his way over to the drinks' cabinet in the corner.

Arthur filled him in, finishing with, 'But as Iggy's rightly pointed out, it'll be more work not less.'

'I think it's great. Especially if we're thinking in the longer term. If we want to offer something like annual admittance passes for the grounds, for example, people will enjoy seeing how things change over the months and years.' He caught Iggy's eye 'And, it gets you off the hook trying to get everything finished in time.'

She frowned. 'What do you mean?'

'Think about it. Photos are all well and good, but if you leave some parts of the garden wild like they are now, the visual contrast will have even more impact. And don't worry about the work, I'll take on the responsibility for the displays.' Tristan turned to Lucie. 'Would you be able to give me a hand with the copy? Maybe a few nice quotes about the gardens if you've come across any in the family journals?'

Lucie beamed. 'Oh, what a good idea! I'm sure I can come up with something.'

'That's settled then.' He clapped his hands together. 'Now all we have to do is decide what you're going to put right and what can wait.'

'You make it all sound so easy; I don't know what I was getting stressed out about.' Iggy couldn't help the hint of sarcasm in her tone. An uncomfortable silence settled over the room, making her feel awful. They were all only trying to help, and she herself had approached Tristan in the first place.

'Come now, I'm sure no one is underestimating how much you've taken on with this, darling girl.' The gentle reproach from her uncle sent heat rushing to her cheeks.

'Sorry, I'm being a brat.'

'No, you're not.' Arthur reached over to pat her knee.

'Yes, you are,' Tristan insisted. 'But we love you anyway.' He settled himself more comfortably, back resting against one of the two leather Chesterfield sofas which dominated the centre of the room. 'Why don't you tell us where you've got to so far, and then we can decide on the rest.'

Lucie curled her legs beneath her on the opposite sofa. 'I've got my notebook so I'll just listen in and make some lists.'

Iggy closed her eyes for a moment and thought about where to start. 'Okay. We all agreed the walk we set out for the Easter egg hunt worked really well.'

The others nodded.

'It'll be a nice family walk whatever the season,' Lancelot said.

'Exactly. And there are a couple of points where we can spiral off from that straight-forward loop – down towards the lake, for example, and another one which we could link up to the existing path that runs along the boundary wall parallel with Tumbledown farm.' She scrabbled amongst her papers and drawings until she found the large photocopy she'd had made of one of the more recent plans which showed the castle and its surrounding lands. 'Look, I'll show you.'

She traced an approximate loop of the route through the woods that led walkers to the replica stone circle their ancestor Thomas had created in a large glade, and back towards the castle. 'That's route one.' Swapping her pen for a different colour, she drew a line leading away from the loop towards the lake and back towards a point at the edge of the Lady's garden. 'This could be the second one.' With a third pen she traced a meandering path around the formal gardens which connected to the lake walk, passed up to the castle and back down again. 'This would be an easy stroll for anyone who didn't fancy tromping through the woods, or if they want a more strenuous walk they can then pick up this one—' she tapped the end of the pen to the second route '—and head down to the lake.'

Arthur angled the paper towards him. 'I see what you're doing.

If we try and interconnect as many of them as possible, visitors can explore as much or as little of the grounds as they want to.'

A warm glow started in her belly. He really did get it. She tugged the sheet back and drew a bold line running from the far end of the formal gardens loop and out towards the dales. 'For the hikers.'

Lancelot leaned forward, elbows resting on his knees. 'If I can make a suggestion?' When she nodded, he continued. 'Rather than having them tramp all over the place, we could easily mow in a path along the edge of the gallops, encourage them to cross the park land that way.'

'That makes sense.' She amended the proposed route. 'Although we're bound to get a few people who stray.'

'Of course, but I think if you give them the option of a path to follow, most people will use it. Most British people, anyway. We love a bit of order, form a queue and all that.'

Iggy laughed. 'Good point. People don't have to stick to the routes, but if we mark them clearly, it should be quite straightforward. And perhaps we should consider whether we want to offer them maps.' She looked to Arthur for guidance.

'I'll have to cost it out, make sure it's built in when we decide on an admission fee.' He glanced up at Lucie. 'Can you highlight that as a job for me to do?'

'It's on the list, don't worry,' she assured him, tapping her pen on her notebook.

'And, again, we don't have to do all of this in one go.' Tristan pointed out. 'We can post large maps at starting points of each of the walks and come up with a less intrusive way to mark the routes along the way so we don't spoil the views.' Her brothers launched into a discussion over the pros and cons of costing in everything up front versus adding value at a later date.

After a few minutes of the two of them going back and forth Iggy held her hands up. 'These are all great ideas, and I'm feeling so much more positive than I was yesterday, but we're getting a bit bogged down in the details. The more I think about it, the more I like the idea of leaving parts of the gardens as they are. It will certainly make life easier for me.'

'It's a shame we can't get one of those garden makeover shows in to do it for us,' Lancelot chipped in.

'How strong is that whisky and soda?' Arthur cast a meaningful look at the amber contents of her uncle's glass.

Tristan laughed. 'I can't see the BBC licence fee payers giving them the thumbs up for spending their hard-earned cash on an ancestral pile like ours.'

'Well fine, not the BBC, but it'd be nice if you could find some way to get people to help you out.' Lancelot sounded disgruntled.

'It's called money.'

Iggy coughed to cover a laugh at Tristan's wry comment. 'It's a nice idea, but no one's going to turn up and do the garden for free.'

'Don't be so sure about that.' Lucie, who'd been quiet up to then, sat forward on her seat. 'My mum loves gardening. One of the worst things about moving to our flat was her losing our lovely back garden.'

Her face clouded for a moment, and Iggy's heart went out to her and poor Constance. Lucie and her mum had been left with nothing when her father had been arrested as a fraudster when Lucie was still a teenager. Constance had been to stay with them a few weeks previously, and Iggy had adored her almost on sight. Seeing her and Lucie together had been bittersweet, reminding Iggy of how much she'd missed out on thanks to the selfish actions of her own mother.

When Constance had taken an interest in the gardens, it had been a highlight of her visit for Iggy. 'Phone her and tell her to come visit us again, I'm happy to exploit her for a bit of free labour.' She was joking, of course, although Constance was welcome any time as far as Iggy was concerned.

'But she wouldn't see it as being exploited, she'd be over the moon,' Lucie said, excitedly. 'Imagine a little army of enthusiasts given the opportunity to play a part in restoring the gardens to their former glory.'

'It could work,' Tristan mused. 'They get volunteers for all sorts of things – archaeological digs, people acting as guides for the National Trust around their properties, local projects to clear rubbish from canals and waterways. We could give them a few perks. We'd feed them, of course. Perhaps throw in a nice after-noon tea and a behind the scenes tour around the castle. We could call them The Friends of Ludworth Castle, or some such thing.'

Iggy looked around at her family. This was why she needed to stop and ask for help more often. It would be the perfect reason to leave some parts of the garden untouched, and offer an incentive for people to feel invested in the future of the castle. An unexpected lump formed in the back of her throat and she had to swallow around it before she could speak. 'I love it.'

Before she could say any more, she heard a muffled thump followed by a cacophony of barking from the great hall. Arthur pushed to his feet with a groan. 'I'd better go and see what that's all about.' He checked his watch. 'It's about time for their evening walk.'

'I'll come with you.' Lucie looked to Iggy. 'Unless you still need me?'

She shook her head. 'No, you go ahead. Now we've got a way forward, I'm feeling much more positive. Tristan can help me decide which sections we can leave for later restoration projects.'

Down on hands and knees. Iggy and Tristan studied the large plan of the grounds. 'So, I definitely need to focus on the Lady's garden and reinstating the original central design.' She circled the area in green.

'What about the maze? It'll be a good distraction for kids.'

She circled that too. 'Yes. It needs reshaping and new gravel for the pathways, but is definitely doable.' She paused. 'I haven't been inside it for years so probably best to assume the benches in the centre will need replacing.'

The door behind them opened again. Glancing back over her shoulder, Iggy saw Arthur pop his head around the door. 'Umm … Iggy? You've got a visitor.'

Before she could scramble up, her brother pushed the door wide to reveal the tall man standing next to him. The biker jacket he was wearing registered first. A distinctive, vintage piece with two grey bands around the upper arms of the sleeves had been paired with a plain grey T-shirt, jeans and trainers, though she'd seen photos of it worn over everything from outlandish board shorts to formal eveningwear complete with black tie. Her brain refused to compute the information it was receiving as she finally shifted her gaze higher, past the five o'clock shadow scattered over a firm chin, the rakish scar cutting into his right cheek she'd always found fascinating, and up to a pair of steel-grey eyes.

Handsome as he was on page and screen, Will Talbot was a stunning presence in the flesh. Heat rushed to her face, as well as a few unmentionable places. The connection between her brain and her mouth finally kicked in. 'What the hell are you doing here?'

Chapter 5

As first impressions went, the sight of Iggy Ludworth's bottom clad in skin-tight denim was right up there as far as Will was concerned. The tempting patch of pale skin above the waistband of those sinful jeans revealed where her top had ridden up made a damn fine second impression; the cascade of dark mahogany curls spilling down almost to meet it, a third. Before he'd even taken in the fine features of her heart-shaped face, he was more than half in love with her. In lust with her might be closer to the mark, he corrected, as he swung the backpack off his shoulder to hang conveniently in front of his body in what he hoped was a casual gesture. For a woman like this he might be willing to break his 'work and play don't mix' rule. More than willing from the urgent signals the rest of his body was sending to his brain – ready and able, too. And, then she snapped at him in that glorious ice-maiden voice of hers, and Will knew he was a goner.

When the furrow between her brows deepened, he realised she was expecting him to respond. Didn't the woman know what she'd done to him? 'You asked for my help.'

She sat back on her haunches, making him want to sigh with regret at the loss of his view of her deliciously plump backside. 'And if I recall our conversation from this morning, you told me in rather graphic terms that you weren't available.' It was wrong just how much that frosty disdain turned him on.

'I shuffled a few things around,' he said, shrugging like it was no big deal. He knew he was stoking her anger, but he couldn't help it. There was something about that frozen façade of hers that made him want to smash through it and find the real woman he could sense behind the icy mask.

His team back in the office might have something to say about his dismissive attitude, too. Having raced back from the Cornwalls with his head full of those haunting images Iggy had emailed to him, they'd spent a gruelling two hours holding an emergency meeting to run through all their scheduled jobs for the summer.

Thankfully, they'd not only seen but understood his passion to abandon the roof terraces and back gardens of London for the chance to tackle something on the epic scale of Bluebell Castle. Even so, he'd needed to be convinced they had everything in hand before Will gave himself permission to follow the craving need the photos of the castle gardens had set itching beneath his skin.

A quick dash from his office to his flat to throw some essentials into a bag, and he'd been on the road. His traffic app had told him he could make it in four hours, but an accident at the Dartford crossing and some hellish roadworks on the A1 had stretched it to six. Plenty of time to debate with himself over the rashness of his actions, and more than once he'd been tempted to veer off onto a passing slip road and turn around.

As he took in the looks he was receiving – from Iggy's barely contained fury to the amused grin from an older man sitting on one of a pair of enormous leather sofas – Will questioned once more the wisdom of acting on impulse. Showing up at this time of the evening was inexcusable, but it couldn't be helped. He'd considered finding himself a hotel or B&B for the night and postponing his arrival until morning, but with every mile he'd drawn closer to the castle the doubts had compounded until he'd known in his gut that if he waited, he'd change his mind. The imposing stone wall guarding the castle had almost been the final straw, but then he'd found the entrance gate standing open as though in invitation and, well, here he was.

Iggy folded her arms across her chest, highlighting to him that she was as pleasing from the front as she was from the back. 'You shouldn't have bothered. We've managed to sort things out without your *esteemed* talents.' She flicked a handful of that glorious hair over her shoulder, an act of dismissal if ever he'd seen one. 'If only you'd called first, it would've saved you a wasted journey.' So much ice, so much disdain in those words that another man might have withered before them.

Not Will, though.

He'd not forgotten that little exhalation she'd made over the phone, that combination of relief and self-doubt when she'd still had hope she might be able to hire him for her project. Tiny as it had been, it had been a chink in her armour none the less. Remembering it made him want to prod and push and dig until he won another glimpse of it. 'Well, I'm here now, so it won't do any harm to take a look, will it?' He gestured towards the stack of plans behind her.

Shifting her weight, she moved as though to block his view of them. 'Like I said, everything's sorted now, thank you.' He'd never heard anyone who could make thank you sound so much like eff you. God, she was marvellous.

Side-eyeing Iggy, the man sitting next to her butted in. 'Bit of an exaggeration there, sis.' Unfolding himself, he rose and offered his hand. 'You must be Will. I'm Tristan Ludworth, it's a pleasure to meet you.'

His informal, friendly manner told Will he had a least one ally present. Time to up the charm offensive and see if he could get the rest of them on side. 'Cheers,' he said as they shook hands. 'You've got a hell of a place here.'

'Not my place, as such.' He turned to include the man who'd

greeted Will in the enormous entrance hall. 'Everything you see belongs to Arthur, here.'

'Oh, yes, of course. Hi there, Arthur, sorry to burst in on you like this.' As they shook hands, Will's mind raced as he worked out the relationships between everyone. Tristan and Arthur were alike enough it was obvious they were brothers, and even if Tristan hadn't referred to her as 'sis', Iggy had the same colouring and striking features.

The man on the sofa was an older version of the brothers – their father, perhaps, although if the castle belonged to Arthur, more likely an uncle. Tucking his free hand in his pocket, Will apologised once more. 'I'm sorry to just rock up like this, but I was blown away by the photos of the gardens your sister sent, and I knew I had to see for myself.'

'We're getting used to unexpected visitors around here.' Arthur curled his arm around the shoulders of the pretty redhead beside him, smiling down at her as though sharing a private joke.

'At least I told you I was coming,' she protested with a laugh. 'It wasn't my fault your internet was broken.' Having accepted a quick kiss from Arthur, she turned to Will, eyes still sparkling in amusement. 'I'm Lucie, by the way.'

With a flush of embarrassment, Will yanked his hand from his pocket and quickly shook hers. 'Hi, I'm Will.'

Lucie bit her lip, casting a sly glance towards Iggy. 'Yes, yes you are.'

'Well, we were just going to take the dogs out, so I'll track down Mrs W, our housekeeper, and get a room sorted out for you. You're probably tired after your drive up so perhaps we can sit down after breakfast and talk things over?' Arthur glanced towards his sister. 'How does that sound?'

The look on her face was decidedly frosty. 'Fine.'

Arthur raised a brow at his sister before turning back to Will with a smile. 'I can see about some supper for you, as well, if you're hungry?'

He shook his head, conscious once more of just how disruptive his arrival was to these people. 'I'm fine, honestly, although if you could point me in the direction of the kettle, I wouldn't mind a cup of coffee.' As soon as he said it, he wondered if people like this even knew where the kettle was. Arthur had already mentioned a housekeeper, and a place the size of this probably had an army of staff to fetch and carry. An image of Downton Abbeyesque servants scuttling about in neat black and white uniforms sprung to mind.

'I'll sort you a coffee,' Tristan offered. 'If you give me the keys to your car, I'll get your bags taken up to your room as well.'

Perhaps he was too quick to judge. He hated people making assumptions about him, had been on the wrong end of enough stereotyping that he should try and avoid doing it himself. Apart from Iggy, they'd all been incredibly polite and charming so far. Retrieving them from his pocket, Will dropped his keys onto Tristan's outstretched palm. 'Thank you.'

'And I'll come out with you, Arthur. One of the mares took a knock to her leg earlier, I'd like to give it a final check before I turn in for the day.' The older man placed an empty tumbler on a side table, then stood and approached Will. 'I think we got lost in the introductions. I'm Lancelot. You're that gardening chap Iggy was talking about at dinner, I gather?'

'Lancelot?' Will couldn't help repeating as they shook hands. His eyes strayed to the other two men in the room. 'Arthur ... Tristan ...?'

'Yes, it's exactly what you're thinking,' Lancelot said with an amiable grin. 'Old Thomas, the ninth baronet, has a lot to answer for.' His smile widened as he turned his attention to Lucie. 'Although he brought you into our lives, my dear, so perhaps the silly names are worth it.'

Baronet? Wow, he really was hobbing with the nobs.

Lucie blushed, the glow of colour bringing a warmth to her pale, almost porcelain, skin. 'Charmer.'

Clearly delighted, Lancelot bussed her cheek with an affectionate kiss.

'You can cut that out.' Arthur said, muscling his way between the two of them though it was clear from his tone that he was joking. All smiles, they moved towards the door.

Lucie paused on the threshold to look back at Will. 'Welcome to Bluebell Castle, Mr Talbot. I'm so glad you changed your mind.'

Will felt his mouth twitch as the slightly odd group left the room. Lucie seemed amused at his arrival. If he could get her onside she might help him work out the lie of the land with the rest of the family.

Filing the knowledge away for later, he focused on the main sticking point in front of him. He moved to occupy the space Tristan had left, dropping to his knees beside Iggy. A blown-up photocopied map lay on top of the pile of documents. Not bothering to ask permission, he pulled it a few inches closer to study it. Looking past the various lines and coloured circles drawn on it, he tried to identify locations for the images she'd sent him.

'Do you mind? Iggy made to move the drawing away from him, but he shifted one knee to trap a corner of the paper.

Will captured her gaze. As he'd suspected, there was a hint of uncertainty buried deep within their hazel depths. 'Please, just let me have a look.'

Disarmed by his plea, she stared uncertainly for a moment before drawing her dark brows down into a frown. 'What's the point? You've already made it clear you think I'm trying to achieve the impossible.' She let go of her end of the drawing, though. Was the ice melting just a fraction?

'You caught me off guard this morning, so I might have overreacted a little bit.' She might have overreacted a bit, too, hanging up on him the way she did, but he left that unspoken in the air between them. 'Were the photos you sent recent? They really blew me away.'

Her scowl softened a little. 'I took them a couple of days ago.'

'So the bluebells are still out? I'd love to see them.'

She nodded. 'The woods are at their peak right now. You can have a look around tomorrow morning, if you want.' The concession, offered with a grudging lift of her shoulder, felt like a major victory. He was still a long way from persuading Iggy to let him stick around, but at least she wasn't trying to kick him straight back out the door … for now.

Deciding not to push his luck too far, he cast around for something else to talk about, the gardens likely to be a flashpoint for her temper. 'Lancelot mentioned someone called Thomas? Is he the reason everyone in your family's got unusual names?'

'What?' The change of topic seemed to catch her off guard. 'Oh, yes. He's my several-times great-grandfather. He became obsessed with the idea that Camland stands on the original site of Camelot.'

Will frowned. 'I thought it was supposed to be somewhere in the west country?'

Shifting from her knees, Iggy sat cross-legged, her body angled more towards him. 'The most popular theories are linked to Tintagel in Cornwall and Glastonbury in Somerset,' she agreed. 'But there's also one suggesting Arthur was a warlord from the north. Thomas seized on the idea, even went as far as naming his children after characters from the legends. Lucky for us, it's a tradition that's continued through the following generations.' Her eye roll told him exactly how lucky she thought it was.

She was definitely loosening up now he'd steered them away from the delicate topic of the gardens, and he couldn't resist teasing her. 'I don't recall Sir Iggy having a seat at the round table.'

She wrinkled her nose. 'It's short for Igraine.'

Her name was beautiful … unique. Much like his first impressions of her. Why she'd choose to shorten it was beyond him, though at least he wasn't stupid enough to say that to her face. 'I like it.'

'Try being stuck with it for a few weeks and then see how much you like it. Half the time people don't pronounce it properly, and nobody can spell it.'

'Not ideal, then.'

'Not really. And not something you'd have any experience of, with a sensible name like Will.'

He shrugged. 'I've been called plenty of choice things in my time, but you're right, none of it had anything to do with my name.' Just his behaviour. After his folks had split up, Will had gone off the rails a bit. He'd stayed with his dad, his mum's new boyfriend not being keen on having a sullen 14-year-old around to cramp his style.

They'd done all right together at first, but the recession had hit the construction sector hard, leaving his dad short of work. To try and make up the shortfall, he'd resorted to picking up evening shifts as a taxi driver, leaving Will alone for much of the time. Never very academically inclined, Will fell into a spiral of missed homework, detentions, letters home he intercepted and threw away. Eventually he'd been skipping school on a regular basis. Hanging around the estate, he'd fallen in with a rough crowd and started drinking and fighting. Following the nasty encounter with a broken bottle, Will had ended up with a face full of stitches, a police caution and a referral to social services.

The injury had shocked some sense into Will, and he'd returned to school, only to find himself even more out of his depth. He might have drifted back into trouble had one of their neighbours not had a nasty fall. Coming home from school one day, Will had spotted Mrs Tyler sprawled on the path of her spotless little front garden. A smashed up hanging basket next to a stepladder lying on its side told him plainly enough what had happened when he rushed to her aid. Not wanting to move her, Will had called for an ambulance before retrieving a blanket and a pillow he'd found on the bed in a downstairs room – he and his dad used their equivalent one as a dining room. As he wasn't a relative, they hadn't let Will go with Mrs Tyler to the hospital. To this day he could still remember how small and frail she'd looked wrapped in a red blanket as they loaded the stretcher onto the back of the ambulance.

Not wanting her to come home to a mess, he'd dug around in their junk-filled garden shed for a broom and swept the soil and broken plants off the path. With his dad's help, he'd made a trip to the local DIY-cum-garden centre next to their local superstore and he'd done his best to replace the damaged contents of the hanging basket. Returning a few days later with her wrist in plaster and a spectacular rainbow bruise on one cheek, Mrs Tyler had been delighted with his efforts and the wonky basket complete with clashing blooms of red, purple and orange had hung from the wall the entire summer.

It'd started off with a trip to the shops to pick up a few bits for her, then progressed to helping her keep her beloved front and back garden tidy while her wrist was healing. Before he knew it, Will was calling in every afternoon after school because the sweet-natured widow had this or that chore that needed doing. Will soon caught on that she was inventing little jobs for him to do, and though he wasn't sure if it was for her own benefit or his, they'd struck up an unlikely friendship born of their mutual loneliness. When he'd confessed to her one afternoon about how hard a time he was having at school, she'd persuaded him to get his books out and helped him with his homework. Over endless cups of tea and slices of homemade cake, Mrs Tyler had slowly imbued her love of gardening in Will. In the weeks and months that followed, Will had grew up a lot. He'd apologised to his dad, and knowing Will had someone to keep an eye out for him had given his dad the freedom to look further afield for better-paying work.

The spring after they'd first met, Will decided it was time to tackle the straggly weeds and bits of rubbish littering their own front garden, and with Mrs Tyler's help he'd transformed the space over the course of the school Easter holidays. Looking back now, two patches of brownish grass and a few pots stuffed with petunias and fuchsias was a modest start for a future Chelsea medal winner, but the sense of pride he'd experienced when his dad had come home from a few days working away to see what he'd done had yet to be equalled. They might not be a family in the conventional sense like the Ludworths, but between the three of them they'd muddled along together very nicely.

The door thumped open just then to reveal Tristan staggering in under the weight of an overladen tea tray. Forgetting his little trip down memory lane, Will jumped up to give him a hand and together they placed it down on a nearby coffee table. 'I thought you might be peckish,' Tristan said with a shrug as Will eyed the piles of sandwiches and cakes.

'There's enough here to feed an army.'

'I'd better help you out then.' Tristan bit into an enormous wedge of Victoria sponge.

It had been a long time since the sausage roll Will had picked up during a five-minute refuelling stop on the journey up. Lifting a sandwich from the plate, he raised it in acknowledgement towards Tristan before taking a bite. 'Thank you.'

They munched in silence for a few minutes, Will content to watch Igraine as she gathered the drawings scattering the floor. Now she'd told him her full name, he couldn't seem to think of her as anything else. With a supple grace which spoke of the strength gained from hours working out of doors rather than slogging away on a treadmill, she flowed from sitting to standing with the drawings bundled under one arm.

Abandoning his half-eaten sandwich, Will moved to intercept her when his phone started to ring stopping him in his tracks. Seeing Chris's name on the screen, he excused himself and hurried into the echoing chamber of the great hall before he answered it. 'Hello?' Silence greeted him. He stared at the 'Call ended' message on the screen then noticed it said No Service in the top right.

He took a couple of steps towards the front door and the phone started ringing again. 'Hello?'

'Whe … uck … are you?' Even with his voice cutting in and out, it was clear Chris was very unhappy.

'I'm in Derbyshire, looking at a new job.'

'… byshire? You've stood up … elody bloody Atkins!'

Shit. In his rush to get everything sorted at work and then the journey up here, he'd completely forgotten about the last-minute invitation to Clay Given's party. 'I told you I wasn't going,' he yelled, but the phone had gone dead again.

Will was still stalking around the enormous room trying in vain to pick up a signal when the front door opened heralding the return of Arthur, Lucie and their motley assortment of dogs. A greyhound bounded over to nudge at Will's hand, while a Jack Russell yipped and scrabbled at his calf. With the difference in their heights, it was impossible to pet both dogs at once, so Will crouched down to fuss over them both until Arthur shooed them gently away.

'Sorry, they're a bunch of unruly beasts.'

Having always wanted but never had a pet of his own growing up, Will was quite happy to lavish them with attention. 'I'm not bothered, really.' He straightened up and waved his phone at Arthur. 'I can't seem to get a signal.'

Arthur pulled a face. 'It's a nightmare around here. I'm going to sort out a signal booster before we open to the public, but it's one of about a million things on the to-do list. You're welcome to use the landline, and I'll give you the Wi-Fi password so you can access your emails, hang on a minute.' He returned a few moments later with the code scribbled on a scrap of paper. 'The phone's in my study …'

The adrenaline which had buoyed Will on his drive up vanished in a sudden rush, leaving him drained. The last thing he wanted was to get into a shouting match with Chris, especially in front of anyone else. He'd already caused enough disruption by showing up unannounced. 'This'll be great,' he said, holding up the paper. 'I can sort everything out with an email.'

'Well, if you're sure?' Arthur didn't sound too convinced but let the point drop. 'Did they get your room sorted out?'

'I haven't had a chance to find out. Your brother very kindly fetched me a coffee and something to eat, and then my phone rang.'

'Let's see, shall we?'

Will allowed Arthur to escort him back into whatever the posh person's equivalent of a front room was. To his surprise and disappointment, Igraine had made herself scarce, taking all the drawings with her in the process. Only Tristan remained, lounging back in the corner of one of the sofas, coffee cup in hand. Will sank down beside him and reclaimed his own cup and the remains of his sandwich.

'Did Mrs W sort out a room for our guest?' Arthur asked his brother.

Tristan nodded. 'We've put him in the green room.' He aimed a quick grin at Will. 'Thought it'd be appropriate.'

'Anything with a mattress suits me, honestly, I'm sorry to put you to any trouble.'

'No trouble at all, we're delighted to have you here.' Tristan slid his empty cup onto the tray. 'If you've had enough to eat, I can show you up?'

*

They said good night to Arthur and Lucie at the bottom of the sweeping staircase in the great hall. 'The baronet's rooms are in the opposite wing,' Tristan told him as they briefly watched the couple stroll off hand in hand. 'The rest of the family rooms are along there.' He indicated a corridor leading off from the top of the stairs. 'And your room is down here in the guest quarters.'

'I might need a map to find my way back,' Will joked as they followed several twists and turns. There was so much to look at, it was hard to keep track of the directions. Paintings hung in almost every space between the doors which he assumed led to other bedrooms. From the size of the gaps between each door, he got the impression each room must be enormous.

'Don't worry, I'll come and give you a knock in the morning and take you down to breakfast. It's a bit of a maze at first, but you'll soon find your way around.' Tristan came to halt before a dark wood door, indistinguishable from all the rest.

'That's assuming I stay.' Will adjusted the backpack on his shoulder, conscious once more of the less than warm greeting Igraine had given him. From the way the brothers deferred to her, it was clear the gardens were her baby. If she didn't want him here, he had little doubt he'd soon find himself out on his ear. *She called you for a reason.* 'Your sister's apparently changed her mind about wanting to employ me.'

Tristan laughed. 'Don't worry about, Iggy. Her bark is worse than her bite.' With one hand on the doorknob, Tristan met his gaze, his expression turning grave. 'It takes a lot for her to let her guard down and ask for help. Unless you're a hundred per cent serious about seeing this through to the end, maybe it'd be better if you did go home tomorrow.'

Will opened his mouth to argue, then closed it again. He'd rushed up here on little more than a whim, after all. Although Anna and Nick had assured him they could keep things running smoothly, had he actually given them much choice? 'I'll sleep on it.'

'I think that'd be a good idea.' Tristan brightened, giving Will the impression that nothing kept him down for very long. 'Well, this is you.' He pushed open the door and stepped back.

'Wow.' There was literally nothing else that Will could think of to say as he drank in the opulent décor of his room. The floor was covered in a carpet so thick his foot sank into the pile. A shade of midnight green, it matched the colour of the ivy climbing over the creamy wallpaper lining the walls. In amongst the pattern of twining vines perched images of exotic birds of paradise, their sweeping jewel-toned tails and bright button eyes so vivid he wondered for a moment if he was looking at a painting. A huge bed frame dominated the centre of the room, swagged with thick velvet curtains a few shades lighter than the carpet. Two large wardrobes bookended the bed; a dressing table and matching chest of drawers in the same burnished wood sat to the right of the room, and a pair of bottle-green leather armchairs faced each other beneath a set of leaded-glass windows.

'Not bad, eh?' Tristan crossed the room and opened a concealed door. 'There's an adjoining room here which you can use as an office.' Leaving the door ajar he gestured beyond the left-hand wardrobe. 'And there's a private bathroom through there.' He turned in a quick circle as though giving everything the once over. 'Right, I'll leave you to it. Shall we say eight-thirty for breakfast?' Still a little dumbstruck, Will couldn't do much more than nod.

As the door closed behind him, Will sank down into one of the armchairs. The crisscross pattern in the leather beneath him spoke of its age, and like everything else around him, he supposed it to be an antique. So different from the sleek, cold lines of his modernist apartment. He let his eyes drift over to the large window beside him, the dark glass reflecting his own image back to him. 'One of these things is not like the others,' he murmured to himself, recalling an old song he'd heard on a kid's programme. If he was going to stay, he had a choice to make – trying to blend in had never really worked for him, but was he brave enough to try and leave his mark on somewhere that breathed history from every stick and stone?

Chapter 6

Pride could be a terrible thing, Iggy mused to herself as she stared at her gritty-eyed reflection in the bathroom mirror. A fitful night spent conjuring a hundred different ways she could've responded to Will's surprise arrival, interspersed with the most embarrassing dreams she'd ever experienced, was making it difficult for her to muster even a pinch of enthusiasm for the day to come.

There was no way around it, she was going to have to find a way to apologise to him for her reaction the previous evening. Or, she could admit to herself her in the privacy of her room, for her *overreaction*. She could blame it on lots of things, but mostly it had been her bruised pride speaking.

She'd long been an admirer of Will's work, and to have him laugh and then dismiss her had struck the sorest of sore spots. The rational part of her said it was foolish to hold a grudge over a response she'd likely have received from almost any other expert in his position. But the tiny part of her which had been formed and honed before Iggy even understood such a thing as rationality existed had taken the inadvertent hurt straight to heart.

Telling herself to embrace her inner Elsa and just 'Let It Go', Iggy dragged the silver-handled hairbrush through her thick curls. Part of a set gifted to her by her great-aunt, Morgana, the

61

brush was akin to a medieval torture device. It tamed the natural wildness of her hair better than the dozens of bottles and tubs of littering the back of the cupboard beneath her sink, so she always returned to it.

The bristles caught on a stubborn tangle, making her wince at the sharp shock of pain in her scalp. She needed to stop mooning over what had and hadn't happened last night and focus on the here and now. Time to swallow down that stupid pride and accept Will's change of mind for the gift it was. He was clearly excited about the project – why else would he have jumped in the car and driven over a hundred and fifty miles only hours after seeing those few photos she'd sent him?

Ten minutes later, Iggy paused outside the dining room for another quick pep talk. *Smile, say good morning, stick to polite enquiries and maybe everyone will pretend you didn't make an absolute fool of yourself.* Fixing a bright smile, she swung open the door. 'Good morn … oh,' she said to the empty room. A quick glance at her watch confirmed it was past eight-thirty and that everyone else was late rather than her being early. Feeling disgruntled that she'd built herself up for no reason, she helped herself to a cup of tea from the sideboard, poured some cereal into a bowl and settled down to wait.

She was halfway through her cornflakes when the swing door leading to the servant's area opened to reveal Maxwell, the butler. Neat as ever in his dark pinstriped trousers matched with a crisp white shirt and a black waistcoat, he carried an armful of newspapers. 'Ah, Miss Igraine, good morning to you.'

'Good morning, Maxwell. Have you seen anybody else up and about?'

Placing the papers down on the sideboard, Maxwell laid them out in a precise pattern, Arthur's edition of *The Times* at the top of the fan, as always. 'Miss Lucie has been and gone. She's got a call with the restoration team at Witherby's at nine and wanted to do some last-minute preparation. Sir Arthur is out with the dogs and I'm expecting him back in—' he checked the plain gold watch on his wrist '—ten minutes. As for Master Tristan and—'

'We're here, we're here. Sorry we're late.' Tristan entered the room with Will on his heels.

Maxwell snapped into immediate action, ushering them both to the table and fetching coffee for both men. They tried to keep things low-key at breakfast with the family helping themselves as much as possible, but with a guest present they might as well ask the butler to dance a jig as not see to their comfort.

'It's all my fault,' Will said, accepting the napkin Maxwell shook out for him. 'I got so mesmerised by the view from my window this morning, I lost track of time.'

Tristan grinned at him after also accepting a napkin with a murmur of thanks. 'No kidding.' He glanced over at Iggy, eyes dancing with bright amusement. 'When I stuck my head around his door he was sketching away, completely oblivious to everything – including the fact he was still only half-dressed.'

'Could've been worse, at least I had my pants on.' Will's rich, deep laugh did something funny to Iggy's insides, as did the unexpected mental image of him clad only in his underwear. Nope! She was not going there. Not today, not *any* day. Forcing the image from her mind, Iggy stared down at the soggy remains of her breakfast until the fluttering in her stomach subsided enough for her to spoon up a mouthful.

Once Maxwell had departed with hot food orders for the men, she concentrated on her breakfast. Tristan and Will seemed content to carry the conversation, and it would've been easy enough for her to let them chatter away. A raised eyebrow from her brother put paid to that notion. He'd never call her on it in public, but she could tell he wasn't impressed with her behaviour. Their father had raised them to always be polite and welcoming towards their guests – even those who hadn't been invited. Remembering her little pep talk, Iggy rested her spoon beside her bowl and pasted on a smile as she met Will's gaze across the table.

Breathtaking.

She wasn't sure if it was the right description to give a man, but it was the one that came to mind. Four feet of burnished mahogany table was not a wide enough barrier when facing a man as good-looking as Will Talbot. This close, she could see the curve of his black lashes, and could name any number of women who'd kill for a set like them – herself included, and she wasn't one for fussing over much about her looks.

The hint of stubble that had darkened his jaw the previous evening had been shaven clean, leaving nothing to conceal the deep scar stretching from near the corner of his right eye to bisect his cheekbone before curling to the corner of his mouth. It should've marred his beauty, but somehow emphasised it. When he raised a hand to skim it over the inch of dark hair coating his scalp, she became conscious she was staring. Fighting the heat of a blush, she reached for her tea as an excuse to break the eye contact. Swallowing down the cold mouthful, she repressed a shudder and told herself it was her deserved punishment for mooning over Will. She set her cup down with a firm click against its saucer, and forced herself to look up, though she focused on the bridge of his nose rather than the unsettling depths of his storm-grey eyes. 'I hope you slept well.'

'It took me a while to unwind, but once I got into bed, I slept like a baby.' His eyes skated over her face as though taking in the dark circles beneath her eyes. 'What about you?'

Refusing to acknowledge the indecent images from one of her dreams about Will threatening to creep back into her mind, she widened her smile. 'Oh, I slept fine, thanks.'

The corner of his lips twitched, as though he knew he'd caught her in a blatant lie, but when he spoke it was only to say. 'The photos you sent me don't do the gardens justice.'

She considered the location of the green room with its view over the rolling rear lawn towards the ivy-covered stable block and the woodland beyond. 'There's something special about the light here, makes the colours seem richer, more vivid.' She lifted one shoulder. 'Well, that's what I think, anyway. Maybe I'm just biased.'

'There's lots of things that are special here.'

Iggy glanced up at the surprising comment to meet a heated grey stare. Was he implying that she was one of those special things? She melted just a little at the unexpected compliment, before giving herself a shake. Will Talbot might be one of the most attractive men she had ever met, but he had the reputation and ego to go with it. Flirting would be like breathing to a man who had a different girl on his arm, and no doubt in his bed, every week. She didn't judge him for choosing to live his life that way, but it wasn't and never would be for her. Besides, the papers had been making a big thing recently about his relationship with a reality TV star – not that she made a habit of reading about him the gossip columns. Well, not *much*.

Her response to him was natural; nothing more than her body chemistry reacting to a stimulus. It would be strange if she didn't find him attractive, given her propensity for sexy, and entirely unsuitable men. Feeling better, and a little more settled, she stood. 'I'm getting another cup of tea. Would you like some more coffee?'

'Yes, please.' His smile was as warm about the thought of coffee as it had been about everything else. He was just one of those men imbued with a natural charm.

Knowing that didn't stop her stomach from fluttering though. *Attractive man plus nice smile equals physical reaction, that's all it is.* Taking a firm grip on that reminder, Iggy went to refresh their drinks.

She'd just set her own tea and a silver coffee pot for Tristan and Will to share on the table when Arthur entered the room.

'Morning all.' Pausing to brush a quick kiss on Iggy's temple, he eyed the pot with a gleam. 'Is that coffee?'

'Guests, first,' she said, giving the hand he'd outstretched towards the pot a playful slap.

His pout switched to a grin when she shooed him to his seat

at the head of the table then returned to the sideboard to pour her brother a fresh cup from the large urn. When she set it down in front of him, Arthur reached for her hand. 'I don't care what they say about you, Iggle-Piggle, I think you're great.'

The teasing she could take as nothing more than the usual banter of an annoying brat of a brother. But she couldn't believe he'd actually used that wretched bloody nickname in front of Will! Wishing her eyes could shoot lasers and set him on fire, Iggy mouthed 'I'm going to kill you,' while he grinned at her like he'd said something hilarious.

Deciding revenge was better than murder, Iggy resumed her seat and took a considering mouthful of her tea. 'I think we should have a movie night tonight,' she said, keeping her voice light and conversational. 'What do you say, Tristan?'

Two against one had always been the favourite game between the three of them, the pairings ever-changing. Catching on at once, Tristan beamed. 'I think that sounds like a splendid idea, sister of mine. What did you have in mind?'

Iggy pursed her lips as though giving the matter much thought. 'Oh, I don't know, how about a musical? I bet Lucie loves musicals.'

Tristan covered a snort of laughter with a cough. 'I bet she does,' he managed to choke out.

'*Iggy.*'

Ignoring the warning note in Arthur's tone, she turned her attention to Will. 'Do you have a favourite musical, Will?'

'I find them all equally diverting.' A hint of mischief glittered in his expression. 'Do you have a favourite?'

He might not know exactly what was going on, but he'd picked up the undercurrents and she wanted to grin in delight that he'd chosen to go with it. Keeping her face straight, she nodded. '*Joseph and the Amazing Technicolour Dreamcoat* is a big hit in this family.'

Tristan began to sing quietly. 'It was red and yellow and green and brown and—'

'I hate you,' Arthur said, as both Iggy and Tristan giggled.

'What's the joke?' Will asked as Iggy's giggles subsided and she pressed her napkin to the corners of her eyes.

Biting her lip, she cast a quick look at the glaring brother, before turning back to Will. 'There was a brief period when Arthur was enamoured with the school choir.'

'Enamoured with a member of the school choir, is what she means,' Tristan butted in.

'Genevieve had a very nice voice,' Arthur muttered.

'Must've been something to do with her well-developed chest,' Iggy said, drily, making Tristan sputter over his coffee and start laughing again. She was about to pick up the story when Maxwell returned carrying three silver salvers on a large tray.

'Everything all right there, Master Tristan?' he asked as he set the first salver in front of Arthur and raised the lid with a flourish.

Tristan coughed then nodded as the butler placed a second plate down in front of him. 'We were just telling Will about Arthur's starring role in *Joseph*.'

'Ah, yes. Mrs Walters spent many hours sewing those coloured patches onto one of my old overall jackets.' He turned to Arthur once more, features deadpan. 'I believe you still have it in the back of your wardrobe, Sir Arthur.'

Oh, that was a delicious titbit Iggy had never realised. Wanting to kiss the butler for dropping her brother well and truly in it, she clapped her hands together. 'You can wear it tonight when we watch the production!'

'What a splendid idea, Miss Igraine,' Maxwell agreed, placing the final plate before Will then returning to Arthur's side. 'You'll be delighted to know that I had all the late baronet's old home movies transferred onto DVD.'

'You're fired, Maxwell.' Arthur scowled at the butler before breaking into a chuckle.

'Very good, sir.' Lips barely twitching whilst the rest of them howled with laughter, Maxwell swept up the empty tray and left the room.

'The joy of siblings, eh, Will?' Arthur said with a rueful smile as he tucked into his breakfast.

'I wouldn't know. My parents had the good sense to stop after me.' Though he said it with a smile, there was a hint of wistfulness about it. It reminded her of the way Lucie, also an only child, sounded sometimes.

'Lucky you. Imagine being stuck with these two from birth.' Iggy took no offence at Tristan's comment, knowing he adored being a part of their triumvirate as much as she did. Maybe she wasn't the only one who'd caught that note in Will's voice.

'So, what's the plan for today?' Arthur asked her. 'Are you going to give Will the guided tour?'

Dark-grey eyes met hers and those stupid flutters were back again. 'I'd really like that, if you have the time. I know the deadline is tight, but the sooner I can get to grips with what we're facing, the better.' Well, someone had certainly changed their tune. *What we're facing* sounded a lot like he was serious about staying.

'I'll show you around the Lady's garden first. As the most formal part of the garden it needs the most work. Other than getting a tree surgeon in to inspect the routes for the walks we have planned, the woods will take care of themselves.'

Will nodded. 'Sounds like a plan. Speaking of which, perhaps I can sit down later with those plans you had last night?'

'If you like.' As much as she wanted to accept his change of heart at face value, she was still wary of it. This was all too easy, so what was the catch? 'We'll also need to discuss your fee.'

'Let me work out first what contribution I think I can make to things, and then we can talk about it.' He shrugged, like money was no big deal.

Maybe it wasn't to him, but regardless of the good fortune Lucie's discovery had brought them, it still meant a hell of a lot to Iggy. Though she'd sworn to herself earlier she would take his presence as a gift, she couldn't shrug off the tiny kernel of suspicion that somehow this was all some enormous joke, and the punchline would be at her expense. 'What made you change your mind?'

Setting down his knife and fork, Will held up his hands to her, palms towards him. 'Look at these.'

She looked. They were large hands. Big square slabs of flesh with broad fingers and neat, squared-off nails. No distinguishing marks beyond a few scattered freckles, no doubt from the hours they'd been exposed to the sun. 'What am I looking for?'

'Now look at your hands.'

Surprised, she raised them in front of her face. Though she'd soaked them last night in the bath, and scrubbed them again in the shower this morning, a couple of her nails still had some ingrained dirt beneath them. Flustered over her behaviour the previous night, she realised she'd forgotten to apply her sunscreen-infused hand cream leaving the skin looking wrinkled and tight. 'Not as pretty as yours,' she mused.

'Exactly. I'm a gardener, Igraine, or at least I'm supposed to be.' His use of her full name surprised her. Almost as much as it surprised her how much she liked hearing him say it. She'd always thought it too girly, but on his lips it sounded like a woman's name; one she might finally be ready to grow into.

Not quite ready to think about that, she tried to concentrate on what he was saying. 'The medal from Chelsea says plenty of people think you're a gardener.'

He shook his head, ignoring her attempt at levity. 'A gardener who can't remember the last time he got his hands dirty.' His derisive snort told her what he thought of that. 'Replanting the Chelsea garden was probably the last time I wielded a trowel.'

Iggy blinked. Surely that couldn't be right. His win at Chelsea had been two years ago. 'I thought you were run off your feet.'

'I am, but that's with designing. I have a team who do all the real work. I try to get more involved, but it's a nightmare because the clients spend so much time coming up with excuses to chat that we don't get anything done. If I send Nick, my planting supervisor, in to run the job, it's done in half the time.'

She'd never considered the flip side of his fame before. Though she wanted to work with him because he was one of the best young talents in the field, there was no getting around the fact that some people probably hired him just so they could tell their friends they'd had their garden designed by Will Talbot. They wanted the celebrity, not the man whose innovative mix of traditional with shocking splashes of urban realism had caught her eye and imagination. 'Surely your team are going to need you back in London?'

'There'll be things I have to go back for, I'm sure.' He lounged back in his chair, the lazy sprawl drawing her attention to just how big a man he was. Big and capable, and just a little bit dangerous. Just as well he wasn't her type. Or rather, just as well she refused to be drawn to what *had* always been her type anymore.

Deciding she had time for one more quick cup of tea while the others finished eating, Iggy carried her cup to the sideboard. The large water boiler had gone into stand-by mode so she flipped through the newspapers whilst waiting for it to get back up to temperature. Their father had liked to get all the daily newspapers, same as their grandfather had. She supposed it dated to a time when the house was busier, when the family did more entertaining and were more likely to have visitors staying. It also put money in the pocket of the local shop in the village so it'd never felt right to Arthur to reduce or cancel the order – even though she knew he read the paper on his phone app more often than not.

As usual, the headlines grew more dramatic and lurid towards the lower end of the tabloid market. It fascinated her that whilst most of the front pages often carried a variation on the same theme, there'd always be something different on one of the red-tops. The boiler clicked off, and she was just tidying the papers back into a neat pile when she spotted what looked like a cartoon drawing.

Tugging the paper from the bottom of the stack, it took a moment for her mind to register what she was seeing. WHERE'S WILLY? Screamed the banner headline over a photo of Will's face wearing a photoshopped cartoon red and white stripped bobble hat and matching jumper like the Where's Wally character from the children's books. Feeling suddenly sick and stupid, Iggy began reading the story beneath:

Will Talbot, love-rat gardener to the stars, has left another broken heart in his wake. Bootcamp Babes beauty, Melody Atkins, was distraught when Talbot left her to strut the red carpet alone last night at the new album launch for pop sensation, Clay Givens. 'I thought we had something special, that being with me had finally tamed his wild ways, but he's not the man I thought he was,' she confided to our reporter, barely holding back the tears. 'I just hope he's all right, and can finally get the help that he needs.'

When approached, Mr Talbot's office refused to comment, and his agent hasn't returned our calls. There was also no answer at his exclusive Battersea apartment. So, where's Willy? If you've seen him, you can call our tip line on 0800 444 5597. Turn to Page 5 for our exclusive tell-all interview with Melody Atkins.

Suddenly, it all made perfect sense.

Chapter 7

Will had been prepared to weather a storm that morning, but thankfully Igraine's mood seemed a lot more receptive to his sudden arrival than it had been the night before. He'd taken what Tristan had said seriously and spent a couple of hours really thinking about what his plans were, and whether he could make a difference to what the family was trying to achieve. When he'd eventually slipped between the soft cotton sheets on that monster bed he'd been expecting a night of luxury; alas, though it looked impressive, the mattress had left a hell of a lot to be desired. No matter what position he tried, he'd ended up rolling down into the soggy centre of the bed as soon as he relaxed. His back might never forgive him.

At least the water in the shower had been hot and plentiful, and after a good few minutes he'd started to feel like himself again. Then he'd drawn back his curtains and any lingering discomfort had been instantly forgotten as the castle revealed its true beauty to him. He'd assumed his room had been named for the décor, but as he'd taken in the view beyond the glass, he'd wondered anew. From the deep, almost black leaves of the ivy climbing over the pale stone walls and roof of the outbuildings, to the distinctive shades of oak, beech and elm trees and the dark and pale stripes of the neatly mowed lawn, there were more shades of green than he could put name to.

His attempts to open the window had been thwarted – the ancient-looking metal opener refusing to budge more than half an inch. By pressing his face against the glass, he'd caught the glimpse of a structure beneath his window that looked like it might be some kind of glass house or conservatory. And then the sun had broken through the light clouds, illuminating the pale stonework and enhancing the contrast between the manmade structures and nature's efforts to reclaim the space they occupied. He'd dug immediately for his sketchbook, and might have sat there all day trying to capture the play of the light.

As he set his knife and fork together on his empty plate with the satisfied sigh of a well-fed man, he could only be thankful that Tristan had persuaded him to abandon his sketching for breakfast. 'That was fantastic, who do I need to thank for the food?'

Arthur finished off his last bite of toast then smiled. 'We source as much as possible from the local area and have an account with the local butcher. You can really taste the difference, can't you?'

'Absolutely,' Will agreed. 'Though I'll have to resist the temptation of a cooked breakfast every day, I must say I could get used to a spread like this. It's a far cry from the black coffee and toast I usually have at home.'

'Oh, I doubt you'll have time to get used to breakfast here with us, Mr Talbot.' Igraine's brittle tone drew his attention across the room. She still had her back to them, her attention seemingly fixed on the newspapers spread out in front of her. There was a tension in her spine, the rigidity of her posture a far cry from the laughing, relaxed woman who'd been sitting opposite him not five minutes earlier. And what was with this Mr Talbot business?

Mentally retracing his conversational steps, he tried to work out what he might have said to sour her mood, but came up blank. Perhaps now they were going to be heading outside to survey the gardens, she was just feeling a bit tense about things. Hoping to reassure her, he aimed for a relaxed air. 'I'm sure you're right. We'll be so busy working, the weeks will fly by.'

Igraine turned to face him at that point, her face like thunder. 'You can stop the pretence. It's clear the only reason you've turned up here is to try and escape the press fallout of your breakup with your girlfriend. What did you do to the poor woman, anyway?'

What the bloody hell was she on about? 'I don't know what you're talking about, what did I do to who?'

At the same time as he was speaking, Arthur shoved his chair back from the table. 'Enough, Iggy! I will not have you speak to a guest of ours like this. You were the one who wanted Will to help with the gardens, and yet you've done everything possible to make him feel unwelcome since the moment of his arrival. What's got into you?'

Eyes flashing, she rounded on her brother. 'Ask him why he's here. Go on, ask him!'

A dull flush was rising on Arthur's cheeks. 'I don't need to ask him, he's here to help us. To help *you*, although the way you're carrying on, we'll be lucky if he gives us the time of day!'

Still clueless as to why Igraine was so pissed off, and not liking the fact he was somehow the cause of her and Arthur falling out, Will waved his arms. 'Umm, hey, guys. *He's* right here.'

Jabbing his hands onto his hips, Arthur huffed out a breath. 'I'm so sorry, Will. What on earth must you think of us?'

He waved the apology off. 'It's cool, really. I just don't have a clue what's going on.'

Reaching behind her, Igraine snatched one of the papers from the sideboard and tossed it onto the table in front of him. 'Why don't you read all about it?' Turning on her heel, she marched out of the room.

With a feeling of dread twisting his stomach into knots, Will drew the newspaper towards him. A quick scan over the front page was enough to confirm his worst fears. 'Shit.' He jumped up, almost knocking his chair over in his haste to put some distance between himself and the unpleasant reminder of the worst aspect of his current life. Anger surged in his veins. Melody had done a serious number on him, that was for sure.

'Is this you?' Tristan was leaning across from his seat to look at the front page.

'Yes, but the story's a load of bollocks. I haven't done anything to Melody, it was a purely business relationship.'

'Well, she certainly appears distraught over something, and you can't deny the two of you have been splashed across the papers for weeks now,' Tristan mused as he flipped over to the inside page to reveal a full-length picture of Melody clad in three tiny triangles of material masquerading as a bikini. 'I wonder if the poor girl needs a shoulder to cry on?'

Though he knew Tristan was trying to make light of things to ease the tension, he could really do without it right now. As Will scanned the innuendo-laden text accompanying the photo, his gut sank. As usual, the reporter had been clever enough not to outright accuse him of anything libellous, whilst merrily trashing his reputation in the process. If you read between the lines, the article managed to infer he was a drunken yob with a propensity for violence. They'd even reproduced that awful photo of him snarling at the bottom of the article. Talk about a bloody hatchet job. Furious at Melody for dropping him in it, and with himself for not making sure she was on side before he left, he shoved the stupid article away. 'Like 99 per cent of the trash they publish about me, there's barely a grain of truth to it.'

He started around the table, determined to catch Igraine up and explain, but Arthur shifted to intercept him. 'Why are you here, Will?'

'I'm starting to wonder that myself, to be honest.' As soon as he'd spoken, Will held his hands up in apology. 'Look, I'm sorry. Melody and I were never a couple, we just decided to play it that way because it suited us both at the time.' Even as he was saying it, it sounded ridiculous and he knew it would do nothing to make them likely to trust him.

'I promise you the only reason I came here was because I was captivated by the images your sister sent me, and I wanted to see if I could play a part in restoring your gardens.' Frustrated that once again he'd been judged on crap written about him, Will yanked out a chair and slumped down in it. 'Maybe I shouldn't have come.'

Arthur clapped a sympathetic hand on his shoulder. 'Or maybe coming here was exactly what you needed to do.'

Feeling suddenly tired and a lot older than his 29 years, Will glanced up at him. 'All I want to do is feel the sun on my back, the earth between my fingers and the ache in my muscles at the end of the day that tells me I've spent it doing some good, honest work.' He flicked a resentful glare towards the newspaper. 'I didn't ask for any of this.'

'Then spending a few weeks here out of the limelight sounds like it'll benefit us just as much as you.'

Still not sure whether he should cut his losses and take the chaos that always seemed to be dogging his heels these days with him, Will looked over towards Tristan. 'What do you think?'

Shutting the paper with the snap of his wrist, Tristan rested his elbows on the table and appeared to give the matter some thought. 'I think we might be able to turn this to our advantage.'

Arthur frowned. 'How so?'

'If we can keep Will's presence here a secret, we can wait to unveil his participation in the restoration works. It'd be a great publicity coup – the tabloids can waste their column inches on speculation, and we can make a big announcement a week or two before the grand opening about what Will's really been up to.' He turned to Will. 'Assuming you don't mind us using your name in that way?'

Feeling uneasy, Will shook his head. 'I'd rather avoid any kind of publicity at the moment. I don't have any problem with you using my name to promote your event, but I want it to be focused completely on the work I do in the gardens and not my personal life.'

Tristan gave him a speculative glance, before finally nodding. 'Okay, I can see why you want to distance yourself from this kind of bad press. We'll talk about it nearer the time and agree a statement.'

Shaking his hand, Arthur gave him a wry grin. 'Looks like you're staying, then. Assuming you can convince Iggy, that is.'

*

It took Will the best part of an hour and half to track Igraine down in a hidden corner of the formal gardens. The way she was hacking at the brambles half-choking the statue he'd seen in one of the photos she'd sent him, it was clear that none of her earlier anger at him had faded. He moved into her eyeline and raised his hands in the traditional surrender gesture, hoping for at least a smile. All he got for his efforts was a disdainful curl of her lip before she attacked the brambles with a renewed vigour that was enough to make a grown man wince. Opting for a waiting game, Will began exploring that section of the garden, making sure to skirt wide around the fountain basin which held the statue.

At first glance, it looked to be a dead end – the fountain enclosed on three sides by thick, overgrown box hedges. Though it would take a bit of elbow grease to extract the weeds interwoven with the box, once the brambles had been cleared and the fountain cleaned and restored to working order, it would be a nice quiet spot for visitors to take a breather and listen to the soothing trickle of the fountain. In his mind's eye, he could picture a couple of benches, perhaps with integrated pergolas which would provide a respite from the sun on a warm day. He paced out the area, calculating angles and distances in his head, and it was only as he approached the hedge at the back of the rectangular space, he realised a narrow path had once run through it. 'What's through here?' he asked as he bent to try and peer through the overgrowth.

'I'm not sure it leads anywhere.' When Will glanced back at her over his shoulder, she'd stopped chopping and was frowning in his direction. 'The back wall of the apothecary's garden is somewhere on the other side, so perhaps it's just a gap where part of the hedge died back and then the weeds and stuff took over.'

Not convinced, Will drew a pair of thick leather gardening gloves from his back pocket then hunkered down for a closer look. Yanking free several handfuls of grass gone to seed where the edges of the lawn had been allowed to run riot, he cleared enough space to see a clear break in the two section of the hedge at the base. The box had grown together to fill the gap, but with a bit of effort …

Lying on his belly, Will wriggled forward, ignoring the surrounding plants that tried to snag his clothing as though bent on keeping him out. *One more shove.* His shoulders suddenly broke through and he craned his neck up.

'What are you doing?' A none-too-gentle kick to the side of his work boot jolted through him. 'You'll wreck the hedge!'

Ignoring Igraine's complaint he studied the small wooden door set into a red-brick wall. 'There's a door here.'

'What? Where?' Any animosity she'd been harbouring for him was seemingly forgotten as she tried to wiggle in beside him. 'Get out a minute and let me see.'

Rather than reversing out, he pushed through to the other side of the hedge, scraping a couple of layers of skin off the outside of his arm in the process. He was still wincing down at the graze, when Igraine popped up beside him, half her mass of curls hanging over one shoulder, the rest still tied back in a now lop-sided ponytail. She appeared not to notice, her eyes fixed on the weathered boards of the door. Reaching out, she touched the brick wall beside it, her fingers stroking over a patch of the yellowed lichen spreading over much of the red brick. 'This is definitely the apothecary's garden, but I'm sure there's only one way into it.'

'Perhaps it's obscured from the other side?'

'No, there's nothing growing up the walls.' She shook her head, only then seeming to realise her hair was a mess.

Fascinated, he watched as she stripped the band from the remains of her ponytail, gathered it all together in a couple of swift, sure strokes of her hands and wound it back up in a knot on her head. The movement drew his attention to the lean musculature of her frame, the delicate graceful lines of her neck and throat as she tilted her head back.

God, she was beautiful.

That she appeared unaware of it only added to her allure. She was so unlike the pouting, preening women he met at those awful bloody promotional events. Though he understood why Melody had chosen to alter her appearance, he'd much preferred her more natural look when they'd first been introduced. Though he'd meant to give her time to calm down, he knew he could leave this particular sleeping dog to lie any longer. 'There's no truth to that article in the paper this morning. Melody is with the same promo agency as me and we decided to pose as a couple because it made life easier for the both of us.' It suddenly seemed vital to Will that Igraine understand the truth of that. 'She's not my girlfriend, never has been, never will be.'

Finished with her hair, Igraine stilled then turned towards him, as though sensing his gaze upon her. Worried about what she might be able to read on his face, Will made a big show of studying the garden wall beyond her shoulder. His eyes followed the length of the wall, and he frowned over her previous comment. She'd said there was nothing growing up the walls of the apothecary's garden, but there were thick ropes of ivy spilling over to cascade down the red brick. He turned his attention back to the door. 'Is it locked?'

Igraine twisted the handle and tugged to no avail. 'I can't tell if it's locked or just stuck from years of disuse.'

'Let me see.' Will stepped around to the other side of her and was surprised when she moved away with a scowl. 'Where are you going?'

'I was making room for you to do your macho-man display, because weak and feeble woman that I am, I couldn't possibly be able to open it without your assistance.'

Will rolled his eyes. 'Do you want some brown sauce to go with that chip on your shoulder? What I was going to suggest was you try the handle again and I'll try to see whether the locking mechanism is moving.' He pointed to the narrow gap between the edge of the door and the wall. 'Try the handle again and this time hold it down.'

With a blush, Igraine returned to her previous spot and did as he asked. Leaning closer, Will squinted at the gap. 'Can you release it now?' As she did so, he spotted something moving. 'And open once more.' He tilted his head to look below the lock and then above it before standing up to face her. 'Something is definitely moving, but there looks to be an obstruction beneath it, so I think we're going to have to try and find a key.'

Igraine gave the base of the door a gentle kick with the toe of her boot. 'That's disappointing. I suppose I can ask Maxwell later if he's got any old keys lying around.' She paused a minute before glancing up at him through her lashes. 'I'm sorry I jumped to conclusions, but you must see it from my point of view. One minute you're laughing me off the phone, the next you're on the doorstep acting like it's completely normal for a man as busy as you must be to drop everything for a project you don't believe can be achieved in time.'

She had a point, but he wasn't sure how he could explain his change of heart without going into the embarrassing scene with Phillipa Cornwall. It couldn't possibly do anything other than make his already bad impression with Igraine worse if he was forced to explain he'd been fending off Phillipa's advances when Igraine had called him. 'It's been too long since I got my hands in the soil. I'd been feeling restless for a while, but didn't know what was wrong with me until I saw those photos you sent me. I'm not one given to romanticising stuff, but the land here called to me. Can you understand that?'

She blew out a breath, nodding slowly as she did so. 'Yes. I've been desperate to do something about the gardens for ages, but I had too many other responsibilities to give them the time they needed. If I could spend months and months restoring them, I'd love to, but I simply don't have that luxury. We have to open up to the public if we stand a hope in hell of keeping the castle up and running.'

Damn, those were some very high stakes, and he wondered what it had cost her to admit that to a relative stranger. 'I'll do everything I can to help you. If I commit to something, I see it through, okay?'

'Okay.'

Though he was curious to find out more about the family situation, Will counselled himself to be patient. Turning back to the wall, he tried to estimate its height. He was five foot eleven, and if he extended his arm he could probably just about touch the top of the wall, but he'd not be able to get enough purchase to haul himself up. He cast an appraising glance at Igraine. She was only a few inches shorter, if he gave her a boost up, she might be able to get at least a peak over the top …

'What are you doing?' she said as he got down on his hands and knees, spreading them just wide enough to create as stable a base as possible.

'Giving you a boost up.' He had a decent set of ladders in the back of his truck, but they might as well find out if it was going to be worth the effort before he lugged them all the way down here.

'Don't be daft, we know what's on the other side, the apothecary's garden.'

Tilting his head back, he met her gaze. 'But you said there's no door visible from inside the garden …' Catching a gleam of excitement in her eyes, he pressed his case. 'Aren't you just the tiniest bit curious?'

She laughed. 'You could get a woman into a lot of trouble, Will Talbot.' She edged closer, then hesitated. 'Are you sure?'

'Go for it.' Will dropped his head and braced his arms in preparation for her weight. He swallowed a grunt as she planted her foot near his shoulders and pushed herself up. Within seconds the pressure had eased, as though she'd found a way to take some of her weight from him.

'Oh. God.'

At her breathy exclamation, Will's curiosity spiked, and he cursed himself for not just going to fetch his ladders in the first place. 'Everything all right?'

'There's a secret garden here!' Her weight vanished as she dropped down onto the ground beside him.

Brushing off his hands as he rose, Will couldn't help but grin at the expression on Igraine's face – she looked like a kid in a candy store. 'Tell me!'

'It's not very deep, maybe six or seven feet across but it looked like it ran the length of the wall. I'll need to go back and consult the plans again, because I didn't notice it when I was studying them.' She laughed. 'Mind you, we didn't notice there was a hidden tunnel in the castle until Lucie helped to uncover it. In fact, if she hadn't found it, you wouldn't be here.'

She was squinting as she spoke and Will realised she was facing directly into the sun. He shifted position, propping one shoulder against the wall so she could angle herself away from the bright light and still be facing him. 'Now I'm properly intrigued. Tell me more.'

Igraine mirrored his pose by leaning on the wall next to him. 'I wasn't kidding earlier when I said we need to open to the public to keep afloat. Things here were in pretty dire straits after our father died last year, to the point we thought we might lose everything.'

'Jesus, that must have been awful.'

She nodded. 'It really was, especially on the heels of losing him.'

82

A sweet, sad smile crossed her face. 'He was the life and soul of this place, and I adored him. Anyway, we'd hit rock bottom and were looking for solutions to raise money. Morgana suggested we get someone in to catalogue all antiques and paintings and that's how Lucie ended up here.'

Will frowned. 'Morgana?'

'She's our great-aunt, you haven't met her yet.' A wicked grin lit up her face. 'I can't wait to see what she makes of you.'

He laughed. 'Should I be afraid?'

'Only a little bit, her bark is worse than her bite.'

Sounded like someone not standing a million miles from him. 'I can hardly wait.' He waved his hand. 'Back to the story, what does Lucie have to do with me being here?'

'She came across some old journals of one of our ancestors – the one obsessed with King Arthur, actually – which led to the discovery of the secret tunnel and a hidden masterpiece which had been walled up inside it. It's being restored at the moment, and Arthur is planning on selling it later in the year. The bank has advanced Arthur enough funds we can crack on with the external works which is how come I was able to approach you.'

'Sounds amazing, it must've been quite the adventure.' He was sorry to have missed it.

'No one in the family had any idea about the painting's exist-ence; if it hadn't been for Lucie …' She shook her head, as though to dispel a terrible thought. 'Thanks to her discovery we've got a fighting chance of hanging onto the castle now. Opening to the public should help us get things onto a secure footing.'

It was all starting to fall into place. 'Hence the rush on the deadline to get the grounds sorted out.'

She quirked a brow. 'Indeed. There is a method behind our madness.'

He took the dig about his initial response to her plans on the chin, but couldn't resist a gentle jab back. 'If you'd mentioned any of this when you called yesterday …'

'Yesterday. It feels like an awful lot has happened since then.' Reaching up, she scrubbed a hand over her face drawing his attention to the tired lines bracketing her eyes. 'Do you think we've got any chance at all of succeeding?'

It would be tight as hell, but he could tell she already knew that. 'We can only try.'

Dropping her hand, she raised an eyebrow at him. 'Can *we*? What about ...' She gestured vaguely. '... London?'

It sounded like she wasn't completely convinced about his explanation about Melody earlier. 'My team is looking after my current clients, and other than that, there is nothing in *London* that holds any interest for me. I'm a free agent.' He couldn't put it much plainer than that.

Hoping that was an end to it, he straightened up and clapped his hands together. 'Right, what's on the rest of the agenda for this morning? Are you going to give me the guided tour, or are we going to give in to temptation and explore this secret garden?'

Igraine placed her hand on the wall between them. 'It's not like we were intending to open this up to the public. We don't even know what's in there. All I saw from that quick look was a lot of dead plants and weeds.' With one final pat of the brickwork, she squared her shoulders. 'We should get on with the tour, so you know exactly what you're up against.'

She was right, and he might have let it go had he not seen her give one last yearning glance back towards the wall before she ducked in preparation to wriggle through the gap they'd made. 'I've got a set of ladders in my truck. It wouldn't do any harm to take a quick look.'

The wicked grin she gave him from on her hands and knees just before she crawled under the hedge sent a spark of something dangerous shooting through his blood stream. A gentleman wouldn't have stood there and enjoyed every moment of her delicious bottom disappearing through the gap. But then again, no one had ever accused him of being one.

Chapter 8

As they made their way back through the gardens and towards the castle, Iggy pointed out a few of the things she wanted to work on, as well as a couple of areas she thought would work well for Tristan's idea of later projects for volunteers. Her mind wasn't really on it though, as all she kept turning over was the idea that Will and Melody had faked a relationship for months. They'd always looked so happy together, it didn't seem possible for there to be nothing behind those smiles and touches emblazoned across the papers. She wasn't naïve; there'd been enough press scandals over recent years for it to be clear there were some murky goings-on in certain parts of the media, but even so, it seemed like such a weird thing to do.

Though she'd die before she admitted it, she'd followed everything about Will in the media, curious about the young man who'd come from seemingly nowhere to win one of the most prestigious horticultural prizes going. If her fascination with him had strayed beyond the professional, well, that was her secret and not something she'd ever share.

They made it as far as the edge of the sweeping gravel drive before curiosity got the better of her. 'Was there really never anything between you and Melody?'

He was quiet for a long moment and Iggy cursed herself for putting her foot in it again. They'd just got things easy between them and she'd opened her big mouth and thrown a spanner in the works. If he got in his truck and drove off without a backwards glance, she wouldn't blame him. 'Please don't think I was questioning your honesty, it just all seems a bit ...'

'Ridiculous,' he supplied, and she nodded in agreement. 'Dealing with the press is a stupid game of cat and mouse. If you don't give them something, they'll take it anyway and trash you in the process.' His voice was so quiet she had to strain to hear him over the crunch of their feet across the gravel. 'Trouble is, I was too young and a bit easily led when people first started paying attention to what I was doing. I spent more time with the plants than around other people so I wasn't exactly a social butterfly. The first few parties I was invited to, I didn't know anyone, and the ones I recognised I was too shy to talk to – why would some actor off the telly want to chat with a kid from a council estate? I turned to the booze – not hard when it flows like water at those things – to calm my nerves and was snapped falling out of a door or two. I also met a few girls who kissed and told.'

They'd reached his large black flatbed truck on the driveway by this point and he gave her a self-deprecating shrug before reaching to unfasten the thick tarpaulin cover stretched over the back. 'Before I knew it, I was appearing in the tabloid gossip columns and an agent contacted me offering to help me manage things. He introduced me to Melody and we decided to put a positive spin on the stories being told about us.'

'Until this morning,' she pointed out.

Will grimaced. 'I didn't hold up my side of the bargain. Our agent arranged a last-minute function, but I forgot all about it in my rush to come up here. Melody spun my absence to her advantage, I guess.'

Iggy circled to the other side of the truck to tug free the

opposite corner of the cover. 'It must be awful not being able to trust anyone, even when you're supposed to be friends.'

He flashed her a quick smile, and she noticed for the first time it was slightly wonky where the scar pulled his cheek tight on the right-hand side. It only added to his attraction and she could understand why women who were looking for a bit of free publicity would be happy to be linked with him.

As though picking up on her thoughts, he continued, 'I wouldn't call Melody and I friends – temporary allies, maybe. It's a brutal world if you choose to live your life in the spotlight. I'm pissed off with her, but I can't really blame her. It was an important event for her, and I let her down. I've met a lot of people over the past couple of years and I'm pretty sure most of them would trash me if it turned the story to their advantage. I'd like to say I'd behave differently, but that's only because I don't care about being famous. It's been the worst thing about being successful, even though I know it's the only reason I'm successful in the first place.'

God, it sounded like he didn't have anyone in his life who he could rely on. She'd be lost if she didn't have Arthur and Tristan to lean upon. 'Don't you have any friends you can rely on?'

He gave her that shrug again. 'I've got my team in the office, and my dad, although I don't see him much these days. I gave up trying to make friends once I realised that people weren't the tiniest bit interested in me, only in being seen with me.'

'I can understand why.'

Will paused in the act of pulling free a ladder to throw back his head and laugh. 'Well that put me in my place. I didn't realise I was that bad!'

'What?' Askance, Iggy stared at him for a moment before realising what she'd said. 'Oh, no.' She clapped a hand to her mouth then giggled. 'Sorry, I meant I could understand why they'd want to be seen with you.' When he raised an eyebrow, that piratical smile tugging at this cheek, she blushed. 'Just hand me that spade so I can dig this hole a little deeper.' Will laughed once more, and she found herself joining in, glad that her faux pas had chased some of the shadows from his face. He had a nice laugh, rich and warm and inviting.

She helped him finish lifting the ladder out of the bed of the truck then refasten the tarpaulin. Though she offered to help him carry it, he hoisted it over his shoulder and declared himself well able to manage. They began to head back the way they'd come when she had a brainwave. 'Rather than causing any more damage to the hedge, we should access the garden from the other side, via the apothecary's garden. What do you think?'

'I think it's just as well that you're the brains of this outfit because I'd have likely spent half an hour trying to wrestle this bloody thing through the gap we made.'

Iggy led them away to the left and along a gravel path which skirted the edge of the gardens until they reached the sturdy door set into the red-bricked enclosure of the apothecary's garden. 'It looks to be the same age as the other one but see how the dimensions are different.' She stretched her arms wide, her fingers barely touching either side of the brickwork arch into which the door was set to show him.

'You're right,' Will agreed, resting the ladder down for a moment. 'The one we found is much smaller and set flush into the brick.'

Turning the handle, she pushed the door open then stepped back to let Will through with the ladder. 'We don't keep it locked because there aren't any children around, but we make sure to keep the door closed so the dogs can't get it.' She gestured towards the weed-strewn brick beds. 'I haven't had time to identify exactly what was planted in here, but given what it was used for there are bound to be some poisonous plants in here.'

Hands on hips, she surveyed the area. It really was a mess. 'My initial plan was to try and replicate what was originally here, but it might just be easier to start again.'

Setting the ladder down flat on the ground, Will crouched beside the nearest bed and examined one of the plants there. Pulling back the overgrown leaves, he showed her the green unripe fruit hanging beneath them. At first glance they looked to be small tomatoes, but when she bent for a closer look, she saw a couple of them were starting to turn black at the edges. 'Nightshade,' he said. 'Definitely not something you want getting into the wrong hands.' Releasing the branch, he brushed the palms of his gloves on his jeans and stood up. 'As fascinating as it might be to recreate what's here, I'd err on the side of caution if you're going to make this one of the public spaces. There are plenty of things you can plant with traditional medicinal and health properties without risking a lawsuit.'

It was reassuring to hear they were thinking along the same lines. 'If we add lots of aromatics and herbs we can make it into a proper, sensory experience whilst keeping it safe.'

'Exactly.' He tilted his head, brow creased in thought. 'What's outside opposite the entrance? I wasn't paying attention.' He turned to face towards the door she'd closed behind them.

Iggy shrugged. 'Nothing much. There's another path, which leads back towards the castle kitchens and a large patch of grass that no one has ever done anything with. Why, what are you thinking?'

'Talking about making this child-friendly made me wonder about creating something interactive for them. A safe place where they can get their hands dirty, do a bit of planting even. I didn't have a clue about gardening until my neighbour showed an interest in me. She started my love of everything green, and I just thought it would be something nice to do for other kids.'

The way his voice warmed as he mentioned his neighbour told her this was something very close to his heart – it was also a really lovely idea. 'We could create a couple of different areas, one for flowers and the other for vegetables. Maybe even get the village school involved.' Her mind started racing a mile a minute.

'Perhaps we could find somewhere for the school to have their own space away from the general public areas, something they could use long-term. We've got more than enough land for it.'

She'd have to consult Arthur, of course, but from their own time at the village school – before they'd boarded from aged eleven – she recalled the only outside space had been the concrete yard in front of the school building. 'They don't have any green areas to speak of. I don't know why it's never occurred to us before.'

'It'd be a fantastic legacy for you guys to establish, and a great way to give access to the community. The biggest thrill I had designing my garden for Chelsea wasn't winning, even though that's brought so many opportunities my way. I specifically designed it together with a London charity that supports inner city gardens and works to provide access to green spaces. After the show finished, we donated the garden to an estate a few miles from where I grew up. Most of the kids there were the same as me and had no experience of gardening. It's maintained by a team of local volunteers and apart from a couple of stupid acts of vandalism when it was first installed, it's proving to be a great success. It's something I'd like to do more of in the future.'

'I'll speak to Arthur and Tristan about it later. Come on, let's check out what's over the wall before you come up with any more ideas. You're supposed to be helping me streamline this project, not giving me more to do.' She smiled over her shoulder at him to show she was joking.

Will hefted the ladder up once more and followed her along the stone path towards the rear of the garden. 'That'll be my last bright idea, I promise.' He leant the ladder against the wall, then braced the bottom rung with his boot. 'Ladies first.'

Iggy placed her foot on the rung beside his, then stopped. She knew they didn't have time for this, that they should be doing a full tour of the grounds and then poring over the plans. There were too many things to do with not enough hours to do them, and yet something was calling to her from the other side of that wall. *It's waited this long to be rediscovered, a few more days or weeks won't matter.* That was the practical, sensible response, but she hadn't been feeling either practical or sensible since the moment she'd decided to crawl through a non-existent hole in the hedge after the man beside her. 'Just a quick look,' she said, not sure if she was talking to herself or Will, 'And then we must get on with things.'

'Five minutes,' he promised. 'If we don't look then it'll nag away at us and be even more of a distraction.'

'Five minutes,' she agreed and began to climb.

Will's hand curled around her calf, pausing her progress. 'Sit on the wall at the top and wait for me, we'll pull the ladder up between us.'

'Oh, yes of course.' If her cheeks felt warm it was embarrassment from not considering the practicalities of getting down into the garden – and more importantly how they'd get back out again. It had nothing to do with the heat radiating from where he held her. Nothing at all.

It took a couple of awkward minutes, but they managed to haul the ladder up and over the wall and were soon standing on the other side. Weeds had forced their way through the cracks in the stones lining the length of the long, narrow area, the dandelion heads a mixture of golden-yellow flowers and wispy seed heads waiting for a gust of wind to carry them away to propagate yet more of the stubborn trouble-makers. A wide stone channel ran the length of the wall, perhaps the remains of an old flowerbed, but it was so choked with ivy it was impossible to see anything through the thick carpet of green. A bronze sundial, weathered to a pale green after years of exposure to the elements, stood in what she judged to be the centre of the garden.

What looked to be the remains of a tree filled the far end of the rectangle, its entire mass covered in ivy to the point that tis species was impossible to distinguish. Curious, Igraine went for a closer look, taking care not to trip where some of the flagstones had

91

cracked and come loose. As she neared, she realised the base was too wide to be part of the trunk. Tugging at the ivy, she uncovered what looked to be a stone bench shaped to encircle the tree.

'What have you found?' Will knelt beside her, his strong hands helping to rip the stubborn ivy free in a matter of moments. 'This is beautifully made.'

Iggy brushed her hand over the cool stone, her fingers tracing the carved edge of the bench. She could imagine one of her ancestors sitting out here, relaxing with a book under the shady branches of the tree. 'What a peaceful little spot this must've been back in the day.' Will only grunted in response, his busy hands tugging and pulling at the ivy stretching away from the base of the bench.

She watched him for a few moments, assuming he was just caught up in the act of removing the ivy. It was one of those tasks she found hard to stop once she started as there was something so satisfying about freeing spaces that had been smothered by its spreading tendrils. It was why she'd returned to the fountain this morning; the rip and pull was a great way to work off the frustration and anger – and, she could admit to herself now, the disappointment when she'd thought Will had been using his visit to the castle as nothing more than a means to escape some domestic drama or other. 'I thought we were just taking a quick look,' she said, her tone teasing.

'There's something here.' Will lifted his head briefly, before turning back to his task. 'I think it's a dog.'

Her brain went into full panic mode at the idea one of their beloved pets had somehow found its way into the garden. Scrambling down beside him, she yanked at the ivy. 'Oh, God, did it crawl through a hole in the wall?'

'Hey, steady, steady.' Will's hands closed over her wrists, stilling the frantic motion of her fingers. 'It's a carving, a little statue of some kind, not the real thing.' Relief flooded her veins, so hot and stark she had to sit back on the ground to steady herself from the rush of it. He squeezed her wrists again. 'I'm sorry if I freaked you out.'

'No, no, it's fine.' She gave him a shaky smile. 'Stupid really to think one of our animals might have got in here, I don't know why my brain jumped that way.' The next breath she took was steadier, the one after it almost back to normal. 'I'm okay.' She tugged her arms gently to free them from his grip, and he dropped them instantly, the expression on his face telling her he'd forgotten he was still holding them. Not liking the sudden awkwardness between them, she gave him a smile and an encouraging nod towards where they'd been working. 'What type of dog is it, can you tell?'

Returning her smile, he shook his head. 'Not yet, hang on a minute and I'll find out.'

She sat quietly whilst he worked, her eyes transfixed by the ripple and roll of his thick shoulders where the movement of his arms pulled his T-shirt tight across his back. This close to him, the difference in their sizes was emphasised, but even with his cropped hair and that scar on his cheek, there was nothing intimidating about him. Though they barely knew each other, she had no qualms about being alone with him, hadn't even paused for a second before climbing down into this garden without telling anyone where they were going. Her eyes flicked back to where the ladder rested against the wall, before she dismissed it from her thoughts. Will had touched her several times in the past hour, but only out of care and consideration. He'd given no hint his thoughts had strayed into untoward territories, which was more than could be said for the way she was admiring his physique.

Feeling her ponytail drooping once more against her neck, Iggy adjusted it with a silent sigh. Of course, he wasn't ogling her. He had shapely blondes like the one who'd been pouting from the inside cover of the newspaper this morning throwing themselves at him. Even if he and Melody hadn't been dating as he claimed, she was still the kind of woman men fancied. They didn't lust after women like her with too-big bottoms thanks to years in the saddle, and thread veins on their cheeks from too much time spent out in the sun and the wind. No, she had no need to worry about her virtue around Will Talbot, he was only interested in her professionally. And if that gave her a tiny pang of regret, well, too damn bad. Time to stop daydreaming and get back to the matter in hand. 'How are you getting on?'

'Almost there.' Will brushed a last few stray bits of greenery aside, then swivelled on his heels so she could see past him.

'Oh, it's beautiful.' Scrambling onto her knees beside him, Iggy touched a tentative finger to the floppy ear of the little statue of a sleek miniature greyhound, or whippet curled into a sleeping ball, its nose resting on its rear flank.

'I think there's another one here.' Will pointed to where the end of a carved tail could be seen poking from the ivy he hadn't yet cleared.

'I wonder why they're here?' Iggy couldn't resist stroking the sleeping dog, marvelling at how the sculptor had managed to render a shape and feel her hand recognised from soothing Nimrod or Bella, the family's current pair of greyhounds. 'She's so lifelike, I keep expecting her to sit up.'

Will touched a brief finger to the top of the dog's neck then began to clear the ivy from the second statue. He worked more slowly this time, his big hands gentle and careful as they untangled the knots of vines to unveil a matched partner to the sleeping pup, this one sitting on its haunches, head raised at an alert angle, as though guarding something precious. At first she assumed he was protecting his sleeping mate, but then a glimpse of grey stone behind the pair caught her eye. 'There's something behind them.'

Leaning forward, she pulled more ivy free until the tips of her fingers grazed over an indent in the stone. 'I think it's a carving of some kind ...' A handful of ivy came free all at once, the loss of resistance against which she'd been pulling almost tumbling her back onto her bottom. Will grabbed her shoulder to steady her, his fingers tightening to an almost painful grip as the two of them stared at what she'd revealed.

'Oh.' It was all she could manage before a stinging rush of emotion burned the breath from her lungs. Behind the dogs stood a simple oval marker, the shape clearly that of a gravestone even had it not been etched with heartbreaking lines of text that looked as fresh as if they'd been carved yesterday.

Here lieth Ector and Kay Ludworth
Born and died Dec 14 1893
Thy hearts did not need to beat to steal all love from ours.

Iggy wasn't aware of the tears streaming down her cheeks until Will removed one of his gloves to pull a handkerchief from his pocket and hand it to her. She pressed the neatly folded square to her face. The warm, woodsy hint of his masculine aftershave had impregnated the material, and she breathed in deeply to settle herself as she mopped at the tears. 'Sorry, I don't know where that came from,' she said once she knew she could speak in a steady voice.

'It's heartbreaking.' His gruff response was enough to let her know how deeply affected he was by what they'd discovered. Wanting to offer him the same comfort she needed herself, Iggy grasped his un-gloved hand in her own. He squeezed her fingers in a brief, hard gesture before slackening his hold so their palms rested easy together. They stayed that way for a few minutes, holding a silent vigil to these babies who though forgotten by the family along the way, had never been alone with their carved companions to protect them.

With one last stroke of the sleeping dog statue's head, Iggy untangled her other hand from Will's and pushed to her feet. Now they'd found the grave, she was reluctant to leave it half-uncovered as it was, but she simply didn't have the time to give the garden the justice it deserved.

As though he recognised the conflict in her mind, Will placed a gentle hand on her back and steered her towards the ladder.

'Once you've got everything else sorted, you can come back and restore things here. You know they're here now, and doing what you can to safeguard your family's future means they'll be able to rest here undisturbed forever.' He was right, but placing her foot on the first rung of the ladder and forcing herself to climb back over the wall was still one of the hardest things she'd had to do in a long time.

Needing something to distract her from the aching sadness threatening to engulf her, Iggy persuaded Will to leave the ladder secured in the apothecary's garden and led him along the path towards the castle which led to the servants' quarters. Now she knew of the twins' existence, she was even more drawn to his idea for turning the open ground on either side of the path into a children's learning and activity space. Having this part of the grounds filled with the sounds of laughter and play would be a fitting tribute for those two little souls who'd never had a chance to shine. Her eyes drifted towards the woods farther over on the right and she wondered whether she could find a suitable space there to create a bit of a playground. Something with a rustic feel that would blend in rather than obtrusive metal climbing frames. *Put it on the list.*

As they approached the castle, she pointed out features and explaining the general internal layout in more detail. 'This wing contains the baronet's apartments,' she said as they rounded the end of the castle. 'That's the dining room where we had breakfast this morning, and you can see here the kitchen and the rest of the servants' quarters are positioned directly behind it.' Spotting Betsy, the family cook, bustling around inside, Iggy tapped on the window and gave her a wave which was returned along with a blown kiss.

'You have a fantastic relationship with the staff,' Will observed as he too gave the cook a quick wave. 'I was really surprised this morning when you were teasing Arthur and that butler guy joined in. He looked like a real costume drama throwback in his uniform, and I'm not shy to admit it was a bit intimidating when he swept in, like he might tell me off for using the wrong knife or something.'

Iggy almost laughed, but stopped herself at the last minute. She'd grown up with the protocols and etiquette of the castle and just took everything as part and parcel of normal life – well, what was normal to them, anyway. It'd been a shock to the system when she and her brothers had gone to boarding school and had to learn to fend for themselves. 'You'll probably think me terribly spoilt, but when I first went away to school, I didn't know how to make a bed. It was just one of those things that had always been done for us, and I don't think it even occurred to our father that we might need to know how to do stuff like that.'

'What about your mum?'

Iggy bristled, the way she always did the moment the subject of Helena arose. 'She left when we were tiny, so it was only ever the three of us and Dad. And Uncle Lancelot and Aunt Morgana, of course.' she amended, quickly. 'She already lived here, but Lancelot moved back home after our mother ran off with the man who became husband number two.' She clamped her mouth shut before spilling any more of her family's dirty laundry. Damn him, he was far too easy to talk to.

'Must've been hard for you to grow up without her. I was fourteen when my mum took off. I was old enough to understand why, but it still didn't make it any easier. I can't imagine what it must've been like for you to have her there one day and gone the next.'

'I was too young to remember her.' It was a lie she told herself, a defence mechanism to protect not only her own, but her father's feelings. As she'd grown older, she'd come to understand the crippling guilt haunting him over the failure of his marriage, and she'd so wanted to reassure him that she'd not needed Helena to feel complete.

But there were times, even now, when she could remember

the feel of gentle hands running a brush through her hair, of the tickle of cashmere against her cheek as a smiling blonde woman gathered her onto her lap for a kiss, of the lingering scent of Chanel No. 5 perfuming the dark air of her bedroom after being told to 'sleep tight'. Or perhaps she'd made the whole thing up, a collection of false memories invented by a sad, lonely little girl because the Helena she knew was nothing like the gentle woman from those tender moments.

Feeling Will's eyes upon her, Iggy forced her chin up and gave him a bright smile. 'Let's finish our walk around the castle and then I'll get you the plans for the gardens. We can go out again tomorrow once you've had a chance to study them.' And she could put some distance between them, get things back on a more professional footing and regain her equilibrium. Her eyes strayed towards the rangy stone buildings compromising the stable block. Yes. She'd get Will settled somewhere and take herself off for a ride.

Chapter 9

The sneaking suspicion that Igraine was trying to get rid of him had only grown during the rest of their whistle-stop circuit of the castle. She'd practically dragged him past the enormous round tower abutting the main structure. When he'd wanted to explore it, she'd waved him off without breaking stride, saying there was nothing to see as it was empty inside. He might have thought about taking offence, or at least wondered what he'd said to put his foot in it and make her eager to abandon him, but then he caught his first glimpse of the glass conservatory running along the rear of the castle and he had no room for anything else in his brain other than a desperate need to explore.

Seeing his eyes light up, Igraine had let him into the conservatory via one of several sets of patio-style double doors and left him to go and fetch the plans. From the first blast of heated air hitting his face, Will knew this was going to be his favourite place in the castle. Heavy scents hung in the air – the rich loamy tang of moist soil, the exotic perfume of tropical flowers, even a sweet hint of banana he could almost taste on the back of his tongue. Intrigued, he began to explore, following the sweetness until he found not the shaggy cascading leaves of a banana tree, but a vine clambering along the back wall, its rich dark leaves interspersed with some of the biggest blooms he'd even seen.

Stretching on tiptoe, he pressed his nose close to the nearest yellow-gold flower and drew in a deep breath. Vanilla and banana filled his senses, and he needed to close his eyes to try and absorb the complexity of the scent without the visual distraction of the huge flower.

'It's a cup of gold vine.' Igraine's soft voice at this elbow made him jump, and he glanced down at her with a startled grin.

'I've never seen anything like it.' Reaching up, Will touched a wondering finger to the shiny leaves.

'It's also a beast. If we don't keep it in tight check it'd take over the place. Thankfully, some of the former gardeners put together a guide to everything planted in here. It's been an invaluable guide, though I've added a few updates of my own as techniques have modernised.' She gazed around the room, hands on her hips. 'Eventually, I'd like to install an automatic watering system, but for now we do it all by hand.'

The list of things that needed doing seemed never-ending, no wonder she'd been feeling a bit overwhelmed trying to manage everything on her own. 'Will the new funds stretch to employing some replacement gardening staff?' As soon as he'd asked it, he wondered if she'd think he was being intrusive. 'Sorry, that's none of my business, is it?'

Thankfully, the smile she turned on him was friendly enough. 'It's fine. I was the one who brought up our finances in the first place. And to answer your question, I'd eventually like to set up a small, permanent team here.'

Her face fell, and he could've kicked himself for raising something else on what must be a never-ending to-do list. He quickly pointed to the big roll of documents under her arm. 'Those must be for me.'

She handed them over. 'Are you sure you don't need me to stay and go through them with you?'

Will wasn't sure it was possible for anyone to sound less enthusiastic than she did in that moment. Glancing over her, he noted she'd swapped her jeans for a pair of fitted navy jodhpurs and her work boots for shiny black riding boots. The message was clear, she wanted to get out of there. 'I'll be fine. Besides, I'm not used to a partner when I'm putting ideas together.'

'Okay. If you have any questions, we can go over them after dinner.' She pointed to a set of internal doors. 'The library is just through there if you want some space to spread yourself out a bit. Lucie's taken over the mezzanine floor, but I'm sure she won't mind you using the ground floor.'

'Cheers.' She was still hovering, as though in two minds as to whether she should leave him or not. 'Go away, Igraine.'

Her startled laugh chased the pensive look from her face and her step was light as she strode for one of the patio doors. He watched her go, unable to tear his eyes from her sleek silhouette. He'd never been on a horse in his life – hadn't come close enough to one to touch it. Other than on the television, the only ones he could recall seeing in the flesh was the occasional police horse in central London, and those were definitely not the type you petted – even had he been so inclined.

She'd probably grown up with it, it was the kind of thing posh people did, wasn't it? He watched until she disappeared through the arch in the stable block, then turned away. If riding a horse was what floated her boat, so to speak, then good on her. Will was quite content keeping his feet firmly on the ground.

Following the direction Igraine had given him, Will pushed open the door to the library and called out a greeting. 'Hello? Lucie?'

The redhead appeared at the edge of the wooden railing lining a balcony area at the opposite end of the room. 'Hello, Will! What can I do for you?'

Showing her the roll of drawings, he replied. 'Igraine suggested I could spread myself out down here to go through these garden plans. Is that all right with you?'

The long plait she'd secured her hair with swung as she nodded her head. 'Of course, help yourself. Is there anything I can do to help?'

Will bent to put the drawings down. 'I should be fine, thanks.'

She nodded. 'Well, just shout out if you need anything. I'm boring myself to death organising the accounting ledgers up here, so I'm desperate for a distraction.' Her bright smile lit her whole face, making it clear to Will why Arthur had fallen for this lovely woman.

'Actually, I could do with a hand finding my way back to the main stairs, if you don't mind? I need to get my books and my laptop.' He knew from the view behind them of the stable blocks that his bedroom was somewhere above them, but that was about it. Another day he might like to wander the halls and corridors of the castle, getting happily lost as he explored, but he was itching to crack on with the plans.

'Of course! It's a bit of a maze until you get used to it.'

*

Ten minutes later, he was sprawled on his front on a rich Turkish-style carpet so enormous he didn't dare let his mind think about what it might be worth. Several sets of the garden plans were strewn around him, held flat at the corners with pens, rubbers and other random bits of stationery he'd dug out of the old leather washbag he used as a pencil case. It'd been part of a gift one Christmas from a girlfriend, the grooming products it'd once held long used and discarded, and was big enough to hold everything he needed to carry around with him.

Using the copy plan Igraine had scribbled her own notes on as a reference for the current layout, he traced the history of the development of the gardens back to their origins. It was fascinating to watch what had originally been a defensive outpost slowly transform from functional to decorative. How buildings and features had come and gone, the changes influenced by both necessity and fashion. From the looks of it, there'd once been a dairy in the same vicinity as the walled apothecary's garden, but there was nothing but grass scrubland where it had once stood, as his own eyes could testify.

There was still a huge amount of parkland beyond the existing formal gardens and it was there he kept finding his attention drawn to. Whether she recognised it or not, Igraine had a pretty good handle on the existing gardens as well as the walks planned for the woods. If she wanted his input, he'd be happy to help her sourcing the right contractors to assist her, but he didn't think she needed much else from him other than to act as a sounding board.

He'd checked his laptop and Anna had come up trumps already, sending through several detailed spreadsheets with suggestions for landscapers, stonemasons and general builders within reasonable travelling distance of the castle. He and Igraine could go through them and start the ball rolling. Once they had a few more bodies on deck it wouldn't take long for real improvements to begin to show.

As he went through each stage of development of the garden's history, he noted the significant changes each designer had brought to bear, the signature they'd left as generation after generation tried to stamp their unique imprint on this wild landscape. The need to do the same, to leave a legacy of his own tugged at him. It'd have to complement what was already here, of course, and yet offer a completely different experience too. Mind buzzing, he dug out a soft pencil from his bag and began to sketch.

He barely looked up when Lucie came down to ask if he was taking a break for lunch, he just gave her a brief nod and then a smile of thanks when she returned about half an hour later with a plate laden with thick cut sandwiches, some fruit and a bottle of water. His pencil moved across sheet after sheet in his notebook, scribbling shapes, patterns and designs as he tried to translate what was in his head into something comprehendible. An hour later, he'd abandoned the empty plate and everything else strewn across the carpet and was marching out through the conservatory.

As he retraced his steps past the walled garden, along the path to the edge of the main driveway and then down past the hedges marking the edge of the formal gardens, his heart beat faster. What if the plans had been wrong? What if he'd misinterpreted the topography based on a handful of old drawings? Anxiety pushed his feet faster until he was first jogging and then flat out running. *It had to work. It just had to …*

He didn't pause until reaching the screen of tall poplar trees which had been planted to act as a demarcation line between the gardens and the parkland. Dragging in deep gulps of air to feed his aching lungs, Will slipped between the closely planted trunks and stopped dead. The land before him sloped away about ten feet from the edge of the trees so he was standing on a natural shelf looking down.

The gradient of the hill taking him down to the lower level wasn't too steep and with a bit of work could be adapted to what he had in mind. Thick grass swished around his ankles as he waded through it down the slope to the flat plain expanding out before him. It was better than he'd hoped, and he could already imagine bits and pieces of his rough sketches sitting within this landscape, transforming it into something unique and beautiful. Form and function; fantasy and practicality; the cornerstones of each and every one of his designs could be applied to this space. Excited, he counted his paces, stopping now and then to take photos on his phone and scribble rough measurements down in his notebook. He'd have to come back with some proper surveying kit and map it accurately, but this would do for now to give him a rough estimate of the area he was working to. The most important thing was he could see *how* it could work. All he had to do was convince the others.

*

Though he was itching to keep working on his fledgling plan, Will had found a note slipped under his bedroom door from Tristan informing him everyone would be gathering in the family room at six forty-five, for dinner at seven. Standing at the foot of the staircase, hair still wet from his shower and dressed in a clean pair of chinos and a navy polo-shirt, Will found his progress halted by an enthusiastic greeting from the castle's collection of motley hounds. A lively Jack Russell pushed its way to the front of the pack, scrabbling at the front of his trousers in a demand for attention. Not wanting paw prints all over himself, Will bent down and scooped up the little terrier, laughing as it licked his cheek before settling contentedly in the crook of his arm for a stroke.

'I see you fell for Murphy's signature move.' Craning his neck back at the sound of Igraine's voice from behind and above him, Will drank in the sight of her descending the steps towards him. Her hair had been released from its ponytail to cascade around her shoulders and she'd changed into a pair of cherry-red trousers and a blue-and-white striped top with a wide neck which showed off the top of her collarbones. Sinking onto the step beside him, she lifted the Jack Russell from his lap to nuzzle at the ecstatic pup before handing him back. 'Now you've picked him up once, he'll never leave you alone.'

Thinking he would quite fancy a nuzzle of his own, Will set the terrier down before standing and offering Igraine his hand. She took it with a smile, but any idea he might have had of keeping hold of her arm and providing a gallant escort were scuppered by Murphy. Apparently part kangaroo, the dog was bouncing up and down in front of Will, refusing to be ignored.

'Told you,' Igraine said with a grin as she slid her fingers from his, leaving Will no choice but to scoop up the annoying terrier once more. 'Cheers, mate,' he muttered into the dog's ear before succumbing to imploring licks, settling Murphy into the crook of his arm and following Igraine towards the door of the family room.

A warm wave of greetings met their arrival, including a part-smirk, part-consolatory grin from Tristan. 'Suckered by an expert, I see,' he said, reaching to scratch the unrepentant Jack Russell behind the ear.

'Your sister already pointed out the error of my ways, shame it was about thirty seconds too late to be of any use.' He glanced around at the rest of the family arrayed around the room, noting an elegant, if stern-looking, older woman who though her brown curls had long since faded to silver, bore the same spark of strength in her hazel eyes as he'd noticed in Igraine's.

Tristan followed his gaze. 'Ah, you didn't get a chance to meet our Aunt Morgana last night, did you?'

He led Will over to the high-backed armchair set opposite the fireplace and at a right-angle to the two enormous matching leather sofas. Dressed in a black, crepe dress with floaty sleeves gathered tight at the wrists with a single large gold button, her silver hair swept into a neat coil at the nape of her neck, Morgana had the poise and posture of a woman half her age. A small slender glass filled with a straw-pale drink sat on the occasional table at her elbow. Tristan leant down to press a kiss against a cheek showing remarkably few lines. 'Aunt Morgana, you are looking gorgeous as always. May I introduce you to Will Talbot?'

The gaze she swept over him left Will under no doubt he'd been weighed, measured and found a little wanting. 'You're here to help Igraine, is that correct?'

'Yes …' What exactly did one call the matriarch of a titled family? He had no idea of the correct protocols. Other than the butler, he'd not heard anyone else give Arthur his honorific of Sir and Arthur had certainly not indicated he expected Will to use it. Did any of the others have titles? Was Igraine a Lady, or Tristan a Lord? Completely flummoxed, Will let the silence hang, hoping like hell someone would fill in the gap for him.

Those fierce hazel eyes so like her great-niece's bored into him for a long moment before the corner of her lips twitched. 'You may call me Morgana.'

Bowing his head to acknowledge what felt like a privilege reserved for family, Will went to offer his hand only to remember it was still filled with Murphy's warm, compact body. Trying to pretend he hadn't offered her a dog, Will quickly withdrew his arm and hoped like hell he wasn't blushing. 'It's a pleasure to meet you, and an honour to be welcomed into your family's home.'

The merest arch to her brow was the only acknowledgement of his near cock-up, and when she reached for her glass of sherry, Will assumed their brief audience was over and started to move away.

'I remember your garden from Chelsea.'

Stopping in his tracks, Will turned back to Morgana as he considered how to respond. Both her tone and the statement had been neutral, and he knew from experience that not everyone had warmed to his mix of modern urban touches with more traditional planting. He'd been dismissed by some as gimmicky, lambasted by others for bringing the RHS into disrepute by adding features such as skate-boarding rails, graffiti and replicas of the little brick walls he and his mates had hung around on when he'd been a bored teenager. Deciding from the directness of her stare that she'd favour an honest conversation, he took a couple of steps closer to her chair. 'It wasn't to everyone's taste, what did you think?'

That little twitch of her mouth returned. 'I wasn't sure at first, but once I heard your interview and you explained the inspiration behind it, I thought it was a brave and beautiful choice by the committee to award you the prize. Growing up, I was taught to appreciate the absolute privilege I had of so much green space to roam around and play in. I'm so pleased Arthur is giving new generations of children the chance to enjoy it too.' She placed a hand to the back of her neck. 'You're giving me a crick, dear, do sit.'

With no obvious chair to draw up, Will settled for sitting on the floor at her feet. Crossing his legs, he settled the little dog into the hollow created between his thighs and stroked his wiry fur. 'Was it very different here when you were a child?'

Morgana took another sip of sherry. 'It was a lot busier – more staff than we have now, and several of them had families who lived on the estate so between them and my brothers, I had lots of playmates. We didn't suffer the same privations as children in the towns and cities did during and after the war as the estate was self-sustaining, so it really was an idyllic existence for those first few years.

'I was only a baby during the war, but Agravaine – my elder brother – used to tell me stories of the soldiers who billeted here. Father stayed here to maintain the estate, but his twin brothers both enlisted in the Sherwood Foresters and saw action. When their unit was evacuated through Dunkirk, Father offered the regiment the estate as somewhere they could use for rest and recuperation breaks. There are some photographs in the archives from those days, including some of Agravaine being shown how to do drill exercises.' The smile on her face faded. 'The only memory I have of my uncles is from a photograph of the two of them holding me at my christening. The regiment was sent back overseas, and they perished in action in Italy in 1944 just a few weeks before my first birthday.'

A hard lump formed in Will's throat, not just from the emotion in Morgana's voice but because it sounded like this was the second set of twins the family had lost. First, the pair recorded on the little memorial he and Igraine had uncovered earlier, and later Morgana's uncles. 'I'm sorry you didn't have the chance to know them.'

Her smile deepened, and some of the sadness faded from her eyes. 'Oh, you are sweet to say so. And you really must forgive me for raising such a maudlin topic.'

Will shook his head. 'Not at all. When you're surrounded every day by so much history I imagine the past must feel a lot closer than for people like me who've lost their connections.' His grandfather had moved to London for work, and his grandmother, like his father, had been an only child. Although he knew there were Talbots down in the west country, he had no links to any of them. He'd got the odd birthday card from an aunt on his mum's side when he was younger, but those had tapered off as he'd grown up and he'd not pushed to maintain the link. It'd all felt too awkward and messy given the estrangement from his mum.

That lack of roots had never been an issue for him. He couldn't say he'd really even thought about it much at all until meeting a family like the Ludworths who were so entrenched in and influenced by everything their forebears had done. Whilst he could imagine there were some advantages from knowing where you've come from, there must be an equal – or likely heavier – burden of expectation and responsibility. If Will's dad had harboured any particular ambitions for his son, he'd never shared them. Thinking about it, he must've been so relieved when Will's passion for gardening had been sparked because prior to that he'd been on a collision course with trouble.

'I suppose there are advantages and disadvantages to both.' Morgana echoed his thoughts. 'But I wouldn't change my lot in life.' Her gaze roamed the room, softening as it touched on where Arthur, Tristan and Igraine were chatting next to the drinks' cabinet. 'For all the sorrows that inevitably come when you've lived to my age, I'm blessed that the joys have outweighed them tenfold.'

Tristan drifted over to join them, offering Will one of the two cold bottles of beer threaded through the fingers of one hand. Accepting it with a nod of thanks, Will was content to sit quietly as he watched the teasing interaction between Tristan and his aunt. There was a rhythm to it, a familiarity that said to Will the younger man was being deliberately outrageous precisely because he wanted to provoke the stern responses Morgana clipped out.

The twinkle in her eyes said she knew exactly what her nephew was doing and was happy to play her part. Tristan was clearly a favourite and the source of many of those joys she'd spoken about. As he sipped his beer, Will sent a silent toast to the woman and hoped that when he reached a similar age, he might be able to say he'd enjoyed the same balance in his own life.

Chapter 10

The next few days passed in a blur of phone calls, spreadsheets and tours of the gardens as Iggy worked her way through the list of specialist contractors Will's magician of an assistant had put together. When he'd handed her the list and told her to choose whichever of the contractors she thought best for each task, it had rankled. There'd been no discussion between them before he'd instructed his assistant and Iggy had half-wished she'd been prepared enough to counter with a list of her own.

To make matters worse, the lists were detailed and included several companies she'd already heard good things about through local connections. She couldn't say why it had irritated her other than the high-handed way Will had already marked up his preferred choices, as though she was incapable of making such decisions for herself.

Given Will's desire to keep his profile as low as possible in the hopes the tabloids would soon lose interest in him, they'd at least agreed that Iggy would carry out the discussions and interviews on her own. Quotations were starting to come through, and with a copy of his company's job pricing spreadsheet Will had told her to use – *told her,* not asked her, the arrogant swine – she was feeling much more in control of everything other than her temper.

She knew it was ridiculous to be annoyed when she was the one who'd asked Will for his help in the first place, she just hadn't known how hard it would be to let him do it. It was just the way he assumed he knew best – even if he probably did – that grated upon her. She wasn't one of his employees to be ordered around, he was supposed to be working for her!

If anyone had asked her before she'd started the project, Iggy would've scoffed about needing any more confidence than she already had, but the weight of expectation had proven surprisingly heavy. As much as she hated his domineering attitude, she also desperately craved Will's approval for her decisions. When he gave her that smile – the lopsided one that tugged at the scar across his cheek – to show his approval, her insides melted like ice cream on a summer's day.

Other than the hour they spent over breakfast reviewing her plans for the day, which often felt like he was a teacher checking over her homework, and a debrief after dinner where they discussed the pros and cons of the job bids coming in, Will had proven frustratingly elusive. When she didn't want his opinion, there he was shoving it under her nose, but when she did need to ask him something, he was off around the grounds somewhere, or hiding away in his bedroom.

She knew he was working on something but was refusing to say what until he had it all worked out. She'd spotted him a time or two in the distance, but always in a different part of the grounds so she'd been unable to pinpoint what had captured his imagination. Never one to enjoy being left in the dark, Iggy had begun plotting to steal his ever-present notebook away.

Just thinking about it sent her eyes straying across the room to where Will was currently curled in the corner of one of the big Chesterfield sofas, pencil flying as he sketched away at something. Why wouldn't he talk to her about it, already? It didn't make sense to her for him to invest so much time in a plan she – or the others – might not approve of. Iggy gave herself a mental pinch at that thought. She couldn't let her impatience cloud her judgement, especially where Will was concerned. This tendency to overreact to him was beyond disconcerting when she'd always prided herself on her self-control.

The family had taken to postponing tea and coffee straight after dinner, opting instead to gather or scatter after the meal as desired before meeting up around nine-thirty to round off the day together. Some evenings saw everyone migrating straight to the family room. Tonight, everyone else had something to do, and Iggy had expected to have the place to herself. When she'd walked in to find Will already ensconced on one of the sofas, she'd had little option other than to take up position on the one opposite and try to focus on the handful of quotations in front of her.

Who'd known the sound of a pencil could be so loud? Every time she tried to concentrate on her own work, that scrit-scrit-scrit of graphite on paper hypnotised her until the figures on the quotes swam before her eyes and all she could think about was finding out what Will was working on. What if she hated it? Or worse, what if she loved it and everyone else in the family hated it?

It had been her idea to get Will involved with the restorations, but what if his ideas were a step too far? Tristan might be on board with a modern installation, but Arthur could be a bit of a stick in the mud when it came to these things. She couldn't blame him. Being the Baronet wasn't just a title, it was a legacy of mistakes and triumphs, and she knew he desperately wanted to end up on the right side of the ledger when his current decisions were looked back upon by future generations. He'd been brilliant so far in giving her and Tristan free rein to do what they thought would help set right the family fortunes, but if she made a decision which fundamentally altered the landscape, it would be judged against Arthur's name, not hers, because he had the title thanks to his correct combination of chromosomes.

Mrs W entered the family room at that moment, her arms laden with an enormous tea tray. Grateful for the distraction,

Iggy was ready to jump up to assist, but a quelling look from their housekeeper kept her glued to the butter-soft leather of the sofa. She watched as Mrs W set down the tray and laid out the tea things just to her liking. A quick circuit of the room followed – a twitch to one of the long velvet curtains, here, the plumping of a squashed cushion there – before she judged the room worthy of her standards with a nod. 'Is there anything else you need before I turn in?'

Iggy shook her head, returning the other woman's warm smile. 'No, that's perfect, thank you. One of us will clear the tray away when we're finished.' She held out a hand to their housekeeper, urging her to come closer. 'Will you be seeing Betsy?' The housekeeper and the cook often shared a pot of tea in Mrs W's parlour before bed.

'Yes. She's got me hooked on a new boxset, so we're about to start the next episode. Did you need me to pass something on to her?'

'Can you just let her know the hedge contractors are starting tomorrow. I'm sure they'll have their own provisions, but if she could fix a flask or two after she's finished with breakfast, I'll drop in and pick them up.'

'Of course, dear. It's going to be a hot one according to the forecast, so we'll get one of the cold boxes made up with some soft drinks as well.' She gave Iggy a mock-stern look. 'Don't let me catch you outside without a hat, either.'

During one particularly scorching summer in 2003, Iggy had spent too long playing outside and ended up with horrible sunburn. 'Come on, Mrs W, I haven't had sunburn since I was ten years old! I peeled for weeks and learnt my lesson.'

'And, I still remember the look on your poor father's face when he carried you in from the garden.'

Iggy frowned. 'I don't remember that.' All she remembered was the terrible itch in her skin and the relentless teasing from her brothers as her arms, shoulders and most of her face had flaked and peeled leaving her skin patchy as a piebald pony.

Mrs W placed a hand on the top of Iggy's hair, smoothing it down in a gesture that had always made Iggy feel safe, warm and loved. She'd been feeling out of sorts ever since she and Will had discovered that heartbreaking little memorial in the secret garden. How her many-times great-grandparents must've loved those poor babies, even without getting the chance to do much more than hold them for a few moments.

It was the kind of love her own mother was apparently incapable of. With Mrs W's touch grounding her, Iggy felt the sadness easing away. A mother's touch could come in many forms – and from many different hands.

'You had the worst case of sunstroke I've ever seen.' Mrs W continued the rhythmic movement over Iggy's hair. Each stroke carried the echo of so many such comforting moments with it. 'Luckily, we got your temperature down, but you were quite poorly for a few hours. Gave us all a dreadful fright.' The gentle hand shifted from her hair to her cheek, tilting Iggy's head until she met the housekeeper's warm gaze. 'So, you'll have to forgive me if I sometimes make a fuss.'

Leaning her cheek into the touch, Iggy counted her blessings. She hadn't had one mother, she'd had four. The one who'd birthed her, and three others in Morgana, Mrs W, and Betsy. Between the three of them they'd kissed every scraped knee, soothed away every nightmare and given her a proper sense of herself as an individual as well as helping her to recognise the unique gift being one of three with Arthur and Tristan truly was. Helena might have carried her, but the other three had shaped her into the woman she was today. Trying not to choke on the thick emotion gathering in her chest, Iggy captured Mrs W's hand and pressed a kiss to the back of it. 'You can always make a fuss. *Always.*'

The look they shared was threatening to get a little teary. Mrs W drew in a deep breath. 'Darling girl, I must get back to Betsy or she'll have started without me. We'll sort out plenty of drinks and snacks for tomorrow.' She glanced over her shoulder to where

Will was still scribbling away in his notebook. 'And you make sure you've got a hat tomorrow as well, young man.'

Will's eyes flicked from the page to the pair of them in a way that told Iggy he'd been aware of the conversation but had been trying to give them privacy. His grey eyes sparkled from beneath his thick, dark brows, a dimple Iggy had never noticed before creasing his unscarred cheek. God, that smile did something to her insides. Made her think things she had no business thinking. If he looked at her like that, Iggy feared she might dissolve on the spot. Thankfully, he was directing all that charm elsewhere. Raising two fingers to his brow, Will gave a small salute. 'Yes, Mrs W.'

The singsong note to his reply made the housekeeper laugh, though Iggy couldn't help but notice a slight flush on the house-keeper's cheek. It seemed no woman was immune to the power of Will Talbot's smile. 'Cheeky boy. Right, I shall wish you both a goodnight. Don't stay up too late working.'

'No, Mrs W,' they chorused together, their eyes meeting in gleeful delight at the unexpected connection of their words and tones matching.

'Terrible, the pair of you.' Shaking her head, a broad smile fixed firmly in place, the housekeeper left the room.

The moment she left, a frisson of tension settled over the room, and Iggy felt the grin on her lips slipping as the warm humour in Will's eyes shifted into something deeper. They'd sat together in this room on plenty of occasions over the past few evenings, both with and without other people around, had sat side-by-side at breakfast only that morning, but she'd never felt truly alone with him until right then.

His gaze dipped from her eyes to her mouth, drawing Iggy's attention to the fact she'd pulled her lower lip between her teeth. Horrified, she stopped at once. Iggy was not the kind of woman who nibbled her lip. That sort of thing was for women who had foolish thoughts on their minds; seductive thoughts; *dangerous* thoughts.

Needing to break the connection, she uncrossed her legs from where they'd been curled up beneath her. 'Cup of tea? I'm having a cup of tea, I think, or maybe a hot chocolate.' Knowing she was babbling, Iggy broke eye contact and made a beeline for the tea tray which Mrs W had thankfully placed on a table behind Will's back negating the need to look at him again. 'Although it's perhaps a bit warm this evening for chocolate, that's more for when I'm in the mood to curl up with something.' *Or someone.*

No. No. She was not going to allow her thoughts to stray in that direction. With much clattering of spoons against china, she set out two cups on their saucers and flipped open the wooden box filled with a selection of different flavoured teas. Her hand hovered over her usual Earl Grey before she hesitated. Perhaps she'd better stay off the caffeine. Something nice and relaxing. Something to calm the jittery feeling welling in her stomach. Settling for camomile, she tore open the envelope, almost ripping the top off the bag in the process. The fact she managed to get more hot water into the cup and not all over the tray was frankly something of a miracle the way her hand was suddenly shaking. She did not fancy Will. She. Did. Not.

The weight of his continued silence sat heavy at her back, and it took a breath of courage before Iggy managed to turn around. 'Well, what are you having?'

He'd twisted on the sofa to face her, one tanned arm stretched along the back cushion. Dark hair sprinkled his forearm, serving a vivid reminder of the differences between them. His dark skin to her light, his short rough hair to her smooth, flowing curls, his hard plains to her softer curves and hollows. That pricking heat was still in his eyes, tempered now with a hint of wariness, as though he too was uncomfortable at the change in atmosphere between them.

Needing to look away – but not ready to acknowledge that need to either of them – she shifted her attention to the notebook balanced on the back of the sofa next to his hand. It was upside down, and she found herself tilting her head to one side for a better look at the shaded lines. When his thick arm shifted to block the view, irritation pricked her, bursting the bubble of tension which had been threatening to envelope them. She turned away, rattling the tea tray once more. 'Well, do you want a drink or not?'

She hadn't meant to sound so snippy, but honestly, the way he'd covered his notebook like a child in school worried someone was trying to copy his homework sent her annoyance with him through the roof. It wasn't like she'd been snooping. Okay, yes, she might have *glanced* at his notes and sketches, but really, he was acting like he was guarding a national secret. Besides, it was his own fault for looking at her like that. If he'd just kept his eyes to himself, she wouldn't have needed to seek distraction elsewhere.

'I'll have a decaf coffee, if there is some, please.' The utter calmness in his tone only served to heighten awareness at her own foolish behaviour. She had to stop blowing hot and cold like this, before he read too much into it.

Forcing herself to move slowly, she fixed his coffee, adding a tiny splash of milk without having to ask. When had she started paying attention to the way he liked his coffee? How did she know that if she offered him the small plate of biscuits resting on the tray he'd choose the plain digestive over the sugary bourbon or the sweet custard cream? Not wanting to analyse it too deeply, she snatched the digestive from the plate and tucked it onto his saucer before turning back with his drink. 'There you go.'

'Thanks.' He held her gaze for a long moment before drawing back the cup and saucer and gesturing with his free hand towards his notepad which was now resting face down on the seat next to him. 'Sorry, I didn't mean to be precious, I just want to get it exactly right in my head before I show it to you.'

She shrugged, knowing the action was too exaggerated, that it negated her next words before they'd left her lips. 'It's fine, no big deal.'

'Give me another twenty-four hours. I have a handful of final details to check and then I'll be ready.'

'Sure.' *Calm, steady, remember?* 'Sure,' she repeated, this time with a proper smile. Wanting to get things back to normal between them, back to before this uncomfortable awareness of the sheer masculinity of him had settled over her, she turned the conversation to a safe topic. 'The hedge contractor starts tomorrow.'

'So I heard. Who did you go with in the end?'

'Davis and Son.' She'd whittled the choice down to a medium-sized company with several branches across the region, and a local father and son firm. Her head had said go with the larger firm until Davy and Simon Davis had arrived at the castle to carry out a visual survey of the works. The rep from the larger contractor had been polite and efficient, but he hadn't gelled with her. Not in the same way Davy Davis had. From his firm but not too firm handshake as he'd climbed from his truck, to the way he'd not been afraid to stray from the original brief with suggestions of his own as they'd walked the length and breadth of the gardens, Iggy had been impressed with Davy from start to finish.

He'd understood the significance of the gardens, asked pertinent questions about the history of the castle and just given her the sense he would treat the plants with a sympathetic touch. If she'd been asked to put it into words, she would've struggled to articulate it beyond that he felt like a gardener to her. In the same way that Will did, underneath that veneer of brash confidence and the sprinkle of celebrity he brought with him.

When the quotation from Davis and Son had arrived with details of how the vast majority of the cut material they removed would be recycled and sold to a nursery as mulching bark with 40 per cent of the sale coming back to Iggy, she knew they were the right choice. Innovative, but conscientious.

Will nodded, and just like that she felt her temper spike once more. As the person paying the bills, she didn't need his approval.

Oblivious to her mood, he continued chatting. 'Where are they starting?'

It was on the tip of her tongue to snap that it wasn't any of his business, before she realised how utterly foolish she was being. Yes, there were times when Will rode a little roughshod over things, but this wasn't one of them. She was the one who'd started this conversation with him, so of course he would ask her questions about it. *Get a bloody grip, Iggy, drink your damn camomile and stop looking for offence where there's no given.*

Forcing herself to relax, Iggy propped her hip against the edge of the sofa. Sipping her tea, she conjured the list of jobs she'd agreed with the Davises in her mind. 'We decided the maze is the first priority. I can't even get in there at the moment to see what needs doing in the central courtyard, and if the central fountain needs repairing – which I'm assuming it does – then it makes sense to combine that with the other stonemason and plumbing jobs.'

'Agreed. The pathways will probably need re-laying as well.'.

Her shoulders stiffened. 'Yes, it's on my groundworks pricing sheet already.' *Snippy, snippy, Iggy.* Gulping another mouthful of her tea, she prayed for its calming properties to kick in sooner rather than later and ploughed on. 'They're going to concentrate on the box hedging after the maze so I can get the planting team in to fill the central beds, and then they'll work on the larger bushes and hedges. Davy's come up with a nice suggestion to shape that big avenue running from the path to the Lady's garden. A bit of texture and shaping will make it more visually appealing.'

The door behind them burst open, making Iggy swivel towards it as a tumbling wave of fur, wagging tails and happy tongues flooded into the room. Quick as a flash, Iggy dumped her teacup on the sideboard and ran to rescue her pile of paperwork from where she'd set it on the floor beside her seat. From the corner of her eye she spotted Will flipping closed his notebook moments before Murphy took a flying leap onto the sofa, turning in happy circles before the little Jack Russell curled up against his new best friend's thigh.

On the heels of the dogs came Arthur and Lucie, eyes shining, mouths stretched wide in matching smiles of utter contentment. Her brother had his arm around his girlfriend's waist, holding her against his hip as though worried she might slip away from him. The hand she had plastered on his chest, fingers spread over his heart said there was no chance she was going anywhere. It was her left hand, Iggy noticed, and something shiny and sparkly winked from a certain significant finger on that hand. Something shiny and sparkly that definitely hadn't been there an hour previously when they'd been sitting around the dinner table.

Iggy glanced from the ring to Lucie's ecstatic smile and back again. Feeling her lips stretching into a matching grin, Iggy raised her eyebrows. Lucie nodded in return, her smile turning impossibly brighter.

'Oh, I thought everyone would be here by now.' Arthur glanced around the room as though Tristan or Uncle Lancelot might pop up from behind one of the sofas.

'Never mind the rest of them,' Iggy crowed, hurrying over to throw her arms around the couple. 'Congratulations! Oh my God, this is amazing news.' Drawing back, she grinned up at her brother. 'You finally did something right, then?'

'You didn't think I was going to let her go again, did you?' Arthur's arm closed even more firmly around Lucie's waist.

Lucie rolled her eyes. 'You're never going to let me forget about running away, are you?'

Tipping her chin with his free hand, Arthur dropped a kiss on his new fiancée's lips. 'Maybe once I've got you down that aisle and you're Lady Ludworth, I might.'

'I'm ready when you are, Sir Arthur. Just name the day.' The way his expression softened at those words clenched around Iggy's heart like a vice and she turned away before they started kissing again. Surely luck would be with them. Surely a couple as kind and generous and loving as her brother and Lucie deserved the happiest of happy endings so many of their precedents had either been robbed of – or had thrown away in her parents' case. The Ludworths didn't have the greatest of track records when it came to love, but the tide seemed like it was finally turning.

Lancelot arrived at that moment, Morgana on his arm. They'd barely cleared the threshold before Lucie was thrusting her hand towards them. 'We're engaged!'

'That's marvellous, my dear,' Morgana replied, drawing her hand free from her nephew's arm to cup Lucie's cheek. 'Welcome to the family.'

'Well done, my boy!' Lancelot clapped Arthur on the back then tugged him into a tight hug. 'I wish Uther could be here to share this moment with us. He would've loved your Lucie as much as I do.'

Arthur made a choked sound, his arms tightening around their uncle, and Iggy felt her own eyes stinging with tears. Using the tea tray as an excuse, she busied herself fixing teas and coffees for the rest of the family.

A salty tear dripped off the tip of her nose to plop onto the shiny wood of the tea tray. Raising her hand, Iggy fingered the moisture on her cheeks, with no idea why she was crying. This was a good thing, a *wonderful* thing and she loved Lucie to pieces, so why did the idea of her marrying Arthur suddenly hurt so bloody much?

Because it changes everything.

They wouldn't be three against the world anymore. Arthur would put Lucie first above all things – just as he should – but the loss of that unique bond Iggy had with her brothers cut like a blade on her skin. And it wasn't just her place in her brother's affections Iggy would have to surrender, it was her unspoken position as lady of the house.

No more discussing menus with Betsy; no more planning which rooms would be allocated to their guests with Mrs W; no more managing of the estate lands to help Arthur. The first two roles belonged to Lucie by right, and Iggy would find the grace to hand them over with a smile. The last one though, *God*, that was the one that would break her heart.

Arthur would likely argue there was no need for her to stop overseeing their lands, and she doubted it was something Lucie had any real interest in, but still she'd have to do it. The power structure at the castle required a strong, united couple to head it up. There could be no room for confusion as to who was in charge. She would not be a third wheel or do anything that could risk causing an imbalance or make Lucie feel for one second her position was undermined in any way. Intellectually, she'd known this day would come, she just hadn't been prepared for it to be quite so soon.

Arthur was more than capable of managing things for himself, or he could get an estate manager in to pick up anything he didn't want to handle directly. She'd finish her work on the gardens, see the project through and make sure everything was in place for the future. She wouldn't get to see all her other plans put into action, but she would give her brother and his soon-to-be wife a solid foundation to build upon.

And then she would leave. To go where, and do what she had no idea, but that would come in time. All that mattered was acknowledging the painful truth – there was no long-term future for her at Bluebell Castle.

'Everything all right?' She jumped at the soft question. So engrossed in her task and the effort of not letting the swirl of bitter-sweet emotion inside overwhelm her, Iggy hadn't heard Will get up to join her.

'Yes, of course.' The tremor in her voice belied her words and Iggy swallowed hard. 'No, not really, but I don't want anyone to know. Give me a minute.' It shouldn't be possible for a heart to carry so much joy and pain at the same time. Like it would rend not just her heart, but her entire being in two.

Will gave her hand a tight squeeze. 'I've got you covered. Just breathe.' She felt his shoulder brush hers as he turned, angling his body in a way that shielded her from the rest of the room, and the dam broke inside her.

Chapter 11

Will had no idea what the hell was wrong with Igraine, but he'd caught a look of such complete desolation on her face as she'd turned from Arthur and Lucie it had taken his breath away. He didn't understand it, for not moments before she'd been hugging the pair and sounding as joyful as if she was the one getting married herself. Maybe that was it. She hadn't said much to him, but he got the impression she'd been on her own for a while, putting all her attention into her work at the estate. He hadn't considered it before, but it must be quite hard to date casually when you lived somewhere as remote as Bluebell Castle. Everyone in the village would know the family, and there couldn't be that many single guys of a suitable age in the near vicinity. He also doubted Igraine would enjoy being the subject of gossip any more than he did.

So that would leave the bigger towns and cities around, and who wanted to jump in the car and drive for an hour just to reach civilisation on the off chance you might meet someone in a club? Sure, there were plenty of dating apps around – he'd tried a few himself until his public profile had made it impossible – but they even made him a bit uncomfortable, as though all he was looking for was sex rather than something more meaningful.

A soft sob came from behind him, and he flicked his eyes to where the others were still crowding around the happy couple. No one but him had heard the sound, but he needed to get Igraine out of there. 'We can't possibly celebrate news like this with a cup of tea,' he called to Arthur in a hearty voice. 'Surely a place as grand as a castle must have a decent wine cellar.'

Arthur grinned. 'Good idea. I'll ring for Maxwell at once.'

Damn, Will had forgotten about the servants. 'No, no, let's not bother him at this time of the evening. I'm sure Igraine can show me the way. We'll rustle up a bottle of champagne and some glasses and be right with you.'

Before anyone had a chance to protest, he took Igraine by the elbow and whipped her out through the discreet door in the wall he'd seen Mrs W use earlier. The corridor they entered was plainer than the ostentatious family ones he was used to. No paintings adorned the walls, and the carpet beneath their feet was a sturdy, hardwearing type more typically used in offices than homes.

There was nothing to indicate the right direction, and he didn't know the layout of the castle well enough to be able to orient himself in relation to where the kitchens were. The most important thing was to get her somewhere private until he could find out what the hell was wrong with her. Flipping a mental coin in his head, he opted for the left-hand corridor and half-led, half-towed Igraine away from the family room.

After they'd rounded several corners, he judged them sufficiently far away. Not wanting to risk a member of staff coming across them, he tested the handle on the nearest door and opened it cautiously when it turned in his hand. The room was pitch dark, giving no indication of its size or use. Fumbling his hand along the inside wall he found a switch and flicked it, casting what appeared to be a storage cupboard of some kind into pale relief. Deciding it would do, he urged Igraine inside and shut the door behind them.

Stacks of neat white linens lined several shelves on one side, an array of checked tea-towels, dusters and sponges grouped in neat piles beneath them. Cleaning products and utensils crowded the other wall, everything separated into regimental lines. Igraine had sagged against him, making no effort to stifle her sobs.

He braced an arm around her back, digging in the pocket of his jeans with the other to remove the clean handkerchief he'd tucked there earlier. 'Here now.' He pressed the navy cotton square into her trembling fingers, but she made no effort to use it. 'Come on then, I've got you.' Will turned her until their bodies aligned and he could draw her properly into arms. 'It's all right, sweetheart, it's all right.'

Her arms circled his waist and the full weight of her body – such as it was – rested against his. 'S … s … sorry.'

'Shh.' His hand found her hair, stroking it in the way he'd seen the housekeeper doing earlier, recalling how Igraine had relaxed under that gentle touch like a cat uncurling. 'Take your time. There's no rush.'

She drew in a shuddering breath. 'Th … the others …'

'Won't even notice we're missing for a while.' He pressed a kiss to her temple, needing to comfort her, needing her to know that whatever was causing this awful pain, he was there with her, *for her*, in any way she required. 'Let it all out, I'm right here.'

Her face pressed into his shoulder once more, and though she continued to cry, the terrible shudders which had racked her body seemed to have passed. He continued to stroke his fingers through the silken length of her hair, the springy curls in it tangling and catching around them as though to trap his hand. He buried it deeper, seeking the warm column of her nape, holding her face close to him, lending her his strength until she found her own once more. A continuous litany of assurances tumbled from his lips, half of it nonsense, the words not important as long as she continued to calm and settle against him.

The rise and fall of her shoulders beneath his other arm gradually slowed, her heartbreaking little noises of grief fading. He went silent then, focused on keeping his breathing slow and rhythmic until he could feel her chest rising and falling in time with his. The lemony scent of her shampoo filled his lungs, the press of her soft breasts a sweet warmth against him. He wasn't sure if it was his breath which caught first, or hers, but the atmosphere between them shifted unconsciously from comfort to something urgent and needy.

If she hadn't turned her head in that moment, if he hadn't felt the brush of her delicate lips against the column of his throat, he might have been able to quell the desire rising hot and wild inside him. But she did, and he did, and the intensity of the earlier connection he'd felt with her when their eyes had met roared back into life. She was already on tiptoes, stretching up, lips parting to meet his as he tightened his hold on her neck and drew her closer still.

Connection.

He didn't know why that word kept coming into his mind whenever he thought of her, but the moment their mouths touched he felt it shudder through him. This was what he'd been waiting for, what he'd always been seeking and never found with any other woman. Their bodies moved in harmony, her head tilting to just the right angle, his thighs spreading to make space for her to slot against him in a way that seemed to fill in all his empty spaces until they were one continuous point of heat and passion and *rightness*.

'Igraine.' Her name on his lips was a promise and a question both, and he felt the short, sharp nails of her fingertips sink into his scalp as she clutched at him. Not thinking about anything other than the need driving him he slid a hand between them to tug at the buttons of her blouse, popping them free until the material hung open from her throat to the waistband of her trousers where the bottom of the blouse was still tucked in. Warm soft skin filled his hands and he couldn't keep them still, the need to shape and mould and learn her body a primal thing.

Her hands were busy too, tugging and pulling at his back until she could slide her fingers beneath the hem of his T-shirt to skim up his spine with a touch that left him gasping. He wrenched his mouth from hers, and drank the sight of her in. Sparks of gold lit her hazel eyes, her pretty lips were darkened and pink from his kisses, the pale skin of her throat and upper chest flushed to a rosy shade he wanted to trace with his mouth. Shifting his grip, he turned her until her back was against the door. *Good.* With her trapped between his body and the heavy wood, she'd have nowhere to go, and he'd be able to sink even deeper into those soft, sweet curves.

A harsh noise rattled through the room, his foot catching on a large metal bucket sticking out from beneath one of the shelves, reminding him where they were. 'Christ.' He released her hips, bracing his hands on the door above her head as sense finally returned to him. He'd just shared the most profoundly intimate moment of his life in a bloody cleaning cupboard with a woman who'd been sobbing fit to break her heart not moments before.

'Will?' Igraine's voice came out on a shaking breath, her little nails digging into his back a request to continue which he wanted to obey with every fibre of his being. But there'd been a hint of something in her tone, a whisper of uncertainty beneath the breathy desire.

Raising a hand that shook from the vestiges of adrenaline still coursing through him, he rested the pads of his fingers against her cheek. 'Not here, not like this.'

Her lips parted as though to protest before she nodded. 'No, of course, you're right.'

Colour darkened the skin beneath his fingers, and he bit back a groan of frustration as he pressed a sharp hot kiss to her mouth. 'Not because I don't want to. Tell me you understand that.' He kissed her again, a quick demand. 'Tell me, Igraine.'

'I understand,' she whispered against his cheek. 'Your timing is atrocious, though.'

Will laughed, the whipcord tension inside easing enough he could take a small step away from her. The sight of her blouse hanging open, the delicate lace of her bra peeking through the gap, was almost enough to unman him. Cursing himself for indeed having the very worst timing in the world, he began the painful task of rebuttoning her blouse, an act which felt almost more intimate than the hot rush of desire that had had him wrenching it open.

With tentative hands, Igraine reached around his waist to tuck his T-shirt back inside his jeans, smoothing and petting over the heavy cotton once she'd finished, as though she couldn't quite bring herself to draw her hands away. He knew the feeling. His own hand still rested inside the open collar of her blouse to cup the beautiful curve where her shoulder met her neck. 'I don't want you to think I was trying to take advantage of you.'

'Is that what you think just happened?' The languid, liquidity of her body stiffened, and her hands fell away. There wasn't much room, but she took a small step back until she was flat against the door once more. Taking the hint, he tugged his reluctant fingers from her skin and made more space between them.

Damn it, he was going to blow whatever the hell this was between them if he wasn't careful. 'You were really upset, Igraine.' Her sharp little chin rose in a defiant gesture and he gripped it between a gentle finger and thumb. '*Really* upset.' He traced his finger along her jaw until he felt her relax beneath his touch. 'It's very easy to mistake one kind of emotion for another.'

'So, what? You were just trying to comfort me and got carried away?' Bloody hell, she was spikier than a hedgehog. Tristan had warned him it took a lot for her to let her guard down, and he hadn't been kidding.

Not wanting there to be any mistakes or misunderstandings between them, he closed the distance until she was pressed tight between himself and the door once more. 'You're not getting out of this by convincing yourself my feelings towards you are anything other than desire. I want to kiss you again, Igraine. Very soon. I just want you to be a hundred per cent sure of your own feelings before I do.' He pressed a hot, possessive kiss to her lips, then spun her away from the door so he could tug it open. 'Come on, let's find that champagne.'

*

A chorus of cheers and applause went up as they returned to the family room, Igraine clutching a bottle of champagne beaded in condensation, he with seven crystal flutes suspended by their necks between his fingers. Tristan had joined the others by this time, and he came over to help Will set the glasses out on the sideboard whilst Igraine twisted the wire cage off the neck of the bottle and removed the cork in a quick efficient twist of her wrist. If he wasn't already half in love, or lust, or whatever the hell was making his head spin and his pulse pound, that casual gesture might have pushed him over the edge.

He loved the way she took control of things, didn't defer to a man when it was something she was capable of doing herself. It was sexy, in the same way she didn't bother to plaster herself in make-up all the time. He'd noticed some evenings that her lashes were a little thicker and darker where she'd added a touch of mascara, that she might select a lip colour to match whatever outfit she'd chosen for dinner, but he never got the impression she was doing it for any other reason than to please herself. Luckily, this evening had been one she'd chosen not to wear make-up, so at least there were no mascara streaks to hint at her earlier upset.

If anyone noticed how long they'd been absent, or the touch of redness around Igraine's eyes, they didn't say anything as the two of them moved around the room distributing glasses of bubbling, straw-pale champagne until everyone had a glass. There was also no hint of her earlier turmoil when Igraine raised her drink towards her brother and Lucie to toast them. 'Here's to Arthur and Lucie. Long life, love and happiness to you both. Always.'

'Hear, hear.' Will raised his glass and sipped, his eyes closing for a moment at the chilly perfection of the champagne bursting across his taste buds. He still had no idea what had upset Igraine, but now was not the time to pursue it. She'd tell him at some point – or not. Given how quickly she tended to draw up her defences whenever she felt vulnerable, she'd never tell him if he tried to push her on it. If he wanted to give things between them a chance to develop, he'd have to tread carefully. Let her come to him. He dug his nails into his palm, knowing already how hard the next few days were going to test his self-control.

Lancelot and Morgana had taken up occupation on the sofa where he'd been sitting, with Arthur and Lucie ensconced on the other, and Tristan lounging at their feet with his back propped against the end cushion close to Lucie's feet. Most of the dogs had been shooed from the room at some point, leaving only Tristan's little wheaten terrier curled in his lap and the pair of greyhounds snoozing in front of the fire. The only free seat was the armchair, and Will gestured to Igraine that she should take it.

The arm of the chair was wide enough for him to lean against, but that would go against his decision not to crowd her, so he propped his hip on the edge of the sofa nearest to Morgana. His notebook had been tucked into the gap between the seat cushion and the arm beside him, he noticed. Retrieving it, he began to flick backwards and forwards through his sketches and notes. He'd planned to talk to everyone tomorrow, but as they were all here, he might as well get on with it.

Rising, he crossed the room to place the open notebook on Igraine's lap, returning her look of surprise with a surreptitious wink before resuming his casual pose against the sofa arm once more. 'As everyone is here, I thought I'd take a few minutes of your time to talk about a suggestion I have for the grounds here.'

He took a quick sip of his champagne as all eyes in the room turned towards him. 'Igraine has the existing gardens well in hand.' He paused to smile at her. 'I'm not sure she ever really needed my input, but I'm not sorry she wanted it and I'm very happy to be here.' Okay, so that was laying it on a bit thick, perhaps. *So much for self-control.* Theory and practice were going to be two very different things, apparently. Fire sparked in her hazel-gold eyes, a hint of laughter and warning and Will had to make himself look away from the promise of it all.

'Anyway, I was going over the old garden plans and I spotted a feature in the grounds which set my brain whirring, so I've come up with a design that I hope you will all like.'

'You're talking about something new, rather than just tidying up what's already here?' Arthur sat forward a little, one arm sprawled across Lucie's knee as though he needed to keep in contact with her. Will understood the feeling all too well, and wished he was at ease to do the same with Igraine.

Keeping his eyes fixed on the baronet, Will nodded. 'There's a flat plateau of land beyond the stand of poplars.'

'I know where you mean, lad, there's that godawful bank leading down to it. I have to keep the horses away from it so they don't break a leg. When we were putting the gallops in, we made sure to do it well away from that part of the parkland.'

Will swivelled his attention towards Lancelot. 'So, you don't use that part of the grounds?'

The older man shook his head. 'No one does, not unless they're out walking. Whatever you have in mind wouldn't have any impact on my work at the stables.' Well, that was one more tick in the plus column. It hadn't looked to Will like the area was in regular use, but Lancelot's confirmation was more than welcome.

'Fountains,' Igraine said, holding up one of his pages covered in sketches. 'You want to put fountains in the middle of a flat open space no one uses?'

'No.' Will crossed to take the pad from her hand and flipped it over to a double-page concept sketch. 'I want to terrace the slope and turn it into a water garden.' He pointed to the top edge of the drawing. 'It would not only act as a feature in its own right, but also provide a beautiful backdrop.'

'Backdrop to what?' Tristan was up on his knees, leaning forward to try and catch a glimpse of the sketch on Igraine's lap.

Will handed him the notebook. 'To whatever you want. That plateau is almost a natural amphitheatre. You could host open air concerts there, get people to bring along blankets and picnics. Or you were talking about a summer fete to celebrate opening the grounds. It's big enough to take a load of stalls, with room for a display ground in the centre for live music, or whatever.'

'They have companies that tour Shakespeare plays and the like.' Tristan's voice was full of enthusiasm, and Will could tell he already had one supporter for his plan. 'I saw them at a country house on the outskirts of London when I was living there.' He looked up at Will. 'Like you said, everyone brought a picnic and chairs or blankets. It was a great evening.'

'Exactly. And if you decide to do regular evening events, I could incorporate a light display into the fountains. Either something simple where you can set the bulbs to a fixed array of colours, or something a bit more sophisticated so you could have a programmable sound and light display.'

He shifted his gaze to where Arthur and Lucie sat together, another idea forming. 'You could also hire it out as a private space for functions. Link up with a marquee hire place, or one of those firms that does that fancy camping thing like they do at the big music festivals.' He knew there was a term for it, but he couldn't bring it to mind.

'Glamping?' Lucie asked.

'Yes.' Will snapped his fingers. 'You see it all the time in the Sunday supplements. People love that kind of thing, and are willing to pay a pretty penny for it.' His attention slid to the ring on her hand. 'You could even offer it for people who want to hold their weddings somewhere special.'

Her eyes widened and he knew another fish had swallowed the bait on his hook. 'Oh, *yes*.' Clutching Arthur's arm, she turned to him. 'Imagine it! A lovely formal ceremony in the chapel followed by a fabulous party under the stars.'

'You two could do a trial run,' Tristan butted in, grinning at the newly engaged couple. 'I'll organise the whole thing!'

'Steady on, we've only been engaged an hour,' Arthur protested, but he was smiling as he said it. He turned to Lucie. 'Do you think it might be what you want, though? Rather than something a bit more traditional here in the castle?'

'I think it sounds like exactly what I want, and like Tristan said we could be guinea pigs to see if it's a viable business opportunity.'

Arthur glowered down at her. 'We are *not* using our wedding day as an experiment. What if something goes wrong?'

Lucie shrugged, apparently not the least bit concerned. 'What if it does? As long as you put a ring on my finger, and we say "I do" in the right place, I don't really care about the rest of it.' She leaned in to kiss Arthur. 'A wedding is only one day; it's getting to be married to you for the rest of my life that's important.'

Arthur rested his forehead against hers. 'I'll give you anything you want, Luce. Anything as long as it makes you as happy as I am right now.'

Feeling like he was intruding on something very private, Will deliberately turned away to face Tristan. 'You'd be interested in planning that kind of thing?'

Tristan nodded. 'It's my bread-and-butter. What I used to do before I came home last year. I'm already working on some house-party ideas for events we can host in the castle, if we can incorporate external parties in the summer months then it puts a lot less strain on the household.'

'It all sounds great.' There was a flatness to Igraine's statement, and Will felt his excitement wane. She was going to throw some spanner in the works, he could sense it.

'But?'

Her eyes met his. 'How much is this going to cost us? I hadn't budgeted for an exclusive Will Talbot design.'

Indignation hit like a punch to the gut, and Will felt his temper flare as hot and wild as the passion she'd stirred within him not half an hour before. He was about to snap back, when he noticed the stiff way she was holding herself, the way she nibbled at her bottom lip for a moment before pursing her lips as though to stop herself. Every line of her body seemed to vibrate with tension. Perhaps her earlier upset was resurfacing now he'd unintentionally returned the topic of conversation to Arthur and Lucie's engagement.

No.

The little glances from under her lashes weren't aimed at the couple on the sofa, but at him. She wasn't thinking about her earlier tears; she was thinking about the two of them and what had happened in that storage cupboard. She was running scared, he realised, hoping if she insulted him, he'd take offence and tell her where to stick her bloody garden. A sly thread of pleasure wound through his gut. No way was he letting her off that easily. Yes, he would give her time to sort through her feelings, but that didn't mean he was willing to give up before they'd started.

Whether she was ready to acknowledge it or not, there was something special between them. Something with the potential to set roots. Something that if nurtured carefully would bloom and grow. He thought about what Arthur had said to his fiancée, the serious expression on his face and her answering look of adoration. Will had never seen himself as the kind of man who'd want that sort of entanglement for himself, not until right now. The rolling stone of his life had come to a sudden halt, right here in the heart of this wild Derbyshire beauty. 'I'll do it for the cost of the materials and hired labour only.'

'You can't do that,' she gasped.

'It's my company, I can do whatever the hell I want.'

He turned to Arthur. 'I'll work up a full price for you, but there's no charge for my time or the design. Your hospitality and the chance to leave my own mark is payment enough.' He swung his gaze back to Igraine, took in her half-open mouth, the pleading expression in her eyes begging him to change his mind. 'I'll separate the different options out for you,' he said, his gaze unwavering. 'So you can make a fully informed choice.'

Chapter 12

A fully informed choice. Forty-eight hours since he'd uttered them, those bloody words of Will's were still ricocheting around Iggy's head. She stared gloomily at her congealing breakfast. It was enough to put a woman off her cornflakes. He hadn't been talking about the costs for the water garden, either. As soon as she'd understood the details of his vision, she'd fallen in love with the idea. It would be a wonderful complement to the other parts of the gardens, and people who might not have visited otherwise would be drawn by his name being attached to the design.

She'd originally assumed they'd host the summer fete on the rear lawn between the conservatory and the stables – it had certainly worked for their impromptu Easter celebrations with the locals from the village. But as he'd outlined his different ideas for using the plateau, she realised it would be a much better spot. Not only was it a lot larger, it was also well away from the castle itself. The locals had been respectful of the location, but other visitors might not be. They'd wander wherever they could, given a chance. They also couldn't afford strangers snooping around the stable blocks or trying to get into the conservatory unsupervised.

That suggestion of his about hosting weddings there had been inspired. Lucie was already gung-ho for the idea and she and Tristan had talked about nothing but marquees, temporary dancefloors and decorations for the past couple of evenings. Even Aunt Morgana had been bitten by the wedding bug, suggesting to Arthur he should place an announcement in the newspaper, and offering to host a small engagement tea for the women of the household once Lucie's mother, Constance, had joined them later that week. She'd been delighted with the news of her daughter's engagement, and when Iggy had said she'd love some help overseeing things in the gardens, Constance had agreed with alacrity and an extended visit had been planned. Iggy adored Constance and couldn't wait to discuss her plans for the Friends of the Castle projects with her.

Lancelot entered the dining room, whistling a tune that was far too jaunty for 6.30 a.m. Iggy wasn't the only one looking forward to Constance's arrival, it seemed. They'd had something of a liaison at the Easter party, and Iggy for one was hoping the two of them might rekindle the attraction. She couldn't remember her uncle being in a relationship. Not one that he'd shared with the rest of the family, at least. It wasn't that he lived like a monk, but the women he saw all seemed to be on a casual basis, and he never brought any of them home.

He stopped in his tracks when he spotted her. 'Hello, early bird! I wasn't expecting to see anyone else up and about this morning.'

'I haven't been sleeping great,' she admitted. 'Too much on my mind.' Like handsome gardeners who were too damned good at kissing for their own good. Every time she closed her eyes, she was transported back to that moment in the storage cupboard. If Will hadn't knocked against that bucket when he had, she had no idea what might have happened between them. A blush heated her cheeks and she quickly ducked over her bowl, pretending to spoon up a mouthful of soggy cornflakes. Oh, she had every idea about what would have happened. Her dreams the past two nights had shown her in embarrassingly graphic detail. Which was another reason she was up so early that morning.

'You've taken on a lot with the gardens refurbishment, so I'm not surprised if it's weighing you down.' Lancelot paused on his way from fetching a coffee to his seat at the table and bent to kiss the top of her head. 'You will let me know if there's anything I can do?'

Raising her eyes to meet his, she nodded. 'Of course, I will. Thank you.'

He tweaked her nose the way he hadn't done since she was a tiny thing and they'd been playing 'who-stole-your-nose'. He wiggled the tip of his thumb at her from between his fingers his memory obviously taking him back to the same place, and they shared a laugh. 'No need to thank me; that's what uncles are for.'

'Well, I appreciate the offer,' she said as he took his seat opposite, 'But you've got your hands full with the stables.' She cast him a sly grin. 'Besides, I'm hoping I can tempt Constance into helping me out.'

The corner of her uncle's mouth tipped up in a cheeky smile. 'I've got one or two things I'm hoping to tempt her into helping out with myself.'

Iggy sputtered over her cornflakes. 'You can't say things like that!'

Raising one shoulder, Lancelot gave an unrepentant shrug. 'I think you'll find I just did.' He took a sip of his coffee, studying her over the rim of his cup in a way that made her want to squirm. 'Never mind my love life, why don't we talk about yours?'

'Mine?' Iggy squeaked. 'What about mine?'

'Don't play coy with me, my girl. I've seen the way Will looks at you.'

Pursing her lips, she made a rude noise at him. 'Rubbish. He doesn't look at me any particular way.'

Lancelot snorted. 'I'm not sure if you're lying to yourself or just to me, but stop it.' When she didn't respond, his tone turned more encouraging. 'He's a good-looking man, darling. Decent, too, and bloody hard-working. Look at what he's made of himself.'

'I'm not disputing any of that. I was the one who brought him on board here, precisely because of what he's achieved.'

'Then what's the problem? It's not anything to do with that girl in the paper, is it?' Lancelot tilted his head. 'He's only had eyes for you since he walked through the door, if you ask me.'

No one is asking you. She tamped her lips of the cross words, knowing they would reveal far too much of the turmoil inside her. 'I'm not looking for a relationship, right now.'

Her uncle snorted again. 'You haven't been looking for a relationship since forever. There is such a thing as being too independent, take that from someone a lot older, though not necessarily any wiser than you.'

Iggy bridled at that. 'I don't need a man in my life to complete it!'

Lancelot smiled as wide and toothy as a crocodile sighting its prey. 'Maybe not, but there are still lots of things in life that are much more fun if you have someone to do them with.' His expression became serious. 'Unless you don't fancy the man? If that's the case, then by all means tell me to shut up about him.'

Tempting. It was so tempting to do just that, to deny she considered Will as anything other than a hired contractor. Only, they weren't technically paying him to work from them – beyond giving him bed and board – and one extra mouth to feed was neither here nor there. Though it would make her life so much easier if she could, there was no denying the desperate attraction she felt towards him. 'It's not that I *don't* like him ...' She trailed off, not sure how much she was willing to admit to Lancelot *or* herself.

'Then what is it? Are you worried we won't approve? Has someone else said something to you about it? You've never been one to shy away from what you wanted just to try and please someone else.'

She shook her head. 'Nothing like that. It's just ... complicated.' Which said nothing and everything all at the same time.

Lancelot sent her a sympathetic smile over his cup. 'Life is complicated, dearest girl. If you wait for things to be simple, you'll find yourself waiting forever.'

The wistful tone behind those words caught her attention. Beneath the laughing, loving face he'd always done his best to show them, she sensed a deep-seated sorrow. 'Who broke your heart, Lancelot?'

A shadow fell over his face, and he set down his cup. 'It doesn't matter now. It was a very long time ago.'

Feeling like she'd stumbled onto something he clearly didn't want to talk about, Iggy let it go. 'Constance is fab, isn't she?'

He brightened at once, the cloud hanging over his brow disappearing to reveal the jovial, smile she was more used to seeing on his face. 'She's an absolute gem. We've talked most evenings since she was last here.'

Well, it sounded like things were indeed going well between them. 'I'm really pleased for you. For both of you.' Checking her watch, she saw it was approaching 7 a.m. The Davises were due on site in an hour so she would have time now to have a walk around and see what progress they'd made. 'I'm going to make a start on my day.'

Lancelot watched her as she rose from the table and carried her bowl over to the empty tray on the sideboard from where Maxwell would clear it later. 'Give the boy a chance, Iggy. Actually, no, give *yourself* a chance. A summer romance might be just what you need.'

God, he was incorrigible. 'Put your bow down, Cupid.'

Laughing, her uncle mimed drawing back and arrow and firing it at her. 'Love is in the air, darling girl. There's no use in fighting it.'

She held up her hands in surrender. 'I'll think about it, all right? I'm not making any promises though.' His delighted chuckle followed her out of the room.

*

The next few days passed in a blur of activity, giving her little time to do as she'd promised her uncle and properly think about her feelings for Will. More quotes were coming in, and Iggy was steadily filling the various tasks to be done. When she wasn't signing contracts and making phone calls, she was out and about. Will had become so absorbed in his water garden project, he was leaving her more or less to her own devices.

Her normal responsibilities hadn't disappeared either, and she'd spent the previous afternoon over at Tumbledown farm helping them with some emergency repairs to one of their feeder systems. The chute had clogged – not for the first time – and she'd been happy to lend a hand. A small-holding like the farms they leased out ran on a tight budget, so if a bit of elbow grease and time could solve a problem then everyone pitched in Between all of that, she'd had no free time to think about anything other than crossing off the next item on her to-do list.

It was Friday morning before she finally eked out a couple of hours to work in the garden herself, spending the morning finishing the clipping and clearing around the fountain near the entrance to the maze. The contractors were making good progress, and had made it about a quarter of the way around the twisting mass of hedges.

The promised heatwave from the weather forecast had also arrived, and with a high-pressure system sitting firm over the country, looked set to stay for the forthcoming days.

Conscious of Mrs W's dire warnings, Iggy had bound her hair in a knot at her nape and kept a floppy straw hat firmly in place all day. The long-sleeved cotton shirt she wore might have protected her skin from the worst of the sun's rays, but it now clung unpleasantly to every inch of her upper body, the thin vest she'd worn beneath it equally saturated. Her feet in her work boots felt like two boiled hams, and all Iggy wanted to do was stand beneath a cold shower for the next hour. Unfortunately, she had a meeting with the local tree surgeon who was coming to survey the walking routes they'd planned through the woods, so that was going to have to wait. Tugging off her hat, she freed the sticky strands of her fringe which had glued themselves to her forehead and used the brim of the hat as a fan to try and cool her skin.

The fanning didn't do much to relieve the heat, so she plopped the hat back on, wincing a little at the clammy feel of the soaked inner band. Helping herself to one of the remaining bottles of water in the cold box tucked into the shadows of a thick hedge, she tucked another couple under her arm and ventured into the first section of the maze towards the relentless buzz of a hedge trimmer. Making sure to keep well out of the way, Iggy stepped into Davy's sightline and held up one of the bottles of water. His broad, tanned face broke into a grin beneath the Perspex face shield attached to his hard hat and the trimmer fell blessedly silent. 'You must be a mind-reader!' he said, stepping down from the sturdy trestle bench and placing the trimmer on top of it.

'How are you getting on?' she asked, waiting patiently for the contractor to strip off his protective gear before she handed him the bottle.

'Not bad, not bad at all,' he said between deep swallows of water. 'Simon?' He raised his voice, turning to call his son who was working deeper within the maze. 'Drink break!'

Sweaty and red-faced beneath his tan, a grinning Simon appeared from around the junction. Not bothering to remove his gear, he settled for tipping up his own face guard before tilting the bottle Iggy handed him and draining half the contents in a series of gulps. 'I needed that, thanks, Iggy.' A little shyer than his more outgoing father, there was still a hint of hesitancy in his use of her first name.

Never really one for formalities, it made even less sense to her to stand on ceremony when these men would be working with her for several weeks. 'You're welcome. There's still another couple of bottles in the box, so I'll leave it for you and come and pick it up later.'

Davy shook his head. 'No need to bother with that, we'll drop it off on the steps of castle when we've finished for the day.'

Delighted at his consideration, Iggy smiled in thanks. 'If you're sure, that would be a great help.'

'Consider it done. You're finishing up, are you?'

'If only. I'm meeting the tree man in a few minutes to begin a survey of the woods.'

Finishing his water, Davy gave her a sympathetic smile. 'You're really going to town with all this work, aren't you?'

'It's past time we got everything sorted. It's just such a shame so much was left to run wild.'

He nodded. 'It is, at that, but don't you worry, we'll see you right between us.'

'If all my other contractors are as reliable as you, Davy, it'll be a breeze.' She could tell her words had pleased him from the way he ducked his head a little, but it was no more than the truth. Now he and Simon were up and running, she was confident they could be left to their own devices.

'We can't wait to see the place back to its full glory. My wife's already been asking when we can buy tickets to the grand opening.'

'You'll be getting a guest invitation, along with everyone else who helps us, but that is a good point. I'll have to check with Arthur and find out what's going on with the website.'

'Well, you let us know and we'll spread the word. It's an honour for us that you picked our firm, and will be a real boost to the community to have a grand site such as this open to the public.'

'I certainly hope that will be the case.' Iggy took their empty bottles ready to stow them back in the cool box so they could go in the recycling later. 'By the way, if you know any other local firms who might be interested in bidding on the works we're doing, feel free to pass on their details. I desperately need some landscapers to help with all the planting.' She ran a quick mental tally of the other jobs on her list. 'And a firm of bricklayers, a stonemason and a contractor to renew all the gravel pathways.'

'My brother-in-law is a general builder. He's got all his health and safety certifications, same as us, and plenty of references. I won't expect any favours for him, of course, but I'll have a word with him tonight and if he's interested, I'll get him to send you an email with his details, if that's all right?'

Iggy nodded. The repairs to the brick beds and walls of the apothecary's garden could easily be handled by a small firm, and it would be nice to support as many local businesses as possible. 'Great, thanks, Davy.' She checked her watch. 'Right, I'll be off. Sure, you're okay here?'

'Don't worry about us. We'll keep going until six, and then be back again at eight in the morning.' He swatted at a fly that was buzzing around his head. 'It'll be a good few days yet before we're finished with this blasted maze, assuming we don't get lost in it, that is.'

She laughed. 'You'll have to tie a piece of string to follow once you get further in.'

'Might just do that.'

*

Her meeting with the tree surgeon lasted for about an hour, and although she was grateful for the shade, the humid heat felt trapped beneath the trees and the small of her back was soon soaked with a fresh layer of sweat. By the time she'd left him to continue his survey in peace, the need to cool off was pressing. On a whim, she headed further away from the castle and down towards the lake.

It was a relief when she finally broke through the trees near the edge of the lake. A gentle breeze – barely enough to stir the leaves on the canopy behind them – sent a welcome puff of cooler air over her skin. Hands on hips, she stared out over the water.

The mirror-smooth surface reflected the afternoon sun, and it was too tempting to resist.

Sitting down on a fallen log, Iggy unlaced her boots and dragged off her thick socks, draping them over the wood beside her to dry off. Checking over her shoulder, she saw no sign of anyone around, so she turned her attention back to the lake once more and strode down to the edge.

Bull rushes lined the banks, and she had to weave through their tall stems to reach the waterline. The first touch of cool water against her toes was so heavenly she sighed in contentment. Knowing the edge of the lake sloped down gently for the first couple of feet, she waded in until she could stand up to her ankles.

As though they'd been waiting for her mind to be still for a moment, memories of Will kissing her came flooding back. The weight of a phantom grip settled about her hips, and Iggy rested her hands there as though she expected to feel the warm strength of Will's fingers beneath her own. Though he'd only touched her that once, it was like the memory of his hands might be burned into her psyche forever. *What am I going to do about him?* Her uncle was right; ignoring it wasn't going to make the problem go away. Stripping off her shirt, Iggy tossed it towards the bank then sank down on her haunches in the blessedly cool water to think.

Chapter 13

Will stretched his aching back with a sigh, his eyes scanning over the figures on his laptop screen one last time. The final price he'd been waiting for had come in half an hour earlier and he'd slotted it into the pricing spreadsheet before giving everything a final read-through. Satisfied he had included enough detail, he saved the file, attached it to an email and sent it to both Arthur and Igraine. Snapping down the lid of his laptop with a contented smile, he decided to stretch his legs after a long day hunched at the desk in his bedroom.

He told himself he wasn't looking for Igraine, right up until the moment his steps veered from the path that would lead him down to the stand of poplars and the open ground beyond where he'd pinned all his hopes, and he turned instead into the formal gardens. Following the sounds of a noisy duet being played on a couple of hedge trimmers, he entered the maze, frustrated to find only the father-and-son contractors Igraine had hired. They pointed him towards the woods, and it was only then he recalled she had an appointment with the tree surgeons.

Abandoning any pretence he was just out for a stroll, Will retraced his steps back towards the castle and struck out a new path down towards the woods. He hadn't had much time to explore this part of the grounds as it wasn't within his remit, so he could kill two birds with one stone. A stillness settled over the air as he walked beneath the dappled canopy of the trees and into a wonderland of sights, sounds and scents. The path beneath his feet was well compacted in the centre, the edges ill-defined where moss and creepy undergrowth fought a never-ending battle to reclaim the spaces where people had walked for years – centuries most likely from the deep groove which had been worn into the land.

The sound of birds chirping and calling filled the air, and he caught the odd rustle in the grass, a flash of grey brown as he disturbed a rabbit and sent it streaking away into the trees. Oak, ash and beech trees towered overhead, the lower spaces claimed by elder, rowan and patches of thick brambles just beginning to show a hint of the berries which would laden the bushes later in the season. Heat sat thick and heavy, the leaves trapping in the moist air until he felt the back of his shirt begin to dampen and stick to his skin, and he was grateful to be wearing a loose pair of cargo shorts, rather than the heavier jeans he favoured when working outside.

Other than the sounds of nature surrounding him, the woods were quiet. No voices carried through the still air, no sounds of feet other than his own swishing through the grass and under-growth. Deciding it was pointless to keep searching for Igraine and the tree surgeons, he let his feet carry him where they would until he found the remains of an overgrown path leading off the main walkway. Curious, he tramped through the grass until he came across a domed structure in the landscape – too regular and out of keeping with the landscape around it to be anything other than manmade.

The path led to a locked iron gate. Pressing close to the metal bars, Will studied the short slope leading down to a thick wooden door. If it hadn't been for the arch of bricks surrounding the door, he might have thought he'd discovered a hobbit hole for that's what it reminded him of with its thick layer of grass-topped soil covering the structure. Intrigued, he walked around the mound. About halfway round he spotted a glimmer of blue through the surrounding trees and things clicked into place. He must be close to the lake which bordered one edge of the woods. He glanced back over his shoulder, realising the structure must be an old ice house. Before modern refrigeration, it had been common for grand estates such as the castle to build ice houses beside their lakes. Ice could be cut from the lake in winter and stored deep underground. The thick layers of soil and grass piled overhead provided insulation so the temperature could be maintained regardless of the time of year.

Turning back towards the lake, Will tried to judge the distance from the water. It was far enough to make him glad he hadn't been one of the poor sods who'd had to cut and lug great blocks of ice in the dead of winter to fill the ice house in its heyday. The sound of splashing from the water lured him down through the trees towards the bank, and he couldn't help but smile at the sight before him.

Hair slicked down her back like a mermaid, Igraine was cutting through the water in strong, confident strokes. No delicate dog-paddling for her, like the way his mum had swum at the local pool when she'd taken him swimming as a kid. He'd always found it odd the way she craned her neck up, trying not to get her hair wet when diving under the water had always been the best bit in his opinion.

The remains of a wooden jetty stretched out into the lake in front of him, a remnant from the ice-cutting days, he supposed. Though the planks didn't look too bad, he decided he wouldn't try his luck with them and instead circled around the bank until he found the spot where the main path through the woods opened up. A pair of boots and socks sitting on a nearby log told him this was the place Igraine had entered the water and he sat down beside them to tug off his trainers and the short liner socks beneath.

Hands in his pockets he edged into the water, keeping an eye on the sandy bottom beneath his toes. A darker shadow appeared a foot or so in front of him, and he stopped, assuming that was where the bank fell away. He glanced up to see Igraine had spotted him and was moving towards him in a graceful breaststroke that sent ripples across the lake behind her.

She stopped a little way from him, hands sculling at her sides. 'What are you doing here?' There was no censure in her tone, only a curiosity.

'I heard you were skiving off, so I came to find you,' he teased.

Laughing, she scooped a handful of water at him before tipping her head back until her hair floated free like dark strands of seaweed. 'Can you blame me, when the water is so lovely?'

It wasn't only the water that was lovely. Her dark vest and shorts clung to her skin, outlining her curves, and as she floated back in the water, he spotted bright flashes of pillar-box red. Igraine had always struck him as the sensible type of woman, and as he watched her scarlet-tipped toes fluttering in the water, it felt like he'd learned a new secret about her. 'It does look very tempting,' he said, layering a double meaning into his words.

Igraine let her body drop back under the water, her hands stirring at her sides the only movement as she studied him for a long moment. It was impossible to tell what she was thinking behind the smooth mask of her features, so when she said, 'Well, you'd better come in and join me then,' he all but stumbled back in surprise.

It didn't take him long to recover, not when those pretty pink lips of hers spread into a delicious smile of invitation and she kicked her legs to propel herself backwards into the water. Yes, she might have invited him to join her, but he was still going to have to work to catch her. Taking a couple of steps back to give himself room, Will charged forward into the shallow water, raising his hands over his head to dive in as the edge fell away. Her shriek of delight reached his ears before being muffled by the water closing over his head, and when he surfaced it was to find she'd turned and was swimming away from him in that efficient front crawl he'd seen earlier.

Pausing only to shake the water from his head, Will set off in pursuit. *Damn, she was strong.* It took all his effort to make any headway, and he began to wish he'd kept up with those youthful swimming lessons. She paused ahead of him to glance back, flashing him a wide grin before she struck off in another direction. Deciding there was no chance of chasing her down, Will bided his time, circling around her to cut off her escape until eventually they were only a few feet from the opposite side of the lake.

Igraine didn't notice her error until too late, and he gave her a grin of his own as he watched her head turning left and right, working out she had no more room to manoeuvre. Sucking a breath into his lungs, Will sank beneath the water and waited until he was deep enough his movement wouldn't give away his position before he swam at right-angles to where he'd last seen Igraine. As he'd expected, she made a final bid for escape, a long lean pale leg flashing in the water before him. Stretching out, he closed his hand around her ankle, dragging her back in the water as he used his other hand to stroke towards her until he could surface with an arm locked around her waist.

They came up for breath, sputtering and laughing, Igraine twisting in his hold, but not hard enough she had any real chance of breaking free. A patch of her shoulder lay bare between her hair and the thick strap of her vest and he pressed his lips to it, tasting cool water and sunshine on her skin.

'That's cheating,' she gasped, her head falling back to rest against his shoulder, giving him better access to the long smooth column of her neck. Taking full advantage, Will shifted his lips from her shoulder to nibble at a point beneath her ear, earning him another one of those delicious gasps. So distracted was he by trying to tempt another such sound from her lips he didn't pay attention to the way she tangled her legs around his until they were suddenly submerged.

Spitting out a mouthful of lake water, Will surfaced to find a laughing Igraine several feet away from him. She'd found her way to the shallow edge of the bank and was sitting waist-deep in the water, legs stretched out before her. A handful of water sloshed over his head, scooped up in her cupped palms. 'You didn't think I was going to make it that easy for you, did you?'

Paddling over, he slid onto the sandy bank beside her shuffling closer until their bodies touched from hip to ankle. 'I'll admit I had hopes in that direction.'

She nudged his shoulder. 'But where would be the fun in that?'

Will contorted his face into a leer. 'Come sit in my lap and I'll show you how much fun it would be.'

Another handful of water hit him square in the face. 'In your dreams.'

'Every night, sweetheart. Every damn night.'

Her breath caught, a little huff of sound that sent fire shooting through him in spite of the cool water surrounding his lower body. 'Melody …'

Will cocked his head to the side, but she was staring straight out over the lake, refusing to meet his gaze. There was a tension in her body, a need he could tell for one final reassurance that she could trust him. 'Means nothing to me; has never been anything to me, I swear it.'

There was a long silence before she finally gave a quick, sharp nod. 'Okay then.'

Not the most romantic of declarations, it had to be said. 'Okay then?' he repeated, unable to keep the amusement from his voice.

'Yes,' she said, swinging one leg over his hips to straddle his lap, her arms coming up to encircle his neck. 'As of now, you and I are officially seeing each other. No secrets, no skulking around and hiding in dark corners because Lord knows it was embarrassing enough watching Arthur and Lucie trying to pretend there was nothing going on between them.' She cupped his cheek then, her thumb feathering along the scar.

He held his breath, waiting for her to flinch away like so many other women had before, but her touch was a tender caress, as though she was trying to soothe away the long-forgotten pain of his injury. It broke something open inside him, laid bare a vulnerability, a need for total acceptance he hadn't been aware of. It was too much, and yet he craved it like a man starved. Not wanting her to sense how deeply affected he was by her touch, he curled his arm around her waist and hitched their bodies closer. 'I quite enjoyed skulking around in a dark corner with you.'

She laughed. 'Me too, but think how much more fun we can have somewhere comfortable.'

'Good point.' He claimed her lips in a hot, sweet kiss. 'A *very* good point, in fact, and I think we should retire to somewhere comfortable right this minute.' He locked his hands on her hips, ready to carry her off there and then.

She rocked down on him, and suddenly he decided that sitting waist deep in the lake was the most comfortable place on earth. 'There's no rush, is there? We've got the whole summer to enjoy ourselves. Just relax and see where the moment takes us.'

He knew where he hoped it would take them, but for all the sensuality in her movements, he could still sense the reticence in her. She might have lowered the drawbridge to grant him access, but there would still be a lot of defences to overcome before she'd let him near her heart. Right now, he'd take what he could get and, as she'd said, they would see where the moment took them. 'It's quite hard to relax when I've got my arms full of the most delicious woman in the world, but I'll do my best.'

*

They spent another hour or so in the lake, making out like teenagers between bouts of playing in the water. When they finally made their way back to the other side where they'd left their shoes, Igraine was visibly shivering and Will couldn't feel his toes properly. His trainers would be fine without socks on, so he used his to dry Igraine's feet as best as he could before she tugged on her thick socks and boots. He waited whilst she wrapped the thick length of her hair around a fist and twisted to wring the worst of the water from it before looping it into a simple knot. The sun had moved far enough around, there was no need any longer for her hat, so she carried it in one hand, the fingers of the other tangling in his hands as they strolled back through the woods towards the castle.

They didn't say much, which was fine by Will as he had plenty to think about. It was all very well for her to declare they wouldn't hide the fact they were together from her family, but he wasn't sure how welcome the shift in their relationship would be – particularly with her brothers. There'd be a conversation or two to be had with them, his instincts told him that, and he needed to be prepared for it. Well, he had nothing to hide as far as Igraine was concerned so they could bring it on.

Reaching the edge of the woods, Igraine tugged at his hand to bring them to a stop. She stared up at him, a hint of determination in her eyes. 'If Arthur or Tristan say anything to you, tell them to mind their own bloody business.'

He couldn't help but chuckle; clearly they'd been on the same wavelength. 'I can handle your brothers.' Unable to resist the sweet lure of her, he encircled her waist and drew her up against him, ignoring the clinging wetness of their clothing. 'I'd much rather be handling you.'

It was a corny line, but it earned him a giggle and a flurry of kisses which quickly turned into something deeper. Fighting the urge to press her up against the nearest tree, Will clenched a fist in the back of her vest and eased her reluctantly away. Panting, he rested his forehead against hers. 'Come to me tonight,' he urged, knowing it was too soon, but unable to ignore the painful ache in his body.

Her fingers curled into his shoulders, flexing and releasing like a cat kneading him with her claws. 'I'll think about it.'

Closing his eyes, he pressed a brief kiss to her temple. 'Think very hard about it.'

Her cheek rubbed against his, as she nodded in agreement. 'I will. I …' She trailed off, and he forced himself to stand still and be patient while she sorted through whatever was going on in her head. '… I need a little time.' She glanced up at him through her thick lashes. 'If that's okay?'

'Of course,' he answered at once. For all the desire thrumming through his veins, he never ever wanted her to feel pressured into anything. 'Don't ever be afraid to tell me to back off.'

Fisting her hands in his shirt, she dragged him down for a hot kiss then gave him a little shove. 'Back off.' Turning she flounced along the path a few steps before turning to grin at him over her shoulder. 'Just don't go too far, okay?'

She held out her hand to him and he jogged to catch up, taking her hand once more in his own. He liked how she fit there, like all the other ways they fit together, like all the ways they would fit together some night soon. 'I'm not going anywhere.'

*

Other than a few raised eyebrows, and a knowing smirk from Igraine's uncle, their entrance into the dining room hand-in-hand later that evening provoked little response. Lucie's mother had arrived at some point whilst he and Igraine had been playing in the lake, which served as a good distraction. Will couldn't help but notice the way Lancelot's eyes strayed to Constance every few moments, nor the way she lit up when speaking to him and surmised he wasn't the only one with romance on his mind.

The conversation turned towards plans for Arthur and Lucie's wedding. 'The announcement will be in the paper on Monday,' Arthur said. 'So, we really ought to give some thought to nailing down a date.' He glanced across the table towards Lucie. 'Are you sure you want to go ahead with it this summer? We can wait until things are less chaotic around here, if you'd prefer?'

She shook her head. 'Let's get on with. I'll be too distracted with preparing the exhibition to start panicking over flowers and table decorations.'

Not looking convinced, Arthur turned his attention towards Will. 'It's down to you then.'

'Me?'

'Yes. Are you sure you can stick to the timetable you included with the quote you emailed earlier?'

The initial flutter of panic over how he was suddenly responsible for a wedding quickly faded. 'I'll have to get final confirmation from my contractors once you give me the go ahead, but assuming we can get cracking next week, then I'm going to say we can have it all finished by the middle of August.'

'That's cutting it fine.' Igraine was frowning beside him. 'We'd only have two weeks before the summer fete. If you wanted to host the wedding there, it'd have to be the weekend before the bank holiday which wouldn't give us much time to prepare.'

Will reached for her hand. 'I've built in a week of testing and trouble-shooting for the fountains within the timescale I quoted. There won't be any works going on in the field area itself so we can get the demarcation ropes installed and whatever marquees and tents you decide on pitched during that same week.'

He turned to Arthur. 'Depending on how big you want the wedding to be, we could repurpose the marquee for the fete. It wouldn't take the hire company long to strip out the wedding fixtures and fittings.'

'The one we had for my birthday party worked very well, I thought,' Morgana chipped in. 'I think you'd want something similar for the wedding and it would be big enough to site the smaller stall holders you're hoping to attract.'

Lucie nodded. 'The website is going live next week as well, so we should get an idea of numbers of vendors who want to take part in the fete in plenty of time to plot out the final layout.' She tapped her lip. 'The only thing I'm not sure about is how the catering would work when we're so far away from the castle.'

Tristan leaned forward. 'You can hire some pretty sophisticated set-ups these days. As long as there's a water and power source to connect to.' He turned to Will. 'Can we sit down with your contractors and work that out?'

It should've occurred to him before that they'd need to supply the site for more than just the water garden. 'Of course. Why don't you and I go down there first thing and survey it out?'

'Perfect.' Tristan sent Lucie a teasing grin. 'If you fancy something a bit out of left field for the reception, we could get some high-end mobile catering vans in rather than bother with a full kitchen set up.'

Arthur scoffed. 'High-end and catering vans don't exactly go together. We're not having our guests eat off the back of a burger van.'

'Think about it for a minute. I'm not talking about burgers, or fish and chips – well, not exactly. I was thinking more along the lines of someone who could do a hog roast, or a carvery. You're probably not going to want a load of hot food, so something like that with a decent cold buffet to support it would be ideal.'

'And you could get a Mr Whippy van in rather than bothering with desserts.' Will was joking, mostly, but the talk of catering vans had conjured up memories of the excitement around his estate when the chimes of an ice cream van had sent him and all the other kids flooding into the streets clutching a pound coin.

'What a fantastic idea!' Lucie grinned at Arthur. 'What do you say?'

'It'd certainly be different …'

'Well, I for one think it's a capital idea,' Morgana declared, as though that settled the matter. 'Now, if everyone has finished their main courses, I'd quite like some cheese.'

'Oh, we'll need a cheese board for the wedding, most definitely,' Arthur said, and the conversation about the catering went around again as Maxwell entered the room and cleared away their plates.

Deciding he'd caused enough mischief, Will let the talk drift over his head and turned towards Igraine beside him. She had that funny half-happy, half-sad look on her face once again. 'Everything all right?' he asked, leaning close enough to speak at a volume only she would hear.

Meeting his eyes, she quirked her mouth in a little smile. 'Yes, fine. I'm just going to miss all this after the summer.'

Not understanding, he frowned at her. 'What are you talking about?'

She blinked sharply, then sat up straight. 'Oh, nothing. Never mind me.' Maxwell approached then and she turned from Will to pass the butler her plate, entering into a discussion with him about what she might want for dessert.

The butler turned to him next, and Will decided against ordering anything else. 'I'll help myself to something from the fruit bowl.'

'Very good, Mr Talbot.' Maxwell swept his plate away and continued to Morgana who was seated on Will's right.

Planning to return their conversation to before Igraine had brushed him off, Will turned back to her only to find her deep in a discussion with Constance about the plans for the interactive children's area in the garden. He bided his time, but there was no let up in their chatter, even after the family decamped from the table to the family room. A suspicious man might have thought Igraine was deliberately avoiding him, especially when she abruptly decided to turn in at the same time as her aunt, who was the first to excuse herself for the evening. A flurry of activity followed, with Constance deciding she would also go up to bed, and both Lancelot and Lucie jumping up to assist her.

With so many people milling around, Will had to settle for a quick peck on the lips, not the long, lazy seductive kisses he'd been hoping to lure Igraine into. Dissatisfied and disgruntled, he took himself off to his own bed. Igraine was keeping secrets from him, and somehow he knew they all tied into whatever had upset her so much the other week.

Chapter 14

Iggy hadn't known it was possible for someone to say so much with silence, but Will was a master at it. She'd been waiting since her inadvertent slip over dinner for him to ask her what she'd meant, but whenever they were together over the following week, he kept their conversation purely to work matters. When he wasn't talking to her about the groundworkers who'd started digging out the terracing layers for the water gardens, he was luring her into quiet places so he could kiss and caress her until she didn't know up from down and all she wanted to do was grab him by the hand and drag him upstairs to bed. Hers or his, it didn't matter as long as they could lock the door and she could fall into his arms and satiate the desire which had her insides knotted up tight.

She never quite took that step though. Either something interrupted them, or her own doubts got in the way. She couldn't put her finger on what exactly it was that was stopping her. Will was attentive and funny, and the rest of the family seemed to have absorbed him into their whole in the same way they had with Lucie and then Constance. Whatever the topic at dinner, his opinion was sought, his answers given as much consideration as everyone else's. It pleased and frightened her in equal measure because he fit almost *too* well. What she'd intended to be a bit

161

of fun – a lovely distraction, a sexy itch to be scratched over the summer – was rapidly turning into something more serious, at least in her mind.

Will remained as opaque as ever. Oh, she knew he desired her, and he seemed to enjoy the quiet moments when they relaxed together curled up on one of the sofas as much as he did the frantic ones when he cornered her alone and laid siege to her mouth with his own. But she was still never quite sure what he was thinking, especially when he just sat there watching her.

There was an expectation in those silent moments, a quiet push that said he was waiting for her to confide in him, a sense of disappointment when she didn't. But she wasn't ready to talk to anybody about her plans for the future, not until she had something in place. If she told him she was planning to leave, he might think she was intending to follow him back to London. God, what if he wanted her to? Or, even worse, what if he didn't want her to, but somehow felt obliged to extend the invitation? She didn't know yet if they had any kind of a future together, and she wasn't willing to stumble accidently into something neither of them might be ready for. What little she'd seen of his life in the capital was world's away from the peace and tranquillity of Derbyshire. Would he slip back into that whirlwind of parties and gossip columns, and would he expect her to join him if he did? She couldn't imagine anything worse than being under constant scrutiny.

Regardless of all those doubts, she still needed to be ready to move on when the time came. In amongst all the other things filling up her plate, she'd begun to surreptitiously look around at what openings might be available to her. She had her degree from the Ag University, and a wealth of experience but as she'd only ever worked at the castle she'd never had the need to draw up a CV. The examples she'd downloaded from the internet had made her skin crawl with their faux-boastfulness and she'd filed them away in a folder on her laptop to look at on a later date. Right now, she had other things on her mind.

Turning to check the back of her dress in the mirror, Iggy straightened the belt of the jade-green cotton shirtdress and gave her reflection a nod of satisfaction in the mirror. Though none of them really had the time to spare, Morgana's planned afternoon tea to celebrate Arthur and Lucie's engagement was due to start in the next few minutes. Iggy knew better than to be late. Slipping her feet into a pair of flat black pumps, she hurried from her bedroom and around the corner towards the main staircase. The door to one of the empty rooms shot open as she passed it, and a familiar hand shackled her wrist with an insistent tug.

Seconds later, her back was to the inside of the closed bedroom door and Will was bearing down on her with a smile that promised the very best kind of trouble. 'Don't wrinkle me,' she warned him, holding her hands up in protest.

Pressing his weight into her outstretched palms, Will leaned across the gap between them. 'I promise not to mess up anything more than your lipstick,' he murmured against her mouth before proceeding to do just that.

Breathless and lust-addled, Iggy's hands softened against his chest. Heedless of her dress, she yearned to feel him against her and was just curling her arms around his neck to urge him closer when a carriage clock on the mantelpiece chimed the hour in three metallic rings. 'You're going to make me late.'

Stepping back, Will perused her with a satisfied grin. 'Not a hair out of place, not a crease to be seen, just like I promised.'

'You're a menace,' Iggy said, reaching for the handle of the bedroom door.

His big hand braced on the wood above her, his voice silky dark against her ear as he whispered. 'When are you going to come to my bed, Igraine?'

Now. She had to bite down on her lip to prevent the word from escaping. 'Soon,' she managed, her voice husky with the need he stirred up inside every time his big body crowded close like this.

He trailed one finger down her spine, sending a helpless

shiver through her, and she couldn't stop herself from leaning back against him. 'I'll make it good for you, so good you won't remember being with anyone other than me.'

He sounded so sure of himself, so deliciously, infuriatingly arrogant that it irritated her just enough for her to find the will to wrench open the door. 'Don't let your mouth make promises your body won't be able to deliver, Talbot.' And with that she stalked from the room, his warm laughter following her down the corridor and just a hint of a wobble still in her knees.

Two minutes later, she entered the yellow drawing room where her aunt held court as she had for all the years Iggy could remember. Morgana continued her conversation with Constance who was seated at her left, though she raised an eyebrow at Iggy to let her know her tardiness had been noted.

Lucie leaned close as Iggy slipped into the chair next to her. 'Everything all right? You look a little bit flushed.'

'I ran into a spot of trouble on the way from my room,' Iggy muttered, settling her crisp white napkin over her lap.

'Trouble in a tall muscular package, I'm betting,' Lucie whispered back with a knowing grin.

Their eyes met. 'He's driving me crazy,' Iggy confessed softly.

Lucie's brows drew together. 'There's not a problem between you two, is there?'

Pulling a face to indicate her indecision, Iggy sighed. 'He's just a lot to handle sometimes.'

'Lucky you,' Lucie deadpanned from the side of her mouth before reaching for the glass of champagne in front of her. 'I'd say that calls for a toast.'

Smothering a laugh, Iggy reached for her own glass and clinked it against Lucie's before taking a sip. The crisp, dry wine fizzed over her palate and she gave an appreciative sigh. 'You're spoiling us with the good stuff, Aunt Morgana.'

'Well, we have such a lot to celebrate, it only seemed fitting.' Reaching for her glass, Morgana raised it first towards to Lucie, and then Constance. 'I know we've already celebrated with the others, but I wanted to personally welcome you both to the family. Bluebell Castle is a better place for having you both under its roof.'

'What a lovely thing to say, Morgana. Thank you so much for opening your home to us.' Constance smiled across the table towards her daughter. 'If you'd told me at the start of this year how much things would change for us, I wouldn't have dared believe it possible.'

'Welcome to you both,' Iggy echoed, forcing the rather large lump which had formed in her throat back down. 'It's nice to have the gender balance tip a bit more in our favour.'

Mrs W came in carrying two large cake stands; one filled with finely cut finger sandwiches, the other laden with bite-sized squares of cake and colourful macarons. 'If I can get you anything else, just ring,' she said, before accepting Morgana's nod of dismissal.

They tucked in, the conversation turning to the wedding, the way it seemed to every time they sat down lately. Not that Iggy minded one bit. Lucie seemed delighted at the prospect of marrying Arthur, and surprisingly relaxed about the whole thing. 'Mum and I are going dress shopping next weekend,' she said to Iggy whilst topping up both their glasses from the champagne bottle. 'You should come with us.'

It was a very touching gesture, but Iggy wouldn't dream of intruding on such a special mother and daughter moment. Shoving away a pang at the unlikelihood she'd ever share a similar day with her on mother, she gave Lucie a smile of thanks. 'You'll want it to be just the two of you, surely? You can take lots of pictures and show me afterwards.'

'Well, I suppose we could,' Lucie drawled out the last word. 'But I'm sure you'd rather try on bridesmaid dresses for yourself rather than leaving it to me to choose for you. What if I subjected you to Bo Peep ruffles?'

'Bridesmaid?' It hadn't occurred to her for a moment that Lucie would want her to fill that role. 'You never mentioned it before.'

'I was waiting for the right moment.' Lucie reached for her hand. 'Arthur's going to have Tristan stand up with him, and I can't think of anyone I'd want by my side more than you.'

That blasted lump was back in her throat again, and Iggy found herself blinking back tears. 'I'd love to do it, thank you.' She squeezed Lucie's hand back, feeling in that moment like she was really gaining a sister.

Keeping hold of her hand, Lucie glanced across the table to her mum. 'And will you give me away?'

Constance reached beneath the table for her napkin, raised it and dabbed at a tear on her cheek. 'Oh, darling, that's a lovely idea, but you might want someone a bit less emotional than me to lean on during your big moment. Every time I even picture you in a wedding dress, I start weeping.'

'Perhaps you could ask Lancelot to do it for you. I'm sure he'd be delighted, and then your mother and I can hang on to each other in the family pew.' Aunt Morgana was looking more than a little dewy eyed, which was very unusual for a woman who prided herself on her composure. She fluttered a hand in front of her face. 'Such nonsense! I'm blaming the champagne.'

The four of them were still laughing when the drawing room door opened to admit a very pale-looking Mrs W. 'Umm, excuse me for interrupting, but there's a visitor.'

Before they could enquire who, the door swung fully open to admit a swirl of Chanel No. 5 perfume and a slender blonde woman clad in a neat cream trouser suit. The scent hit Iggy's nose, bringing with it a flood of memories as her brain tried to process what her eyes were seeing.

'Hardly a visitor, Mrs Walters,' the blonde declared as she swept past the flustered housekeeper. Taking the empty chair beside Constance, she picked up a spare glass and held it out towards Lucie. 'I hope I'm not too late to join the celebrations.'

'Umm, no,' Lucie replied, faintly, her good manners

automatically kicking in to pour champagne into the glass. 'The more the merrier, I guess.' Her inquisitive gaze flicked from the new arrival to Iggy.

Shaking off her shock, Iggy drained her own glass in one swallow, then held it out to Lucie. 'Fill it up, and yours too, you're going to need it.' She raised the crystal flute across the table, no warmth in her words as she spoke once more. 'Constance, Lucie, may I present Helena Ludworth-Mills-Wexford-Jones. My mother.'

Helena's smile didn't waver, but there was a certain tightness around her eyes as she returned Iggy's toast. 'Always a pleasure to see you too, darling.' Having taken a sip, she switched her attention to Lucie. 'When I saw the announcement in the newspaper, I had to come and meet the lucky woman who'll be marrying my darling Arthur. Though it was naughty of him not to tell me the good news himself.'

'Perhaps if your children heard from you more than once or twice a year, you'd know what was going on in their lives.' Morgana's steely façade was well and truly back in place.

'Perhaps if you'd not forced me out of my home and turned your family against me, we wouldn't be in this situation,' Helena snapped. She reached back to touch the elegant chignon tied at her nape, and then let out a brittle laugh that sent a warning shudder up Iggy's spine. 'But that's all water under the bridge, and I'm here to concentrate on the future, not the past.'

Embarrassment and anger burned through Iggy, and it was only out of deference to Lucie and Constance that she held her tongue. The familiar complaint she'd heard throughout her childhood summed up her mother to a T – whatever happened, it was always someone else's fault.

Her gaze strayed to the head of the table, where Morgana sat ramrod straight, disapproval radiating from every pore. She knew people found her aunt intimidating, though she'd never found her so as her stern nature had been tempered with an equal balance of deep affection she'd lavished on Iggy and her brothers. For the first time, she found herself contemplating whether a grain of truth ran through her mother's accusation. It couldn't have been easy for a young bride to enter a household where a woman as foreboding as Morgana acted as matriarch.

Hadn't Iggy already decided she needed to withdraw from her own position at the castle to make room for Lucie? She adored her future sister-in-law and knew she was surrendering what had always been a temporary role to someone who was wholly suited to taking it on. Though it would break her heart to leave, she'd never, ever let Lucie sense even a hint of resentment at the change her presence had wrought over Iggy's circumstances.

Morgana had never been anything other than scathing towards Helena as far as she could remember, though Iggy had always assumed it stemmed from her disapproval of Helena for abandoning her family. What if she'd felt that way towards Helena from the beginning, and worse, had made it clear how she felt? The unexpected pang of sympathy towards her mother sat uncomfortably. Why was she even questioning her aunt's integrity? Digging her nails into her palm, Iggy did a slow mental count to five. Her mother had been in the room for mere moments and was already manipulating the emotions of everyone present.

'Your remembrance of events differs greatly to mine, Helena.' Iggy didn't think she'd ever heard her aunt speak so coldly to anyone. 'I have no desire to embarrass our guests any further with our dirty laundry, so I'll leave it at that.' Morgana took a delicate sip from her china teacup. 'May we assume this is a flying visit?'

'That's up to Arthur.' Helena paused to send a sweet smile across the table to Lucie. 'And his enchanting bride-to-be, of course. Beaumont is over in America on an extended business trip, and I don't have any particular plans for the summer so I thought I'd come and help with the wedding arrangements.' The look of satisfied malice that flashed in her mother's eyes

168

vanished so quickly, Iggy thought she might have imagined it, but she knew better.

Even if her mother had been dealt a bad hand when she was younger, she'd had the best part of twenty-five years to put things right between them. Recalling the last contact at New Year's Eve when she'd phoned in tears because the allowance she'd been paid by Iggy's father – even throughout her subsequent three marriages – had finally ceased according to the terms of his will, Iggy hardened her heart once more. Helena never did anything out of the goodness of her heart, and whatever had caused her to turn up at the castle like a proverbial bad penny, she'd bet the wedding had little, if anything, to do with it.

*

'I'm not staying a night under the same roof as that wretched bloody woman!'

Iggy banged her head softly against the wall outside her uncle's room as she listened to him yelling in fury. He'd stormed upstairs the moment he'd entered the family room before dinner to find Helena perched on one of the sofas like a queen holding court. From the banging and crashing of furniture, it sounded like he was actually packing his bags.

'Lancelot, please. I know this is difficult but think of the children. If they want a chance to spend time with their mother, then surely you owe it to them to keep your feelings under wraps.' Constance had followed Lancelot to his room, and Iggy had to give her credit for stepping into the middle of their family mess in an attempt to mediate.

Wondering if she should intervene, Iggy edged closer to the slight gap where the door had resisted his efforts to slam it closed. Tristan seemed as ambivalent as she was about their mother's arrival, but kind-hearted Arthur had lit up at the news. He'd

169

always held out hope when it came to Helena, no matter how many times she might have let them down in the past.

Before she could make up her mind, the decision was taken out of her hands by her uncle flinging open his bedroom door and stalking out with a large holdall gripped in one hand. 'She's a poisonous bitch, Connie,' he flung over his shoulder. 'I've spent the past twenty-odd years watching her tear the heart out of those children time and again. I won't stand by and let her do it again.' He stopped short at the sight of Iggy, scrubbing a weary hand through his silvering hair. 'Don't ask me to apologise, because I won't.'

Straightening up, Iggy rested her hand on his arm. 'I don't particularly want her here, but it's up to Arthur.'

Lancelot's features crumpled into a frustrated scowl. 'She'll ruin the bloody wedding. She'll ruin everything, she always does.'

Iggy squeezed his arm. 'We won't let her. Give her a couple of days and she'll get bored and move on. You know what she's like.' It was the hope she had to cling to. Like a magpie, Helena was attracted to anything shiny and new. Right now, it was the idea of the wedding, but she fully expected something else to crop up on the social circuit which would draw her away. 'It's Ascot in a couple of weeks, and you know she never misses that.'

Her uncle placed his hand over hers where it rested on his arm, squeezed her fingers and then gently removed her hold. 'I'm sorry, darling, but for as long as she's staying in the castle, I can't be around her. I'll be in the stables if you need me.' Her uncle kept a room in what had been the old stable hand's quarters in the upper floor of the stable block for the odd occasion where he had a sick horse that needed watching overnight.

With a nod, Iggy stepped aside, feeling as miserable as Constance looked standing in the open doorway of Lancelot's room. 'I'll talk to him later, once he's had a chance to calm down a bit,' she said, giving Iggy a lopsided smile that didn't belie the worry in her gaze.

'Just don't find yourself caught in the middle of it all,' Iggy begged her. 'You're so good for him, I'd hate for the two of you to fall out over this.'

Constance shook her head. 'I'll try, but it's not just me caught in the middle, I have Lucie to think of, too. Nothing's ever easy, is it?'

'Not where my mother is concerned,' Iggy agreed ruefully and they shared a smile.

'Are you all right, though?' The warmth in Constance's voice drew her like a magnet, and Iggy accepted a hug, fighting the urge to cling on when Constance closed her arms around her.

Why can't our mother be like this?

It was a forlorn hope, a child's foolish wish and Iggy pushed it aside. Helena was as she was, and that was all there was to it. 'I'm okay. It's a bit of a shock to the system, but as I said to Lancelot, with any luck, she'll move on again just as quickly as she arrived. We'd better go back down and make sure she's not causing any mischief.' Another forlorn hope, as it turned out.

When the two of them entered the family room, all eyes turned their way. Ignoring everyone else, Iggy caught Tristan's gaze and gave an imperceptible shake of her head in response to his raised eyebrows. Rolling his eyes, he stood and offered his seat to Constance, fussing around her until she was beaming up at him.

'I'll fix some drinks, shall I?' Arthur said, his hearty tone just the wrong side of fake. Iggy wanted to shake him. She understood his conflicted feelings about their mother, but he needed to get over them. She was never going to change.

'A G&T for me please,' Helena tipped her face up to smile at her eldest son as he stood, drawing Iggy's attention to the fact she'd injected herself into the middle of the sofa between Arthur and Lucie. Turning that smile towards Constance, Helena notched it up and said in a sweet voice. 'Poor Lancelot. He's always carried *such* a torch for me. I had hoped he would've got over it by now, but apparently not.'

Watching Constance's brow crease in shock, Iggy glared across the room at her mother. 'How can you possibly say that?'

Helena opened her mouth to respond, but Morgana cut her off. 'Forget about the drinks, Arthur, let's go straight into dinner.' There was no missing the warning look she shot at Helena on her way out of the room.

Completely nonplussed, Iggy exchanged a look of confusion with Arthur who was standing beside the drink's cabinet still clutching an open bottle of Bombay Sapphire gin. Lancelot couldn't stand Helena, so why on earth was she suggesting otherwise?

As the others filed out, she cornered Arthur. 'You can't let her stay here. Can't you see she'll ruin everything?'

To her shock, his expression darkened to a frown. 'You're just like all the others. It can't have been easy for her to come here after all this time, knowing the kind of reception she'd receive.'

'With bloody good reason,' Iggy hissed. 'She's going to drive a wedge between all of us if we're not careful.'

Red-faced, Arthur glanced towards where Lucie was waiting for him by the door before glaring back down at Iggy. 'The only thing that's going to drive a wedge through this family is your inability to let the past go. Mother wants to celebrate mine and Lucie's wedding with us, is that really so bad?' Without waiting for her response, he stalked across the room, took Lucie's arm in his and walked out.

Her heart wanted to break. Not because of his uncharacteristic outburst, although she hated the idea of being at odds with him for even a moment. Beneath his anger, she sensed a terrible need for their mother's love and acceptance. She would give anything to be proven wrong, but she desperately feared her beloved brother was in for a terrible fall. 'Oh, *Arthur.*'

Chapter 15

Will had never seen a family dynamic change so swiftly as that of the Ludworths' in the space of a few minutes. He'd been about to descend the stairs for dinner when a furious Lancelot had rushed past him, with Constance and Igraine in his wake. She'd barely given him a glance, and her worried expression had been enough for him to decide not to interfere and continue on his way down to the family room.

He still had no real grasp on what was going on, but he'd instinctively disliked the way the stranger seated on the sofa had widened her eyes at him as he walked through the door. He knew that look, had seen it too often in the past. He was interesting to them because of what he was, not who he was. After managing a polite introduction, Will had retreated to the opposite sofa and done his best to remain inconspicuous.

The distress and confusion on Igraine's face as she watched her brother walk away from their whispered exchange sliced at him, and he crossed to her side. 'What's going on?' He kept his voice low, angling his body to block out the rest of the room.

'I don't know. I feel like I've woken up in the middle of a nightmare.' Her eyes closed for a second, before snapping open, a fire of determination burning in the gold-flecked hazel. 'Will you keep my mother occupied during dinner?'

He'd rather pet a viper, but understanding she was asking for his help, Will agreed at once. 'Of course, we'll talk later, yeah?'

She nodded, opened her mouth to speak then hesitated.

'What is it?'

'Don't let on to her about us, okay? She has a nasty habit of spoiling things and I don't want what's between us to be any more grist to her mill.' Popping on tiptoe, she pressed a quick kiss to his lips. 'She's trouble, Will, be on your guard at all times.'

Not liking this latest development at all, he hurried from the room to find almost everyone else had disappeared leaving Helena alone in the great hall. Lengthening his stride, he caught up to where she stood with one hand resting on the enormous round table, a look of sadness on her face. She looked so sad and forlorn he felt sorry for her until he remembered Igraine's warning. Turning on the empty smile he'd honed from years of practice, he held out his arm to her. 'Would you do me the honour?'

'How kind.' Her face brightened at once with a smile as fake as his own as her fingers closed over his forearm. 'I had no idea I'd be meeting a celebrity when I arrived today to surprise Arthur and Lucie.' Her lashes fluttered, her smile turning coy. 'You must tell me everything about why you're here.' *Oh, Igraine hadn't been kidding, this one could switch it on and off like a lightbulb.*

Will escorted her into the dining room, giving her a brief outline of the ongoing renovation works for the grounds and gardens, but making no mention of the fact it was Igraine who'd first got in touch with him. 'It's a pleasure and a privilege for me to be able to work somewhere with so much history.'

Noting that Tristan had already taken the seat beside Constance and Morgana the one opposite him besides Lucie, he decided he'd better act as a buffer and pulled out a chair for Helena one further down from Morgana then settled on the seat between them.

Igraine slid into the seat opposite him beside her brother

and he gave her a quick reassuring smile. 'I was just telling your mother about the works in the gardens.'

Picking up his cue, Igraine joined in their conversation and between them they managed to keep the topic going through most of the meal, leaving Helena little chance to switch the topic of conversation until after the plates had been cleared away. 'Have you chosen a date for the wedding?' she asked Arthur, who'd been leaning close to Constance and talking to her quietly.

'What? Oh, I think we've settled on the middle Saturday in August.'

He turned to Lucie for confirmation, and she nodded. 'That's right. The gardens will be ready, and we should have most of the exhibition stuff sorted out by then. I spoke to the team at Witherby's and they've agreed with me that we should push back the opening until the beginning of October. It will give us a couple of extra months to secure the last of the Viggliorento paintings we need to complete the exhibition.'

'Exhibition?' Helena all but leaned across Will, and he pushed his seat back a few inches to avoid her brushing against him.

Lucie's eyes darted to Arthur, a quick flush marring her cheeks. Will watched him take Lucie's hand and give it a squeeze before he answered his mother. 'Thanks to Lucie's detective work, we discovered a quite valuable painting hidden in the castle. It's currently being restored and once that's completed, we're mounting an exhibition of several works by the artist, with our picture as the centrepiece. We're then going to auction it off at the end of the year and put the funds towards the upkeep of the castle.'

'Well, that makes things a little clearer,' Helena said, settling back into her seat once more. 'I was beginning to wonder where all the cash was coming from to pay for all these grand plans for the grounds. And I'm sure a celebrity like Will doesn't come cheap.'

'Mother,' Igraine hissed across the table, as Will sensed Morgana stiffen on his left, though she made no move to turn in Helena's direction as she had throughout the meal.

Apparently undaunted, Helena gave an aggrieved sniff. 'Well, you can't blame me for wondering when your brother was pleading poverty not six months ago.' She let out a brittle laugh that went straight to Will's nerves like nails on a blackboard. 'I assumed Arthur must be marrying for money when I saw the announcement.'

At Lucie's shocked gasp, Helena leaned forward once more, that horribly fake smile on her face. 'But as soon as I met you, I knew that wasn't the case.' She paused a beat too long before adding. 'He's obviously in love with you, my dear.'

Will met Igraine's eyes across the table, and knew he wasn't the only one who'd caught the sly dig in her mother's words. Like him, Lucie had been raised on a council estate in London, although unlike him, she'd also spent some time at a private school and carried no trace of a city accent.

'I don't think I'll bother with dessert,' Constance said, her voice stiff with what Will suspected was outrage. 'If you'll excuse me?'

'I'll come with you, Connie.' Morgana made a move to stand, and Will hopped up to pull her chair back. She gave him a nod. 'Thank you, Will.'

'My pleasure.'

He was about to resume his seat when Igraine stood up. 'Come on, Mother, you're looking a bit tired after a long day of travel.' There was a razor edge to the smile she gave Helena, and Will glanced away before he started laughing at the absolute affront on the older woman's face. Circling the table, Igraine placed a hand on her mother's chair, giving her no option but to stand up. 'I'm sure you'll just want to relax for the rest of the evening. I'll arrange for some tea to be sent up to your room.' With a hand on Helena's lower back, she all but propelled her out of the room.

The rest of the group dispersed; Arthur and Lucie to take the dogs out for a walk as was their usual after dinner routine, Tristan to go and check on Lancelot who'd apparently moved out of the main castle and into the stables in protest at Helena's arrival. Left alone in the dining room, Will took a minute to rotate his neck in an attempt to relieve the tension in his spine. If the triplets' mother was planning a prolonged stay at the castle, it was going to be a very long summer.

*

The knock on his bedroom door came a couple of hours later. Although he'd changed for bed into a T-shirt and a baggy pair of sleep shorts, it was still too hot to be comfortable, so Will was sitting in the armchair as close to the open window as possible, enjoying the light breeze floating in. 'Come in.'

Igraine poked her head around the door, her dark hair caught up in a long plait which trailed over her shoulder. 'I'm not disturbing you, am I?'

Putting down the risk assessment the groundworkers had sent through for the next stage of their works, Will patted his lap. 'Come here.'

With a sigh, she closed the door behind her then crossed the room to curl up against his chest. 'What a bloody day.'

He loved the way she melted into him, could feel her relaxing by inches as he pushed his hand under the base of her plaited hair to stroke her nape, his other curling under her knees to tuck her a bit closer. 'Are you all right?' It was a stupid question, because she clearly wasn't, but he wasn't sure what else to say.

'I just wish I knew why she decided to show up now, it's all so out of the blue.'

Will pressed a kiss to the top of her head. 'Didn't she say something about seeing the wedding announcement? It's only natural she'd want to be involved in that, I guess.'

Igraine stiffened against him. 'She's never shown any bloody interest in what any of us do before now, I don't see why a wedding should be any different.' Her tension drained out on another sigh. 'Sorry, I don't mean to be snappy, it's just not like her to turn up like this.'

She had a point, he supposed. If it was him getting married, would his mum suddenly drop everything to show up unannounced? He hardly thought so. 'When was the last time you saw her?'

'She hasn't been home since she first left when we were little. The few times we saw her, she picked us up from school for a day out. She lived abroad for about six years with her third husband.'

'Third?' Will laughed. 'How many has she had?'

Igraine shifted on his lap so she could tilt her head back against his shoulder and look up at him. He was pleased to see she looked a bit cheerier than when she'd first come in. 'She's up to four, so far. The latest one does something *very important* for one of the big banks. As to your original question, I haven't seen her since I graduated from university, and she only dropped in that day because she was visiting some friends who lived in Gloucestershire at the time. I haven't really thought about it until now, but it's been over five years.'

'You didn't miss her then?' He'd got used to his mum not being about, but he couldn't assume it was the same for Igraine.

'Hardly! You've seen how much havoc she's created in just a few hours. I was more than happy when she married Beaumont Jones the third – he's an American, in case you hadn't guessed by the name – because it meant they were always off travelling because of his work. It became easier for her to stop any more half-hearted attempts at keeping in contact, which was a relief as far as Tristan and I were concerned, though it's always been harder on Arthur.'

Ah. Things were starting to fall into place. If Arthur was the one closest to her, it was only natural he'd want her to stick around if she was showing an interest in his wedding. 'How long is she intending to stay?'

Igraine shrugged. 'I've no idea. She said Beaumont is on an extended business trip, so I'm worried it'll be for the whole summer.' Letting out a groan, she buried her face into his neck. 'God, I hope not.'

He hoped not as well. 'Can I ask why you don't want her to know about us?'

Raising her face, she gave him a challenging look. 'If you're thinking it's because I'm ashamed of you in anyway, you can put that idea right out of your head! I *adore* you. Being with you makes me feel so good.' He accepted the kiss she offered, liking the idea of this beautiful woman adoring him more than was probably sensible.

'*But?*'

She nestled back into his chest, one hand stroking over the thin cotton of his T-shirt. 'You saw the way she sharpened her claws on poor Lucie – well, she's been doing that to me for as many years as I can remember. She can spot a weak spot a mile off, and will exploit it mercilessly.' Her hand pressed over his heart. 'You're a very big weak spot, and I don't want to give her the chance to spoil things between us.'

Holding her close, Will shuffled his bottom along the seat of the armchair to create a bit more space for her to lean against him. 'Don't fret, sweetheart. I won't let her do that.'

'Promise,' she whispered against his skin.

'I promise. Whatever you need me to do, you only have to ask. Even if that means keeping a low profile.'

She fell silent for a long moment, then raised her face to stare up at him. 'Will you hold me?'

'I thought that's what I was doing?' he teased, pressing a kiss to the tip of her nose.

'You're such a funny guy.' Shifting position, she pressed her hips down into the hardness of his lap and all humour between them melted into a deep, throbbing need. She stretched her neck up to capture his lips with her own. 'I want.' She kissed him again. 'You to take me to bed.' Another, deeper kiss. 'And make love to me.'

'*Igraine.*' He lost himself in the sweet heat of her mouth, in the promise of those words and all the myriad things he would do to her in the long, slow hours of the night. He tried to pull her

179

closer, but soon grew frustrated with the awkward angle of their bodies and eventually grasped her hips and urged her to stand.

He didn't drag her to the bed, well not *quite*, but she didn't seem to mind his hurry as he tumbled her back across the crisp, dark sheets. Bracing himself with his hands on either side of her head, he wriggled his hips against hers until she widened them to let him settle exactly where he wanted to be. The heat of her scorched through the thin layers of their clothing, his mind racing as he tried to decide which of the many delicious things, he wanted to do to her first.

'What's the matter?' she asked, when he didn't immediately move.

'Nothing, just savouring the moment now I've finally got you beneath me.'

'Mmm.' Her little hum of pleasure shot sparks of pleasure through him. Hooking a foot over his hip, she locked their lower bodies together. 'I've been thinking about us being together like this ever since you waylaid me on my way to tea this afternoon.'

Her hands slid up his back beneath his T-shirt her short nails teasing against his skin. 'Now what was it you promised me earlier? That being with you would be so good I'd forget any other man.' A sly smile teased around her mouth. 'Perhaps you're the one having second thoughts. Worried you won't live up to those big words, are you?'

The challenge in her eyes tipped him over the edge, and soon there was no more room for words, no more doubts about whether they were ready to take this next step, only the need driving him on, and hers rising to meet and match it. Only the secret whispers of lovers meeting in the dark.

* * *

The next couple of weeks passed in a blur of back-breaking days working on the water garden and sweet, sultry nights with

Igraine in his arms. Everyone was so busy, the lack of public contact between the two of them had gone unnoticed – or at least uncommented upon. Helena had taken herself off to Ascot for a few days, giving them all a brief respite from the tension her presence at the castle was causing, but she'd arrived back again the previous evening, arms laden with wedding magazines.

Lancelot was still living above the stables, and his continued absence from the dinner table was a constant point of unspoken stress. The continued hot weather wasn't helping, either, and there'd been a few frayed tempers, especially from Arthur. The poor guy looked miserable as sin, and it was clear to Will he felt torn between the women in his life. The only one who seemed oblivious to it all was Helena. She was either a consummate actress, Will had decided, or she had a hide thicker than a rhino and zero self-awareness. Probably a combination of all three.

Some nights Will and Igraine found themselves too exhausted to do anything but sleep, but that didn't matter because waking in the morning to find her curled up next to him was a simple joy in itself. Glancing down at her now in the early dawn light, Will couldn't resist running a finger across the shadowed line of her cheekbone. Grumbling in her sleep, Igraine raised a hand to swat him away before rolling onto her other side and wriggling back until her bottom slotted neatly against the curve of his hips.

Curling his arm round her waist, Will settled down against her back, content to hold her until the alarm went off in another hour or so. She wasn't a morning person, as he'd learnt to his cost when he'd attempted to wake her early the previous week with a kiss and earned a mouthful of choice words. No, he schooled himself to patience, best to leave her to sleep and let the alarm catch the brunt of her early morning grumpiness.

The next thing he knew, the phone on his bedside cabinet was beeping and Igraine was elbowing him in the stomach. 'Turn it off,' she muttered, dragging her pillow over her head.

Rolling over, he swiped off the alarm then rolled back to tug her pillow away. 'Come on, sleepyhead, you've got a busy day ahead of you.' She was going dress shopping with Lucie and Constance – and now she'd returned, Helena had decided to tag along with them.

'Go away and let me sleep.' She made a grab for her pillow, hair tumbling all over her face in tangled waves, but he reached it first, tossing it off the bed with a laugh.

'You told me I had to make sure you got up on time.'

'Well, I changed my mind,' she said, stealing his pillow and curling up with it. His phone started to beep again, and she let out a groan. 'You're determined to torture me, aren't you?'

'That's not my alarm.' He reached for the phone. *Who the hell was texting him at that time of the morning?* It beeped again just as his hand was closing around it. And again, before he had chance to tap in his unlock code.

The first message was from Anna, his assistant. *Have you seen the papers yet?*

'Bloody hell, now what?' There'd been a sporadic flurry of more of those stupid Where's Willy articles, with claims of sightings from all sorts of unlikely places, including a couple of blurry photos of some poor rando on the beach in Ibiza. They'd soon lost interest, though, and Will had begun to believe he'd heard the last of it. Melody was stepping out with that singer whose party he'd forgotten about and looked for all the world to be as in love with him as she'd appeared to be with Will. There was an Oscar in that woman's future, for sure. It had taken the heat off him, so he wished her nothing but well.

Igraine propped herself up on her elbows. 'What is it?'

'Dunno,' he said, tilting the phone to show her the message from Anna. 'Some rubbish in the press again by the looks of it.'

'Don't they ever get bored of it?' she sighed, flopping back against the pillow.

His phone beeped again. 'Apparently not.' The next message was from his agent, asking him to call urgently and not to make any statements until they'd spoken. His gut started to churn, and he ignored the rest of his messages to open his web browser and type in the address for the most notorious of the red-tops.

WILL CHEATSPEARE! Screamed the headline above a photograph of a man in a biker jacket staring down at a woman clad in a white dressing gown. It took the familiar twin grey bands encircling the arms of the jacket for Will to register he was looking at a picture of himself with Phillipa Cornwall.

Feeling sick now, he flicked to another tabloid homepage WILL NICKS TONY'S JULIET. If anything, the photo they'd used was even more damning than the previous one, as it showed Phillipa standing on tiptoe to kiss his cheek.

'Shit.' Will tossed the phone onto the bed, then raised his hands to cover his eyes, as though he could somehow shield himself from what he'd already seen. 'Shit, shit, shit.'

'What's the matter?'

He opened his eyes to see Igraine reaching for his phone. 'Leave it!' he snapped, but it was already too late.

'Is that you?' Igraine frowned at the screen. 'And who's the woman you're with?' He watched in silent dread as her eyes flicked back and forth as she took in the lurid details and innuendo in the story below the image. When she met his gaze, her expression was incredulous. 'Phillipa Cornwall? *The* Phillipa Cornwall?'

'She was a client, nothing more,' he said, crossly, trying to take the phone back off her. 'It's all bollocks.'

'Just like Melody wasn't your girlfriend, right? It doesn't look like bollocks,' she retorted, tucking the phone behind her back when he made a snatch for it. 'It looks like you're snogging a married woman on her bloody doorstep.'

'Not snogging! She kissed me on the cheek, for God's sake. Bloody hell, you're as bad as they are, reading more into something than there is.'

Her brows shot up, and when she spoke, her tone was icy. 'Don't speak to me like that. There's a photo of you being kissed by a famous actress wearing nothing more than a dressing gown splashed across the front page of a national newspaper, so I don't think you're in any position to take the moral high ground with me!'

Throwing back the covers, he jumped out of bed and reached for a pair of shorts. Yanking them on, he turned to face her, hating the look of distrust on her face. 'Christ, if that's what you think of me, you'd better get the hell out of my bed.'

'Good idea!' She tossed his phone down and got out, marching towards the bedroom door.

She'd almost reached it, when common sense crashed through the anger and he ran to catch her, shoving the door shut just as she'd tugged it open. 'I'm sorry, I'm sorry. I shouldn't be taking it out on you.'

Igraine stayed with her back towards him, shoulders high around her ears. 'You said she was a client ...'

'And only a client, I swear to you. I showed up because she wanted some alterations to a job I'd quoted and she tried to throw herself at me.' Taking a risk, he placed a hand around her arm. 'It was the same day you phoned me, that was why I was so distracted and didn't pay proper attention to what you were saying to me.'

She turned to face him. 'You were in her house when I called?'

Nodding, he reached for her hand. 'You saved me from the most embarrassing situation of my life. Turns out Tony Cornwall isn't the hero everyone thinks he is. He's cheated on her for years, and she thought she might be able to get her own back.' Gesturing behind him towards the phone on the bed, he continued to explain, hoping she'd believe what was sounding ridiculous to his own ears. 'She got really upset and ended up pouring the whole sorry story out to me over a cup of tea. That kiss was nothing, just her way of saying thank you because I didn't embarrass her.'

Igraine's expression softened. 'Poor thing, she must've been mortified.'

The relief flooding through him threatened to make him giddy. She believed him. *Thank God.*

A scowl of suspicion clouded her face. 'Is that why you changed your mind and took the job up here?'

It was on the tip of his tongue to deny it completely, but any lie between them now could spell disaster. 'I won't deny that the chance to escape London had its merits, but I wouldn't use you like that. As soon as I saw the photos you'd taken, I fell in love with the place.' He reached for her hand, deciding there should be total honesty between them. 'Bluebell Castle isn't the only thing I'm falling in love with.'

He could tell he'd taken her by surprise from the way she stared up at him, mouth shaping a little 'O' of surprise. 'Iggy,' he reached for her hand, but his bloody phone started beeping again.

'We'll talk later.' With a smile that could hardly be called encouraging, she evaded his grasp and slipped out of the room.

'Damn,' he said to the empty air, wondering if he should go after her. His phone beeped again, and the next curse which left his lips wasn't so mild. He needed to sorted this mess out first, and just hope his hasty words hadn't inadvertently created another.

185

Chapter 16

Dread had filled Igraine at the prospect of Helena tagging along to Lucie's dress shopping day. It was bad enough feeling like an intruder herself, but her mother had never been one for taking a back seat and Iggy feared she would steamroller over quiet, gentle Constance. Added to that was the constant feedback loop in her brain. Will had said he loved her – well, as near as made no difference – and she'd bolted from the room like a startled colt.

She'd regretted leaving the moment she walked out of his room, but then she'd seen her mother's bedroom door opening and she'd been too busy sprinting around the corner before she got caught sneaking around to worry about it. Showered and dressed, she'd been sucked into the vortex of Hurricane Helena and was still reeling. Though, she'd been an absolute angel to both Lucie and Constance, she'd still taken every chance to have a little dig at Iggy whenever the other two weren't around.

When they arrived at the boutique, Helena immediately ordered a bottle of champagne to be served – making a big show of assuring them she would pay for it – and something of a party atmosphere settled over the private fitting room on the upper floor of the boutique.

Only when Lucie actively sought her opinion, confessing to

feeling hopeless in the face of so many different shapes and styles of gowns did Helena speak up. She pulled the boutique owner into the discussion, and the two of them debated the pros and cons of fishtails, empire and princess lines, most of which had gone straight over Iggy's head. She knew how to dress herself, knew what suited her shape but had never been a follower of any particular fashion trend.

When it came to what Iggy should be wearing, however, Helena showed no such restraint. Not wanting to cause a scene on Lucie's special day, Iggy had grabbed a handful of gowns and retreated into one of the changing rooms for a respite. She should've known it would take more than a curtain to keep Helena at bay.

'What about this one? It's not too fussy and will make the most of your figure.' A hand dangling a drape of sage green satin from a padded hanger thrust through the changing room curtain, followed a few moments later by her mother's face. 'The colour will look lovely and fresh, even on the hottest day.' She waved the hanger towards Iggy, indicating she should take it.

Iggy stared for a moment, waiting for the other shoe to drop, for one of Helena's trademark acid asides to take the sheen off the seeming pleasant façade. It didn't take long.

'You should really invest in some *Spanx*, darling, they're a godsend for women with ample hips like yours.'

It took all of her willpower not to look in the mirror behind her, or to drop a hand to shield the curves of her body. She was fit and healthy and had no issues with her physique, but it still stung her pride. Wordlessly, she took the dress her mother had brought, and hung it on the hook in front of her so she could study the lines more closely.

The simple sheath had spaghetti-thin straps, a scooped cowl neckline which would hint at rather than reveal her décolletage and a flowing skirt created by some cleverly inserted extra panels of material. Though she wanted to reject it out of sheer irritation with her mother, she couldn't stop looking at it. It was gorgeous, and – she reached out a tentative finger to stroke the shiny fabric – soft as a cloud. 'Don't you think it's a little bit strappy for church?'

'There's a jacket that goes with it.' Helena thrust her other hand through the curtain.

Trying to ignore the smug expression on her mother's face, Iggy studied the lace bolero jacket in the exact same shade as the dress. The sleeves looked as though they would come to the middle of her upper arms, and the scalloped edges of the lace would soften the muscular lines of her triceps. It was a more delicate garment than she would have instinctively chosen for herself, but her heart skipped a little at the sight of it.

'I know it's not your sort of thing, but it won't do any harm to dress a bit more femininely even if it's only for one day. All I've seen you in so far is jeans and trousers.'

'I was wearing a dress the day you arrived,' Iggy retorted before she could stop herself. Damn it, she knew better than to let Helena know any of her petty strikes were hitting their mark.

'If you can call it that. It looked like something you'd stolen from one of your brother's wardrobes.' Helena shook her head. 'Your father always did spoil you, letting you run wild instead of ensuring you had the kind of education fitting for a lady.'

Okay, now she'd gone too far. 'Don't you dare say one word against him, Mother. Not. One. Word.'

'I'm only trying to do what's best for you, Igraine, that's all. I'll go and see how Lucie's doing and give you a chance to get a hold of yourself.' Lower lip trembling, Helena flounced through the curtain.

Feeling hot and bothered, Iggy pressed her face against the cool glass of the mirror. 'God, give me the strength not to strangle her before the day is out,' she muttered.

Tempted as she was to hide out in the dressing room for the rest of the morning, there was no way of avoiding Helena forever. Deciding to bite the bullet and get it over with, Iggy reached for the dress. It fit like it had been handmade for her. Clinging where it needed to and skimming over her hips and thighs to fall to her feet. The hem brushed the floor, but once she had suitable shoes on, the length would be perfect.

Taking care with the delicate lace of the bolero jacket, she slipped it over her shoulders and settled the edges so they framed the soft cowl neck of the dress. It instantly transformed the dress from sophisticated to demure and would be perfect to wear in church, and for the official photographs. She could always take it off later once the reception got into full swing. A small smile played over her lips as she imagined the look on Will's face when she removed the jacket before they took to the floor for a slow dance. Panic and pleasure rippled through her. *Will had said he loved her.*

'How are you getting on, darling?' It was Helena again, sounding for all the world as though they shopped together every day, and had fun whilst they were at it.

At least the interruption stopped her mooning over Will. She couldn't think about him now, couldn't give voice to the hopes and fears his earlier declaration had stirred up within her. Today was all about Lucie and the wedding. 'I'm coming out.' Taking one last look over her reflection, Iggy sucked in a deep breath and pulled the curtains open.

'Oh.' She wasn't sure which of the two women seated on the circular banquette in the middle of the room had made the little sound, but they were both beaming up at her, Helena with a hint of triumph, Constance with tears sparkling in her eyes.

'You look beautiful,' Constance said. 'Simply gorgeous.' Dabbing a finger to the corner of her eye, she turned to Helena beside her. 'You really have the perfect eye for this kind of thing. Perhaps you'd like to help me with my outfit, too.'

Iggy gulped, hoping Constance knew what she was letting herself in for. Although, it had to be said that Helena had been on her very best behaviour towards Lucie, so perhaps she'd manage to do the same towards Constance, too.

Helena inclined her head like a queen bestowing her favour on a minion. 'I'd be delighted, Connie, simply delighted. Once we know what the girls are wearing, we can coordinate accordingly.'

'Well, I'm wearing green,' Iggy declared, unable to resist the temptation to turn on the spot, sending the skirt of her gown twirling. She simply adored the dress and she would not say otherwise as much as she might enjoy throwing something back in her mother's face.

It suddenly occurred to her that the most important person wasn't present. 'Umm, unless Lucie doesn't want me to, of course.'

'Doesn't want you to what?' Lucie appeared from the opposite dressing room, clutching the front of a strapless ivory dress studded with twinkling aurora borealis crystals to her chest, the boutique manager in her wake, still trying to fasten the hooks of the bodice together. The bride-to-be stopped dead. 'Oh my goodness, look at you!'

'Look at you!' Iggy echoed, gaze roaming over the acres of net skirts flowing from the bottom of the fitted, crystal-encrusted bodice. 'I love that dress!'

Lucie cast a dubious stare down the gaping front of her gown. 'Do you think so? I'm not exactly filling it out in all the right places.'

Helena was on her feet in an instant. 'Lift your arms out of the way, dear, and let Lorraine finish fastening it up.' With efficient hands, she replaced Lucie's hold on the dress, tugging it here, twisting it a little there whilst the boutique owner fiddled with the tiny hooks at the back. 'There, that's a lot better.' Helena stepped back, then forwards again to pinch a bit of excess material in the bodice tight. 'A couple of tucks on either side, and it will fit you just fine.' She looked past Lucie to the boutique owner. 'Can we do the adjustments without ruining the line of the bodice?'

Lorraine moved to Lucie's other side, taking her own pinch of material. 'If we put them under the arms, they wouldn't show,' she mused.

Lucie caught Iggy's gaze and rolled her eyes. Returning a

sympathetic smile, Iggy said. 'It's your job to stand still and get talked about, you might as well get used to it!'

Lucie giggled, then turned her attention towards Constance. 'What do you think, Mum?'

Constance studied her daughter for a long minute, before looking at the two women still tugging and fussing at the top of her dress. 'You look stunning, darling, but don't forget you have to wear it all day. It doesn't matter what I think, or what anyone else thinks, for that matter.' She cast a significant glance at Helena who'd quietened to listen to her, much to Iggy's amazement. 'If you feel anything less than a hundred per cent confident in it, then I think you should try something else.'

Lucie glanced down. 'I do feel a little bit exposed,' she admitted. 'But I love all the sparkle, and—' she gathered handfuls of the tulle net skirt '—I absolutely love this.'

'Hold on a moment, I might have the answer.' Lorraine disappeared down the stairs leading to the main showroom floor below, heels clacking on the wooden treads.

While the manager was away, Iggy took the opportunity to return to her dressing room and remove her dress. Much as she loved it, she didn't want to risk spoiling it. Returning a few minutes later in her jeans and T-shirt, she took a seat beside Constance. 'Where's Mother?'

'Helping Lucie with her hooks.' She nodded towards the closed curtains on the other dressing room, face pensive.

'Are you okay?'

Blinking away the distant look in her eyes, Constance smiled. 'What? Oh, yes, I'm fine, just hoping I didn't put my foot in it.'

'About Lucie's dress?' When Constance nodded, Iggy continued. 'You know Lucie better than anyone and you could obviously tell that although we were all raving about it, there was something not quite right.' She patted Constance's hand. 'Mother's got a hide thicker than a rhino's so don't worry about offending her.'

Constance tried and failed to give her a disapproving look,

and Iggy wondered if perhaps she wasn't falling for Helena's flannel as much as it might seem. Perhaps Lancelot had confided in her about what lay at the heart of his dislike for Helena, Iggy thought as she settled back on the bench. 'It will take as long as it takes. We've got nothing else to do all day other than find Lucie the dress that's perfect for her – even if it means trying on everything in the shop.'

Lorraine's heels clacked on the stairs once more and she appeared with a huge confection of beads and gauzy net hooked over both arms. 'Sorry I took so long but it wasn't hanging where I thought it was.' Reaching up, she hooked the hanger of the dress on a high hook beside Lucie's dressing room. She fiddled and fussed with it before at last stepping back and giving Iggy a good look at it.

The crystal-encrusted bodice was indeed similar to the dress Lucie had tried on, and it had the same kind of voluminous skirt, though this one had a sheer layer of organza covering the tulle, with an inch-wide band of crystals hemming the base of it. What made it stand out from the other dress was that rather than being strapless, this one had an upper panel of sheer organza connected to the bodice and full sleeves of the same material. Iggy didn't think she'd seen anything more beautiful in all her life.

'Are you ready for me in there?' Lorraine asked before peeking inside the curtain. 'Don't worry about all those hooks, I'll sort it out later. Now, shall we swap places?'

Iggy was relieved when Helena took the hint and retreated from the dressing room and came to sit beside her. Constance leaned across to the table beside her and handed them both a glass of champagne. They sipped in nervous silence as whispers and rustles of material came from behind the curtain. It seemed to be taking an awful long time, which Iggy decided was either a really good sign, or a really bad one.

'Umm, Mrs Kennington, can we borrow you for a minute?' Lorraine called. Iggy held out her hand to take Constance's glass as she rose and hurried over to the dressing room.

More whispers, followed by 'Oh, darling, don't cry.' Iggy's heart sank until she heard a giggle from Lucie.

The curtain swept back and Iggy suddenly understood why not only Lucie, but her mum and Lorraine all had tears in their eyes. Looking like something out of a fairy tale, Lucie walked out of the dressing room and turned in a slow circle before them. Choked by the beautiful picture she made, Iggy couldn't do anything other than bite her lip and smile enthusiastically when Lucie's eyes met hers.

'It's the one, isn't it?' Lucie glanced around at them all.

'When it makes everyone cry, I know I've found a winner,' Lorraine agreed, then laughed. 'Goodness, look at the state of us all.' Bustling over to the banquette, the manager reached for a box of tissues on one of the side tables and handed it around to everyone.

Still clutching two glasses, Iggy gave her a helpless look which Constance caught. She hurried over with a smile. 'Let me take that back from you.' Constance took a sip then dabbed at her eyes once more with her tissue. 'Goodness me, what a day.'

'Someone help me out of this so I can have a drink, for goodness sake!' Lucie's plaintive cry set them all laughing and Lorraine ushered her back into the dressing room.

*

'It's all going very well, isn't it?' Lucie nudged the stack of boxes beside her which contained shoes, a sparkling tiara and a cloud-like veil. The dress itself required a couple of minor alterations and would be ready for collection in a couple of weeks. Constance and Helena were downstairs browsing through the racks of mother-of-the-bride outfits Lorraine also stocked, giving the two of them a chance to sit and relax after the excitement of the morning.

Iggy glanced down at the box beside her containing her green dress and the matching bolero carefully folded into acid-free tissue paper and couldn't resist smiling. 'It's proving to be a much better day than I thought it was going to be when I woke up this morning, that's for sure.'

Lucie wrinkled her nose. 'We saw the papers. I wasn't sure if I should say anything, but I just wanted to make sure everything is all right with you and Will.'

'I think so.' When Lucie raised an eyebrow, she shrugged. 'He had a more than plausible explanation for the photo so it sounds like it's just another lot of baseless muck-raking like that stupid Where's Willy article.'

'But ...?'

Iggy flashed a sidelong glance at her friend, wishing like hell they hadn't made the sensible decision to switch to Buck's Fizz which was a good three-quarters orange juice. 'He told me he loves me.'

Lucie laughed. 'Not the best of timing!'

'Indeed,' Iggy agreed, wryly, before the weight of Will's words settled heavily upon her once more. 'I kind of wish he hadn't said it at all, though.'

'Oh, dear.' Lucie winced. 'You don't feel the same way?'

Iggy sighed. 'I think I do.' And that was the crux of the problem. She'd been quite happy to ignore that part of her that had started to get over-excited about how well things were going between the two of them. The part that had caught her off guard once or twice with daydreams about her own wedding. Will was sexy and funny, and oh so easy to be with, and she'd been happy with that, flights of romantic fancy be damned.

A summer of fun, that's what they'd agreed to, but then he'd gone and broken the rules. The worst part was, she didn't know why. Had he said it just to placate her? To try and convince her there'd been nothing going on between him and Phillipa Cornwall? Not that it was Iggy's business who he'd been involved with before they'd met, but when she'd first seen the headline and those photos, there was no denying the idea he might mess around with a married woman had unsettled her.

There was also still that little seed of doubt that perhaps there was some truth to the scandal and he'd only come to Derbyshire in the first place in order to escape scrutiny. 'I'm worried he's using the project at the castle as an excuse to hide out,' she admitted to Lucie.

Her friend huffed out a breath. 'I'm not exactly one to judge him for that, now, am I?'

'Sorry.' It was Iggy's turn to wince. It had completely slipped her mind that Lucie had applied for the conservator's position at the castle precisely because she'd been trying to run away from a scandal at her previous employer. Things had been resolved, eventually, and Lucie's name had been cleared, but it had nearly had serious implications for the discovery of the lost Viggliorento painting.

Lucie waved her off. 'I'm only teasing.' Half-turning on the bench, she propped her elbow on the back of the seat, rested her temple against her fist and stared at Iggy. 'Do you honestly think that Will is the kind of guy who'd screw up somebody else's marriage?'

It certainly didn't sound like the man Iggy had come to know these past weeks, but who could tell anything about anyone in such a short space of time. 'No.' Not liking the doubt she could hear in her own voice, she repeated herself in a firmer tone. 'No. Will's not like that.'

'I agree.' Lucie reached for her with her free hand. 'And what does it matter what brought him to Bluebell Castle in the first place, only that he's here now and he makes you happy.'

'You're right. I know you're right; I'm just feeling a bit off balance.'

Lucie grinned. 'It's not every day that a super-hot man tells you he's in love with you, you're allowed to have a little wobble.'

*

By the time they returned to the castle, they were all laden down with boxes and bags. Both Constance and Helena had found outfits they liked, and after a trip to a nearby department store they'd found shoes, fascinators and handbags to match. The excited barking of the dogs notified the men of the castle to their arrival, and Tristan and Arthur hurried over to relieve them of their burdens. A laughing Lucie had refused to surrender her boxes to Arthur, even after he'd promised not to peek inside. With an imperious finger, she'd sent him back to his office and with Tristan's help, they'd secured all Lucie's accessories in the wardrobe in her mother's bedroom.

Leaving Constance and Lucie to put their things away, Iggy sent Tristan to stow her purchases in her room and escorted her mother around the corner. She took charge of Helena's bags whilst she opened her bedroom door then they paused on the threshold facing each other. 'Thank you for finding my dress for me.'

Helena smiled. 'It was the least I could do.' She reached out and for a moment Iggy thought she was going to brush her cheek, but instead Helena's fingers tugged at a lock of her hair. 'Next we'll have to do something about your hair,' she said, her lips pursing in disapproval. 'It's in shocking condition, and probably full of split ends. And you'll need to stop messing around in the garden before the wedding, or your nails will never recover in time.'

Twitching her hair free, Iggy folded her arms across her chest knowing it was a defensive gesture, but damn it, she was tired of the constant barrage of criticism. 'My hair's fine as it is, and I'm not messing about, I'm doing my best to contribute to this family's future which is more than can be said of you when you were in my position.'

'But I wasn't in your position, was I, darling?' Helena's voice was acid now. 'I was the Lady of the house. That's never been your job, and it definitely won't be once Arthur and Lucie are married. Ludworth is never going to be yours, and it's time to stop pretending otherwise.'

The truth of it struck Iggy like a slap in the face and she reared back a step. Quick as a flash, Helena followed her, her voice lowering to a concerned hush. 'Let me smarten your appearance, darling. Who knows, you might even attract the attention of one of your brother's friends at the wedding.'

Shaking with a combination of hurt and fury, Iggy clenched her fists. 'The idea I'd change myself just to catch a man is disgusting. I'm not like you, all surface and no substance! I'll have you know that Will likes me just the way I am!'

She knew she'd made an error the moment Helena's brows twitched up in astonishment. 'Will? *You* and Will Talbot?' Her tone made it clear such a thing had never occurred to her.

'Yes, me and Will Talbot. We've been seeing each other for several weeks.'

Helena's lip curled into nothing so friendly as a smile. 'Well, lucky you. I suppose a man like that would need some amusement whilst he's away from home.' She arched a brow once more. 'Oh dear, you didn't think it was more than that, did you, darling? Haven't you seen today's papers?'

'He's not like that!' Iggy snapped. 'You don't know what the hell you're talking about. God, I wish Arthur and Lucie could see this side of you, they'd have you out of this house in a minute.'

'You never were good at handling the truth, Igraine,' Helena said before turning back towards her bedroom. 'I think I'll have a lie down before dinner.' Pausing at the threshold, she glanced back over her shoulder. 'Don't let your jealousy get the better of you. It's not Arthur's fault he inherited the title over you, any more than it's his fault that you aren't as close to me as he is.'

Jealousy? She honestly thought Iggy was jealous of her so-called relationship with Arthur? The woman had a bloody nerve. Before she could respond, she heard footsteps behind her, and Iggy turned to find Will standing a few feet from her, deep lines furrowed across his forehead.

He looked exhausted, and all she wanted to do was go to him, to comfort him and offer whatever support he would take from her.

'Well, here he is, the inconstant gardener.' Helena let out a titter. 'I always *knew* the Cornwalls were too good to be true. Nobody's marriage can be that happy.'

Will spun on his heel and walked off, but not before Iggy had caught the look of hurt on his face. Furious, she rounded on her mother. 'What on earth did you go and say that for? I already told you that nothing happened between him and Phillipa.'

Helena's brows rose. 'Oh, come on, darling, don't tell me you're that naïve.' When Iggy didn't answer, she shook her head and sighed. 'Apparently you are. Well, I just hope you're right, but remember that old adage. With a man as good looking as that, there's very rarely smoke without fire.'

Iggy stepped back because if she didn't put some space between them, she feared she might slap the knowing smile right off her mother's face. 'Not another word, Mother, or I won't wait for Arthur to see you for what you really are, I'll throw you out of the house myself.'

Chapter 17

Humiliation and anger surging through his veins, Will stomped back to his bedroom. After a hellish day spent holed up in Arthur's office, using the landline to consult with his agent and dodging WhatsApp messages from members of the press who'd managed to trace his mobile number from somewhere, all he'd wanted to do was find Igraine and hold her. At least the terrible mobile phone signal had prevented any of them from actually calling him.

Arthur and Tristan had been polite and sympathetic at his plight, both offering to do whatever they could to help out. Tristan had spent the day supervising the groundworkers and had assured Will on his return that the contractors would be discreet about his whereabouts. They recognised the kudos their reputation could gain from being involved in a prestige project like the water gardens and had sent their assurances via Tristan that their loyalty lay with Will. He could only cross his fingers and hope that was the case.

Picking up a cushion from one of the chairs, he tossed at the wall in frustration. He had no choice other than to try and ride it out; he had no power to do anything else.

The bedroom door flew open and Igraine threw herself into his arms. 'I'm sorry. I'm so sorry for what she said.'

As the familiar weight and shape of her body settled against his, Will felt some of his tension seep away. 'It's okay,' he said, kissing her hair. 'She's only saying what everyone else is probably thinking.'

'She doesn't know you.' Tipping up her head, she pressed a kiss to his chin. 'I was chatting to Lucie earlier, and she didn't think for one moment there was any truth to it.'

He sought her eyes. 'And what about you? You didn't seem so sure this morning.'

'I'm not good with anything that hints at infidelity.' She ducked her head into his shoulder. 'I got engaged briefly when I was at university. I thought Marcus was everything I wanted – or at least everything I was supposed to want. We had similar backgrounds and upbringings and he was due to inherit an estate similar to ours. Our families were acquainted, I think there was even a marriage connection several generations back.'

'Sounds like the perfect match.' Will couldn't help the little pang of jealousy over this unknown and clearly long-distant ex of hers. Though none of the family had ever made an issue of it, there was no escaping his life experience and Igraine's were classes apart.

She lifted her head to look up at him once more. 'He was unfaithful to me. Not just a one-off fling, either, but to an almost pathological degree. He'd decided to marry me because of who my family was, of what I could bring to him in terms of good breeding and station, rather than because he loved me.'

Anger flared in him at the old pain he sensed in her words. Whoever this Marcus was, he'd better never get within arm's length of Will. 'Bastard.'

'Yes, he was.' Igraine said in a fierce voice. 'But he did me a favour.'

Arms around her, Will backed towards the bed until he fell back onto the mattress, pulling her down on top of him. 'Is that so?' He couldn't help the smug smile he could feel tugging at his lips.

'Yes.' Leaning down she kissed him. 'If he'd been a better man, I'd never have had the opportunity to meet you.' She kissed him again. 'To get to know you.' Her fingers touched the scar on his cheek. 'To fall in love with you.'

Heat curled inside him, burning away the last of the cold fear which had been twisting his guts into knots all day. Lifting her into his arms, Will turned and carried her towards his bed. Lying beside her, he twined one of her gorgeous mahogany curls around his finger as he stared into her eyes. 'I never expected any of this.'

'Me either.' Her breath hitched. 'Promise me this is real, Will, that I'm not making a fool of myself.'

'Why would you even think that? You're the most beautiful, the most *real* woman I've ever met, Igraine, and I'm crazy about you.'

Catching her lip between her teeth, she glanced away before meeting his eyes once more. 'I'm sorry, I shouldn't let her get inside my head.'

'Who? Your mother?'

Igraine nodded. 'She thinks you're only with me because it's convenient.'

Those bloody stupid newspaper articles again. 'Because of what she's read about me, I suppose?'

Her nose wrinkled up. 'Not just that. She doesn't see why you'd want a scruffy woman with dirt under her nails and a fat bottom when you've got your pick of pretty, glamorous girls like Melody back in London.'

Christ. Igraine had warned him about Helena, but he'd had no idea she was so utterly poisonous as to openly criticise her own daughter like that. Reaching for her hand he placed a kiss on the tips of each of her fingers. 'Your hands are perfect because of the way you use them to tend to the land.' Letting it drop, he tangled his fingers into her curls and drew a handful to his nose to inhale the clean, zesty fragrance of her shampoo. 'I love your hair because it's wild and untamed, just like you.'

'*Will.*' There was a hint of embarrassed laughter in her voice, but the blush on her cheeks told him he'd said what she needed to hear. Good. He would tell her each and every day how beautiful she was, how sexy he found her, and how damn grateful he was to have her in his life.

Her fingers found his scar, tracing the puckered edges of it with that infinite tenderness that would have driven him to his knees had they not already been horizontal. Leaning down, he claimed her mouth in a searing kiss, wanting to drive away any lingering doubts she might have about his feelings towards her. When he finally broke for breath, her lashes had drooped to shade her hazel eyes, a look of languid need shining in them.

Flipping her onto her side, he leaned down over her and sank his teeth into the denim-clad roundness of her bottom in a playful bite. 'Next time I see your mother, I'm going to tell her this is my very, *very* favourite part of you.'

Shrieking and laughing, she wriggled away. 'You wouldn't dare!'

Will pounced, pinning her hands over her head and her hips down with his own. 'Oh, you know I would.'

*

When they walked into the family room before dinner, Will made a show of keeping his hand on her hip, his fingers splaying out to cover as much of her lovely curves as he could reach. Igraine was beautiful, and he never wanted her to doubt his attraction to her, though to be fair he'd just spent a very happy hour proving it to her. Helena was sitting on the nearest sofa so he made a point of steering Igraine straight past towards the opposite one and the pair of them sat down next to Tristan who was frowning over his tablet. When he glanced up to smile at them Will offered him his hand. 'Thanks again for helping out today.'

Tristan shrugged it off. 'Don't mention it, now if you could only think of a way to help me with these dismal ticket sales, we could call it quits.'

'It's still early days, though, isn't it? How long has the website been up and running?'

'Only a couple of weeks, but I placed a load of adverts in the local press as well as via our social media pages, so I was hoping to have more to show for them than we have. The Facebook page has had lots of likes, but nobody seems to be clicking through to the website to purchase a ticket.' He scowled at his screen. 'Not that I can make heads or tails of their data metrics.'

Will wasn't sure what to say. They could put as much blood, sweat and tears into renovating the castle and its grounds, but it would all be for nothing if the public didn't show up in numbers. 'There's a few weeks yet. Perhaps it's a bit too soon for people to be making up their minds. The bank holiday is notorious for bad weather so perhaps they're hedging their bets and you'll get more interest closer to the time.'

Tossing the tablet onto the carpet by his feet, Tristan sank back into the corner of the sofa with a sigh. 'Or perhaps we're not interesting or unique enough to capture their attention. There are plenty of stately homes and amusement parks clamouring for their money, why risk it on a new place they know virtually nothing about. We need a hook, something to draw them to us.' His hazel eyes settled on Will. 'Something like you, perhaps.'

'You must be bloody joking!' Though Will didn't find it funny at all.

'Nope, I'm deadly serious. Your profile is already sky-high so if we want to take advantage of the draw of your name, now's the perfect time. Besides, you can deflect the speculation in the press about you and Phillipa Cornwall by making it clear you've been up here for the past couple of months.'

Will felt sick. He thought Tristan and he were friends, that from the sympathetic response he'd got from both him and Arthur this morning that he understood how much the lies and speculation in the papers upset him. 'Talk some sense into your brother,' he said to Igraine, pushing to his feet.

She stared up at him in confusion. 'What's the matter?' She rounded on Tristan. 'What did you say?'

Tristan shrugged. 'I just suggested we could release a story about Will's work here on the water garden as a way to boost sales.'

'And I told you when I first got here that I wasn't interested in any more publicity.' Will snapped.

'Hey, now. You said you wanted any publicity to focus on what you've been doing here, and that's exactly what I'm talking about. It distracts from the negative stuff going around and will also hopefully get people talking about the castle and what we're trying to achieve here.'

'Yeah, yeah. You're doing it from the goodness of your heart, and all you want to do is help me.' Will couldn't keep the bitterness out of his tone. 'I'm sick to the back teeth of being used.' He stormed from the room, not missing the speculative glance Helena gave him on the way out.

Will kept walking, out the front door and across the crunching gravel of the driveway until he hit the grass and quickened his pace. Anger and embarrassment gave momentum to his feet until he was jogging past the high hedges of the formal gardens. By the time he reached the row of poplars screening the work site for the water gardens, he'd run off the worst of his mood.

Sinking down on the edge of the bank, Will let his legs dangle over the edge. *Shit*! He shouldn't have lost his temper like that. Tristan was only trying to do what was right for the family finances, and they would have to announce his involvement in the project at some point, or what the hell was the point in him doing it? But the idea of having his name bandied about in the papers again, even if it was for a good cause? Will shuddered at the thought of it.

His eyes surveyed the land before him. The terracing works were almost complete, and the plumbers had installed the storage tank and laid the network of pipes which would feed the system. The concrete troughs which would make up the cascading steps of the water garden had been poured and were drying in their wooden moulds. Right now, it looked an unholy mess, but he could see beyond that to what would be one of his best achievements in just a few more weeks.

'Hi.'

At the sound of Igraine's soft greeting, he turned to see her settling down beside him. 'Hi.'

Curling her knees up, she rested her chin upon them, eyes fixed out upon the land beyond them. 'Tristan's sorry for being so crass.'

'I shouldn't have lost my temper.' He hooked a hand around her ankle, needing the anchor of her touch. 'It's been a really shit day.'

She leant into his side, head resting on his shoulder. 'Tell me about it.'

'It's getting better all the time now you're here.' He pressed a kiss to her temple. 'I'll talk to Tristan about doing a statement, let's just let things die down a bit first.'

'Of course. He understands. We all do, don't worry about it.'

If only it was that simple.

* * *

Although he and Tristan had apologised to each other, things were still a bit awkward between them for a few more days. As they moved into July, the hot weather continued and work around the gardens was starting to take shape. The maze was cut and ready and the Davises were finishing off the last of the big hedges. The woods had been surveyed, the walks cleared and marked out ready for the first explorers to tramp their way beneath the leafy boughs.

In an effort to boost interest in their website, Tristan had started blogging about the ongoing works around the grounds, and the mission of the three siblings to save their ancestral home. Interest was starting to build, and Arthur had done a couple of interviews with the local press looking every inch the baronet as he'd posed on the steps of the castle, flanked by Nimrod and Bella, the two greyhounds. Will kept his head down and his mind focused on getting the water gardens finished.

Tristan had agreed to wait until the fountains were farther along enough so they could include some images of them as part of any press release they put together, 'wanting to make a splash' as the other man had joked. Will had pushed his team hard and they were ahead of schedule so he reckoned it would be a day or two more at most before they'd be ready to test the fountains. Pleased with the progress he was making, Will decided to take a break and check on how Igraine was getting on with the planting in the apothecary's garden.

As he approached the open door to the garden, the sounds of laughter and women's voices greeted him. Stepping inside, he grinned at the sight of a row of bottoms lined up along the length of one long flower bed. 'Looking good, ladies!'

Igraine peered over her shoulder at him, her laughing eyes shaded by the wide brim of a floppy straw hat. 'Come to lend us a hand, have you?'

He waved a hand towards the others around her. To her left, Lucie and Constance were working together to plant several clumps of lavender, to her right, Mrs W and Betsy were planting what looked like verbena. Heavenly scents came at him from all sides, the majority of the red brick beds already bursting with plants and shrubs. 'It looks like you've recruited everyone else already.'

Tugging off her gloves, Igraine rose from the little rubber pad she'd been knelt on to protect her knees from the paving slabs and came over to join him. 'We're almost there.' Pulling off her hat, she wiped her brow with her forearm then glanced up at the sky. 'This heat is a killer. We're going to have to water in here every day to make sure everything survives.'

There was one noticeable absence from the gathering. 'Where's your mother?'

Igraine rolled her eyes. 'A friend of hers in London invited her to stay, apparently. The first we knew about it was when a taxi rolled up to take her to the station, but she said it had been arranged for ages.' She shrugged. 'Maybe she told me, and I forgot. I do try hard to forget most of what she says.'

'How long will she be away for?'

Apparently catching the hopeful note in his question, Igraine laughed. 'A couple of weeks.'

Not long enough, but better than he could've hoped for. Leaning down, he whispered in her ear. 'Long enough for Constance to persuade your uncle to move back in for a bit?' Lancelot was still stubbornly refusing to move out of the stables, sticking to his word about not being under the same roof as Helena.

'I doubt it. The two of them seem quite cosy in there. I hear he's cleared out one of the other rooms and been appropriating bits and pieces of furniture to create a cosy little lounge. Now Arthur's got the internet booster sorted out, Lancelot told me he and Constance are quite happy to Netflix and chill out there together.'

Will grimaced at the euphemism. 'Do you think he knew what he was saying when he told you that?'

She grinned. 'Oh, I'm very sure he did. I'll be surprised if he moves back to the castle even after Mother eventually leaves for good. He was making noises about getting the stables properly converted into a self-contained apartment, although he might have his work cut out convincing Constance to put up with the smell of horses.'

Will turned to watch the older woman working side by side with her daughter. 'Do you think she'll stay then?'

'I think so. I know Lucie wants her close, and Arthur wants whatever Lucie wants. Things seem pretty solid between her and Lancelot, so I really hope they give it a go.' She glanced up at him. 'Did you come here for any particular reason, or just to catch up?'

Casting a quick glance towards the flower bed, he noted the others were all busy working away with their backs turned to them. 'I came here to give you this,' he said, swinging Igraine into his arms and planting a kiss on the soft, yielding warmth of her mouth.

A slow handclap came from behind them, joined quickly by others until it became a full round of applause complete with a couple of cheers and a very piercing wolf-whistle. Releasing Igraine with a grin, Will swept a bow towards the other women who'd all turned to watch them.

Red-faced and more than a little flustered, Igraine bent to scoop up her hat which had fallen from her head when he'd swung her around. 'Right. Well, we can continue this discussion later.'

'I'll hold you to that,' Will said with a grin before blowing a kiss at their audience. 'See you later, lovely ladies!'

*

His chance to pick up their 'discussion' came a lot later than Will hoped. Having returned to the water garden's site, he'd found a scene of absolute chaos. One of the small dump trucks they'd been using to shift the last of the excess soil away had driven over the pipe which had been filling the storage tank, sending water shooting into the air, and soaking everything in sight. The protective plastic shielding over the pipe had given way under the weight of the loaded truck, from the looks of things so work had had to stop to not only carry out a repair to the water pipe, but to hold a full investigation and safety inspection of all the equipment they'd hired from the same supplier to ensure nothing else was at risk of failing.

It was getting on for ten-thirty by the time a tired and filthy Will finally trudged up the front steps to the castle. He'd sent a message earlier to say he wouldn't be back for dinner, and was delighted to find a note waiting for him propped up in the centre of the round table next to a covered tray holding a cold supper for him. Collecting the tray, he decided to head straight up to his room as he would need a shower before he could do anything else.

The door to his bedroom stood slightly ajar, and when he edged around it, he was greeted by the arresting sight of Igraine dressed in a silky looking vest and matching shorts fast asleep across his bed. The TV was still on, tuned to a news channel. Putting his tray carefully down on a side table, he used the remote to turn the sound down, but left it on.

Igraine didn't stir in the time it took him to shower and pull on a clean set of boxers and a T-shirt, nor did she do much more than mumble and turn over when he settled himself against the headboard beside her with the tray upon his lap. With only half his attention on the TV Will let the headlines scroll past as he tucked into the selection of cheese, cold meats, pickles and several thick slices of Betsy's wonderful homemade bread and butter. He was just finishing off his supper when he accidentally dropped his fork, the clatter of it loud in the quiet room.

Igraine lifted her head. 'What? Oh, it's you,' she said with a sleepy smile. 'What time is it?'

'Almost eleven, I didn't mean to wake you.' Reaching out, he smoothed her messy curls from her forehead 'Go back to sleep, sweetheart.'

She pulled a face. 'I'm thirsty.'

He couldn't help but laugh at the way she'd scrunched up her nose, like a sleepy child not quite sure where they were. 'Here, sit up then.' He handed her the glass of water he'd filled from the sink in his bathroom.

She drained over half of it, then wriggled off the bed to go and refill it before he could stop her. Looking much more alert when she returned, she handed him back the glass before clambering onto the bed to sit cross-legged beside him. 'Are you eating that?' She gestured towards the chunk of sharp cheddar cheese on his plate.

'Apparently not.' He nudged it towards her with his fork, knowing it was her absolute favourite.

With a happy grin, she swiped it through the remains of the piccalilli in the corner of his plate and popped it into her mouth. 'Heaven,' she mumbled around the mouthful, eyes closing in sheer pleasure at the taste.

Will shifted the tray from his lap, stood and crossed the room to place it on the table beneath the window out of the way. 'You'll have to clean your teeth again now,' he said, pointing towards the bathroom.

As they stood next to one another, he marvelled at how intimate an act so ordinary as brushing one's teeth could be when you did it next to another person. Most of Igraine's toiletries had migrated to his bathroom over the past weeks. She hadn't slept in her own bed since the first night they'd been together, and as far as he could tell she only used it to get dressed and for the occasional shower – when he wasn't fortunate enough to persuade her to share his in the mornings.

He liked the sight of her things jumbled in together with his. He'd never been a neat freak, and it appeared Igraine was also missing the tidy gene from the way her clothes from that day were hanging half-in, half-out of his laundry hamper. Having never shared a domestic space with anyone since leaving home, he hadn't expected it to feel so comfortable so quickly. He'd brought women home before, sure, but they'd been sent on their way again with all their belongings intact the next morning.

This though, he could get used to. What would it be like to sit across from Igraine at the breakfast bar in his kitchen as they served each other coffee and toast and ran over their plans for the day? Or to come home in the evening and curl up in their pyjamas on his enormous corner sofa with a takeaway in their laps, and a boxset on the TV. It appealed to him on the most visceral level, but how on earth could he expect her to uproot herself from her family and everything she knew and loved to join him in a soulless high-rise apartment in the heart of Battersea?

He couldn't stay here, that was for sure. He'd already stretched the limits of his team's patience by throwing them in at the deep end when he'd upped sticks to come up to Bluebell Castle. Besides, he had a living to earn, and once the water gardens were finished there was no place for him here. Would he be able to tempt Igraine with the proposition of going into business with him? And could the idea of living with him ever be enough to tempt her away from not only her home, but her family? He wasn't ready to ask. He wasn't ready to face the prospect of her rejecting him – not that he'd blame her. These past months in Derbyshire had spoiled him to the point returning home held little appeal. How on earth would it feel to someone who'd lived in these wild, open spaces all their life?

'You're very deep in thought,' Igraine said, having rinsed her mouth and stowed her toothbrush in the little cup next to his.

'Just got a lot on my mind, that's all.' Taking the towel she offered, he wiped his mouth. 'Come on, let's get you back into bed, we've a long day tomorrow.'

'Every day is a long day at the moment,' she grumbled as she settled next to him beneath the thin sheet which was all they were using for cover in the lingering heatwave.

'I know, but we're getting there. The apothecary's garden was looking fantastic today.'

'Yes. It feels really good to have another thing ticked off the list. I'm almost starting to believe we can have it all ready in time.'

He settled down beside her then held still until she'd wriggled herself into the right position for sleeping. As she tugged her pillow an inch or two one way, and then the other, he couldn't help but smile. She was like the princess and the pea, seeming to feel every little lump and bump until she finally found that one perfect position that suited her. He flicked off the bedside lamp, leaving only the glow of the TV to illuminate the room with its ghostly glow. 'Are you turning off the telly?' she murmured into his chest.

'In a minute. Ssh, go to sleep.' He kissed her hair, then settled one hand on his favourite spot where her hip curved out into the cheek of her bottom.

He was in that awkward headspace; physically and mentally exhausted, but his brain was still too full of the day's events to switch off enough to let him sleep. As he listened to Igraine's breathing deepen and slow into the gentle rhythm of sleep, he tried to match the pace of his breath to hers, feeling his body ease and relax as he did.

The weather came and went on the TV showing no signs of a break in the temperatures and he was just reaching over for the remote to turn it off when the newspaper review came on. The news anchor introduced her panel of journalists and the early front pages flashed up one by one. It was all the same stuff, the endless political fallout from the referendum seeming no closer to a solution. The broadsheets came and went, and the images shifted to the brighter, bolder photo-splashed front pages of the tabloids.

His pleasant sense of drowsiness vanished as the most notorious of the red-tops flashed up. 'You have got to be fucking kidding me!'

Chapter 18

Iggy shivered as she tugged the shirt she'd pulled on over her pyjamas closer around her. She wasn't cold – even at close to 1 a.m. the temperature was still oppressive – but she was beyond that point of tiredness to where her body couldn't seem to stop shivering. It didn't help that her bare legs kept sticking to the leather of the sofa. Glancing around the room at the collection of equally tired faces, she sighed. 'This isn't getting us anywhere, why don't we try and get some sleep and we can sort things out in the morning?'

Will looked up from his laptop only long enough to glare at her before he was head down once more, fingers flying over the keys. 'We need to find out where the hell this leak came from.' He turned the screen towards her, thrusting the array of images at her. 'Look at this and tell me it doesn't bother you to have our private life splashed all over the papers.'

She turned her head, not wanting to see again the array of images of her and Will kissing. They'd been taken a couple of days earlier when the two of them had been walking in the grounds. She'd been able to work out the date by the colour of the T-shirt she was wearing, but how the photos had been obtained was a mystery to her. The spot where they'd paused to kiss before departing to their own tasks was not far from the edge of the formal gardens. It was an open space, and she couldn't recall anyone else in sight. 'Of course it bothers me! How can you possibly think otherwise?'

'You seem to be very calm about it,' Will snapped.

'Only because you've been ranting enough for the both of us! Bloody hell, you roused the whole household, and to what aim? We can't change anything.'

'We can find out who betrayed us.'

Her head started to thump, an unwelcome partner to the queasiness in her stomach. 'Betrayed us? Have you heard yourself?' Her tired brain finally caught up with what he was saying. 'Oh my God, you think it was one of family who did this, don't you?'

She held his gaze for a long moment, willing him to refute what she'd said. 'Where else could it have come from?' he muttered, turning his eyes back to the screen.

'I don't believe this!' An outraged Tristan was on his feet. 'Look, I had every sympathy for the situation when you got us out of bed, and of course we want to help do whatever we can to contain this, but I can't believe you're holding one of us responsible.'

Will snapped the screen on his laptop shut with a snap, jumping to his feet to face off with Tristan. 'You're the ones who will directly benefit from this, and how else did they know where the hell I was, never mind get so much detail in the story?'

'You're paranoid. It could've been any number of people. We've had contractors on and off the grounds for weeks now. It might even have been one of the local press photographers when they came to interview Arthur.'

Will shook his head. 'Balls. Those interviews were weeks ago, and I kept well out of the way until they'd left. The contractors have had loads of time to do this, and what do they gain, eh? They're not the ones who were moaning about ticket sales, were they?'

Tristan stepped back, eyes wide with shock. 'Jesus Christ, you honestly think this was me, don't you?'

When Will only raised one shoulder in a negligent shrug, Iggy couldn't believe it. He really did think Tristan capable of such a terrible thing.

'Enough!' Arthur was on his feet, stepping between the two of them. 'This is getting us nowhere, and I've got better things to do than watch you two take lumps out of each other. The story is out, and that's all there is to it. What we need to focus on now, is how we deal with it.'

'How we deal with it?' Will scoffed. 'Jesus, you don't have a clue, do you? There is no dealing with it! These photos—' he swept his hand towards the closed laptop '—were taken with a long range lens of some kind, meaning they were likely taken from outside the boundary wall.'

'How is that possible? You can't mean someone propped up a ladder and shot these from outside.' Arthur sounded as incredulous as Iggy felt. The wall had protected their family for generations, it didn't seem possible that someone could breach their privacy so casually.

'Either that, or they used a remote-controlled drone. You'd be amazed at what technology can do these days.' Will shoved his hands on his hips and blew out a frustrated breath. 'Unless you are prepared to put some kind of patrol out along the external wall, you've got no way of keeping them out if they want to try again, and if they used a drone, even that won't work. As long as they think there's a story here, they're going to keep coming back for more.'

'It can't have been one of the contractors,' Lucie said quietly from the opposite sofa. 'They wouldn't have known about the painting.' In addition to raking over the sordid details of all of Will's other supposed romances over the past few months, the article implied he was wooing Igraine because the Ludworth family stood to inherit a vast fortune.

'So I was right, then. It has to be one of you!' Will rounded on Tristan. 'You couldn't wait, could you? I only needed a couple more days to get the fountains sorted and we could've released

215

the story we agreed upon. Only I don't suppose that would've got you the national coverage you needed, eh?'

Iggy stared in horror as a vein started pulsing in her brother's forehead and she saw his fists clench and unclench. 'Tris ...' she pleaded with him, not because she believed what Will was saying, but because she hoped he was far enough removed from the situation to still be thinking rationally.

His eyes flicked to hers for a moment before returning to Will. 'Fuck you,' he said, his voice all the more awful for its measured calmness, and then stalked from the room.

Will might have followed had she not leapt up and grabbed his arm. 'Stop it, just stop it for God's sake!' She saw Arthur move towards them and shook her head to warn him off. 'No, leave it, Arthur. Go to bed, the pair of you and we'll sort this out in the morning when we've all got clearer heads.'

Though he stared hard at the restraining hand she'd looped around Will's forearm, Arthur didn't do anything more than nod before holding out his hand to Lucie and leading her from the room.

When they were finally alone, Iggy couldn't hold back an enormous yawn. 'Sorry,' she covered her mouth. 'I'm just so tired.' Another shiver racked her, and she pressed herself to the warmth of Will's body. 'Come to bed now, please. There's nothing more we can do tonight.'

Expecting to feel the comforting warmth of his arms closing around her, it shocked Iggy to the core when Will brushed past her and headed towards the door. Pausing at the threshold, he looked back at her. 'I can't be where I don't trust people.'

'You can't be including me in that statement.' *He couldn't be.*

Will stared at the floor for a long moment before meeting her gaze once more. 'You sided with your brothers over me.'

'No!' She hesitated. 'Well, I mean, I believe Tristan when he says he had nothing to do with this, of course I do, but ...'

'Family sticks together, right?' Will's lip quirked up, the twisted smile she'd always loved an ugly caricature. 'Especially families like yours. Pull up the drawbridge, lower the portcullis, repel outsiders, that's how it works.'

'Will, no!' She ran after him, the tiles of the great hall chill beneath her feet.

Refusing to look back, he continued to march up the stairs. 'Go to bed, Igraine. We'll talk again in the morning.'

Her foot froze on the bottom step. *Go to bed*. Without him. Though he'd not said as much, it was clear he didn't want her in his bed that night. Shivering and sad, she hurried in his wake, turning left when she reached the landing along the corridor which led to the family quarters.

* * *

Iggy stared at her hollow-eyed reflection feeling as though the woman she'd been the last time she'd looked in the mirror wearing the pretty green dress was a complete stranger. In less than two months since that day in the dress shop, her life had altered beyond all recognition. She'd had a home, a purpose, a boyfriend with whom she'd begun to dream about building a future. After today, she'd have none of those things.

The gardens were complete. Though they'd argued fiercely about it, Arthur had accepted her reasoning for finding a new job beyond the estate and although she would stay on to oversee the summer fete, she'd stepped down from all her other duties. As for the boyfriend … well, the less said about Will and his Lord Lucan vanishing act the better.

Her mobile phone buzzed, startling her. She still wasn't used to the improved phone signal on the estate thanks to the booster mast Arthur had installed. For a second, hope filled her heart as though thinking about Will had finally summoned him from wherever it was he'd disappeared to in the early hours following his bust up with Tristan.

217

Quelling her foolishness with a hand pressed to her belly, she answered the call to hear the frustrated tones of her uncle on the other end. 'Iggy, darling girl, can you pop over and give me a hand with this blasted cravat? Constance is busy with Lucie and your brothers have disappeared down the pub for a pint without having the decency to invite me, the blighters!'

She couldn't help but smile at the affront in his voice. Tristan had asked her if she wanted to join them, but she'd declined. It would be good for him and Arthur to spend a bit of time together and so many of the locals wanted to wish Arthur well on his big day. Already melancholic, she'd feared she'd start bawling in front of everyone if she'd tagged along. 'I'll be with you in two shakes,' she told her uncle. 'And I'll steal us a bottle of champagne on the way.'

'Now you're talking! Did I ever tell you that you were always my favourite of the three?'

*

'Look at you,' Lancelot exclaimed as he relieved her of the bottle of champagne and planted a smacking kiss on her cheek. 'Pretty as a picture. You'll have to be careful or you'll upstage the bride.'

'I don't think there's much chance of that. The moment Lucie takes her place at the top of the aisle, no one will have eyes for anyone else.' Which was exactly as it should be.

Iggy followed her uncle into the little kitchenette and watched as he pulled a couple of mugs from a cupboard before twisting the cork from the bottle with practised effort. She'd peeked in on Lucie on her way across, just to let her know where she would be if they were looking for her and to check everything was all right. She and Constance had been clad in matching dressing gowns, their hair in rollers as the girl they'd hired to do hair and make-up fussed around them.

She'd been invited to join them, of course, but it was a special moment for the two of them and Iggy had wanted them to enjoy it together. Helena had been given strict instructions not to intrude, and Iggy had commandeered the assistant who'd come with the hairdresser and dispatched her off to Helena's rooms with instructions to keep her there as long as possible.

Offering her one of the mugs, Lancelot rested his hip against the counter behind him and raised his own in toast. 'To the happy couple.'

'Cheers.' Iggy raised her own mug then took a mouthful of the ice-cold champagne. Smacking her lips together, she sighed in appreciation. 'Is there anything better than cold champagne on a hot summer's day?'

'Not at half ten in the morning, there isn't,' Lancelot said with a wink. 'We'll have to pace ourselves. Morgana will kill me if I'm half-cut when I walk Lucie down the aisle.' His expression turned wondering. 'I still can't believe she asked me to do it.'

'I can't think of a better man for the job,' Iggy said, before an image of her jolly, lovely father popped into her head, stealing her breath away.

'Uther would've loved her,' Lancelot said, gruffly, his thoughts clearly having moved in the same direction as hers.

'Yes, he would.' Iggy drew in a shaky breath. 'But it's right you do it.' She'd already seen the way Lucie had begun to turn to Lancelot for support, how the two of them and Constance were beginning to form their own smaller family unit within the bigger whole.

They exchanged wobbly smiles before Lancelot lifted his mug for a bracing draft of champagne. 'Right, enough of that maudlin nonsense, today is supposed to be a celebration.' He set his mug down and gestured to the pale grey cloth dangling over the back of one of the mismatched kitchen chairs. 'Give us a hand with this blasted thing, will you?'

'Stop turning the screen around!' Iggy gave her uncle's hand a playful slap as he tried to turn the tablet she'd propped up on the table towards him once more. The instructions which had come with the cravat had proven incomprehensible, so she'd resorted to looking up how-to videos on the internet. 'And put your chin up so I can see what I'm doing.' Lancelot chuckled, but did as he was told, even managing to sit still long enough for her to gather the complicated folds of the material together. 'Okay, hand me the pin.'

She slid the diamond-tipped pin into the cravat, then fumbled behind the knot to screw on the little end cap which would keep it secure. Stepping back, she gave her work a critical glance, then nodded. 'You'll do. Although why you didn't ask Maxwell to do it, I don't know.'

Rising from the chair, Lancelot moved through the kitchen to the open door of his little bathroom to study himself in the mirror. He made a couple of deft adjustments to the cravat, his hands moving in an assured way which raised her suspicions. 'You didn't need my help to do this at all, did you?'

Having smoothed the ends of the cravat once last time, her uncle turned to face her with an unrepentant grin. 'Not really, but I wanted an excuse to check up on you.'

'Check up on me?' Iggy kept her voice light. 'There was no need.'

Lancelot shook his head at her. 'You can't kid a kidder, darling girl. I know how hard these past few weeks have been for you, and I wanted to see how you were holding up.'

'I'm fine.' The lack of conviction in her voice was all too clear. 'I'm going to be fine,' she amended.

Her uncle closed in on her, taking her hand in the comforting warmth of his own. 'I know you haven't been down to the water gardens since Will left. If you find you're having a hard time at any point during the reception, you come and find me, okay?'

She nodded, not quite able to speak. Arthur had mooted the suggestion they move the wedding reception to the back lawns, but she'd refused point blank. He knew he was doing it to try and spare her feelings, but she would not let the spectre of

Will spoil anything about today. Tristan had taken over project managing when Will had walked out on them, although the groundworks supervisor had proven infinitely capable and had only need someone to nod through his decisions.

'Have you heard from him at all?' Lancelot's question was full of tender concern and it would be so easy to fall into his arms and sob out the grief and loss threatening to split her heart in two.

Stuff that. She hadn't shed a single tear since the moment she'd discovered Will had left – at first, she'd simply been too shocked to properly register it, but then it had become a matter of pride. He didn't deserve her tears, any more than he'd deserved her love. His apparent belief that one of the family had been behind the betrayal had only served to prove she hadn't really known him at all; no more than he'd known her. 'This was always on the cards, Lancelot. It might have happened sooner than either of us expected, but there was no future for us. We were a summer fling that got a bit ahead of itself. It was convenient at the time, nothing more.'

Her uncle frowned. 'I don't know who put those words in your head, my girl, but none of that sounds like you, nor is it an accurate description of the closeness I witnessed between the two of you.'

She looked away. 'I don't normally agree with her, but on this occasion, Mother was right.'

Lancelot barked an ugly laugh. 'I might have recognised her poison behind those words. Haven't you learned by now not to believe a word that comes out of the Hellbeast's mouth?'

Turning away from him, Iggy reached for her champagne and took a sip. 'She's not always wrong.' She indicated to her dress. 'She picked this out for me.'

'Well, that's the only decent thing she's done for you in all her years.'

Perhaps it was the champagne giving her courage, but Iggy couldn't hide her curiosity any longer. 'I know she did *us* wrong, but why do you hate her so much?'

If she'd stuck a pin in him, she didn't think he could've deflated more quickly. Sinking into the chair behind him, Lancelot scrubbed a hand over his face. 'Because she broke my heart.'

Stunned, Iggy sank into the other chair. 'What on earth do you mean?'

Tipping his head back, Lancelot stared up at the ceiling as though seeking divine guidance. 'I always swore I wouldn't talk about it, but perhaps we shouldn't have kept it hidden all these years.' Tilting his head forward once more, he nodded towards the bottle on the table. 'Fill us up, first, and then I'll tell you.'

Iggy did as she was told, then settled back with her mug cradled to her chest as she watched Lancelot wrestle with himself. 'When I was nineteen, I met the most beautiful girl I'd ever seen in my life. Incandescent, she was able to light up a room with not only her looks but her sweetness and charm. She was the life and soul of every party and I fell in love with her before we'd even exchanged a single word.

'Helena led me a merry dance, and I enjoyed every moment of the chase. When I finally got her to agree to go out with me, I was a goner for her. I told her everything about me, all my hopes and dreams for the future, how I was struggling to find my fit in the world as the spare to the heir.'

He sighed. 'I showed her all the parts of me, and I believed she was doing the same. We were inseparable for weeks, and then she had to leave town and go back to her parents as she'd been away from home longer than intended and they were starting to put pressure on her. She said she wanted to take me, but that they were very traditional and would be very upset to find out we'd been all but living together out of wedlock. When she asked me to give her a little bit of time to ease them into the idea of our relationship, I agreed to give her all the time she needed.'

Their eyes met, and the pain in his gaze shattered her heart. 'Oh, God. We had no idea you even knew her before she met Dad.'

His lips twisted into a wry smile. 'Imagine how excited I was when your dad telephoned to tell me he'd met the most marvellous girl at a house party, and he was madly in love with her. It felt like serendipity, the two of us finding our perfect matches at the same time. When he told me he'd proposed, I thought it seemed a bit hasty, but then again, I'd fallen in love at first sight so I knew such things were possible.'

'And he was talking about Mother?' When he nodded, Igraine was baffled. 'But, how?'

Lancelot shrugged. 'She didn't need to go home as it turned out. In fact, I'm not sure anything she'd told me about her background was true. She'd given me the impression her people came from South Devon, that they had extensive landholdings down there. We'd even talked about the possibility of my setting up my own stud in the area, once I'd finished my apprenticeship at Johnny Lassiter's yard. It was only years later that I found out she'd fallen out with her family and they'd all but cast her out.

'Anyway, instead of going home as she'd claimed, she came north and managed somehow to insert herself into the local set. When she met your father, she already knew so much about him because I'd told her all about the family. With that prime knowledge, she was able to present herself as the perfect woman for him.'

Igraine couldn't believe her ears. 'She deliberately sought him out? God, I knew she could be calculating, but I had no idea she was capable of that kind of ruthlessness.'

'The chance at landing the rich heir with the title, rather than his horse-mad younger brother with no real prospects other than those he could earn for himself was too tempting to resist, I suppose. We had no idea at the time how precarious our father's finances were as he'd always hidden it from us. I was young and prideful, and determined to make my own way in life rather than sponge off him.' He laughed. 'It came as something of a shock when he finally sat Uther and your mother down after they were married and told them straight how dire things were.

Crafty old man wanted to ensure the family line was secure for another generation.'

'And what did you do when you found out she and Dad were together?'

'What could I do? She laughed it off, made it sound like we were barely more than strangers to each other, and your father was so smitten, he wouldn't hear a word against her. It caused a rift between us, one that only healed after she abandoned you all and your father called me in tears.'

Lancelot drained his mug. 'After what she did to me, I found it impossible to trust another woman.' His face softened into a warm smile. 'Well, until my Connie showed up, that is. God, when I think about what I have now, that infatuation I had for your mother seems pathetic in comparison.'

Still reeling from it all, Iggy finished her own champagne. 'We'll have to tell the others.'

Her uncle shook his head. 'Your Aunt Morgana knows every sordid little detail already, and as for your brothers, what's the point? With any luck, she'll beat a retreat once the wedding is over and done with, and things will get back to the way they used to be.'

'And if they don't?'

'Helena never has had the attention span to stick to anything for very long. Once the fun and excitement of today is over, she'll get bored and move onto the next shiny thing.'

'I certainly hope so.'

Chapter 19

'Well, you've really gone and done it then?' Tristan said to Arthur as he hooked his arm through Iggy's, linking the three of them into a line.

Arthur raised his eyes to where his new bride was chatting to her mother and Lancelot, the bouquet of dark red roses she clutched a vivid splash of colour against the bright white of her gown. 'I really have,' he agreed, his voice full of pride and adoration. 'She's perfect, isn't she?'

He said it with so much enthusiasm, Iggy couldn't help but laugh. 'Yes, she really is.'

'I'm just going to make sure she's all right.'

As they watched him curl an arm around his wife's waist and tug her close, Tristan squeezed Iggy's arm. 'Poor girl, he's never going to let her go again.'

'Probably not,' she agreed with a grin. 'Oh, look out we're being summoned again.'

The photographer they'd hired for the official wedding photos had seemed like such a genial chap when they'd met him, and he still was to be honest. What none of them had banked on was his officious wife who acted as his assistant and had been marshalling everyone about like a general commanding the troops.

'Just the immediate family now,' she bellowed, pointing them towards the steps of the castle.

It took a bit of shuffling around as no one wanted to stand to close to Helena – not that it was physically possible to stand too close when she'd chosen to wear a hat roughly the size of a satellite dish. She'd needed half a pew to herself to accommodate the enormous brim, and Iggy had already had to duck a couple of times to avoid being whacked with it when her mother had turned to address some comment or other towards her. Since her uncle's earlier revelations, Iggy had barely been able to look at her, never mind speak to her, but thankfully, Helena was too busy being the centre of attention to notice. Claiming Arthur's free arm, she beamed at the camera, for all the world the perfect picture of attentive motherhood. It made Iggy quite sick to look at her.

Thankfully, Arthur's patience with the photographer soon wore thin, and he declared an end to the formal poses. 'That's enough of that, you can take a few more in the gardens, and at the reception.' Claiming Lucie's arm once more, he glanced down at her. 'Are you ready?'

'I just need to change my shoes.' The heels she'd worn for the ceremony itself wouldn't last five minutes on the walk through the gardens.

'Hang on, I'll get your others,' Iggy said, pushing open the front door to fetch the pair of sparkly wedges they'd stowed there ready. The same height as her stiletto heels, they would be much sturdier support on the uneven grass, as well as being a damn sight more comfortable.

With Lucie hanging onto both Arthur and Tristan for support, she and Constance managed to get under the back of her dress to swap the shoes out with a lot of laughter, but not too much fuss. Iggy was just backing out from beneath the wide lacy skirt when she caught a flash going off out of the corner of her eye and she spotted the photographer with a cheeky grin on his face.

'Well, you did say you wanted some candid shots to balance out the formal,' he said with a wink.'

'We might not put these ones on the mantelpiece,' Arthur said with a wry grin.

*

They strolled across the driveway, different groups coalescing, parting and forming up once more as people who hadn't had a chance to catch up at the church exchanged greetings and congratulations with the happy couple. Another round of photos followed in the heart of the Lady's garden – close family only – while Mrs W and Maxwell saw to escorting the rest of the guests on through the grounds towards the water gardens where the marquee was set up for the reception. Though she'd told Lancelot she would be fine, Iggy was happy to pose for as many blasted pictures as the photographer wanted to take, her stomach already churning at the thought of seeing Will's finished creation for the first time.

Once the photos were over, Lucie tugged Arthur down to whisper something, and Iggy watched as he pressed a sweet kiss to her cheek before nodding. When he turned to face her, there was a sheen in his eyes. 'Lucie would like to take a minute to visit the secret garden.'

Feeling her own eyes pool with tears, Iggy pressed her hand over her heart. 'I think that would be a lovely idea.' Rather than keep it hidden away, Iggy had arranged for the hedge cutters to clear a proper gap in the bushes she and Will had crawled through that day they'd first discovered the garden. Though Maxwell hadn't been able to turn up a key to fit the old door, they'd had the lock replaced and a private – no admittance sign fitted to the outside.

As they made their way quietly into the garden, she paused to look around. It would take time to restore the garden to its full glory, but Iggy and Constance had at least had a chance to clear away the old ivy choking up the flower beds and around the tree. It still looked a little barren, but come next spring, the space would be alive with the scents and colours of daffodils, tulips and other pretty blooms. Moving to stand in the shelter of her uncle's arm, Iggy bit her lip as Lucie crouched before the two stone dogs guarding the tiny grave and laid her bouquet next to them.

Feeling a tear escape, Iggy captured it with her finger, and leaned into Lancelot's tight hug with a little laugh. 'What a lovely touch,' he murmured to her. Iggy nodded, still not quite trusting herself to speak.

Their contemplative mood didn't last long when the family group exited the gardens to discover that rather than making their way down to the marquee, the rest of the guests had formed up in two rows to create an honour guard. 'Whose idea was this?' Lucie asked, with a delighted laugh as the guests clapped their hands together.

'You can thank Tristan,' Iggy said before moving to take up her position at the top end of the one of the lines and joining in the applause.

As Arthur and Lucie began to make their way along the corridor, whoops and cheers of congratulations rang out and handful after handful of confetti showered down upon their heads. Tristan had sourced it and handed it around the church as they'd waited for the ceremony to start, so they knew it was totally biodegradable and would cause no harm to the land.

The guests fell into line behind the happy couple, forming a huge, snaking line towards the steps which had been cut into the bank. As gasps of surprise and exclamations of wonder reached her position at the back of the queue, Iggy felt her insides tighten once more. A big hand engulfed hers, and she looked up to find her uncle on side, and Constance taking up position on the other. 'Courage, mon brave!' Lancelot said with a wink as he squeezed her hand. Feeling more determined, Iggy gave him a nod and they followed the crowd towards the gap cut into the screen of poplars.

Bracing herself for sadness, Iggy took her first proper look at the spectacle Will had envisioned, but never seen completed. Showers of water danced in the air, the crystalline droplets refracting the sunlight into a curtain of shimmering rainbows that stretched the full length of the bank on either side of the steps. Desperate to see the whole thing, Iggy dropped her uncle's hand and gathered her skirts to skip down the rest of the steps and join the throng of guests who were all doing the same.

The fountains in each level of the terrace formed different patterns – some shot jets high into the air, others a low bank of murmuring water like a stream bubbling over rocks. As she watched, the patterns of the water shifted in unison to form a new combination, drawing oohs and aahs of delight.

Feeling nothing but joy in her heart, Lucie turned to smile at Lancelot and Constance as they approached her once more. 'The boy did well,' Lancelot said, quietly.

'Yes. Yes, he did.' Bittersweet emotion swelled in her heart. For what might have been, and for the stories her own ancestors might tell each other one day of another failed love story in their family history. Like the long forgotten masterpiece Lucie had uncovered which told the tale of her many-times great-grandfather's heartache, the water garden would forever be linked to the legacy of Iggy's own doomed love affair.

All of a sudden, she couldn't bear to look at it. 'I'd better go and check everything is ready in the marquee before we start,' she said, not missing the sympathetic look her uncle and Constance exchanged before she cut her way through the guests until their backs formed a shield between her and the dancing waters.

*

The reception proved the perfect mix of relaxation and enjoyment they'd all hoped it would be during the planning stages. Thankfully, some kind soul had switched off the fountains after the initial display so Iggy hadn't been faced with the sight of them as she joined the others queuing up outside at the hog-roast station and later on in front of the ice cream van as she waited for a 99 cone with a cone and sticky raspberry sauce drizzled over the soft whipped peaks.

Champagne flowed, the speeches were short and sweet, including a very moving tribute Arthur paid to the memory of their father which had moved more than just Iggy to tears. The evening light was fading, and she kicked off her shoes and left her jacket hanging over the back of a chair somewhere hours before. Thanking her dance partner – an old school rugby pal of Arthur's who'd taken something of a shine to her – Iggy retreated from the dancefloor to sink a little breathlessly into the chair beside Arthur. Like her, he'd shed his jacket and now sat with his sleeves rolled to his elbows, the buttons of his waistcoat hanging open and a slightly lopsided grin on his face. 'Jimmy's got his eye on you,' he said, giving her a nudge.

'Well, Jimmy can keep his eye and all the rest of his bits firmly to himself, thank you very much,' she said, archly.

'Don't tell me you're still pining for that bloody gardener,' Helena slurred a little as he leaned across from the opposite side of the table. Her enormous hat had been removed, and Iggy had last seen it being worn on the dancefloor by Tristan. Fixing her slightly unfocused gaze on Iggy, she pointed a red-tipped nail at her. 'I told you at the time he was only after one thing. Find yourself some nice, filthy rich idiot and settle down, for goodness sake.'

Anger bubbling in her gut, Iggy pushed the wagging finger out of her face. 'You're the last person I'm going to take relationship advice from. Why don't you do us all a favour and piss off back to your own filthy rich idiot and leave us in peace?'

'Iggy, come on now, don't spoil it when we've had such a nice day,' Arthur pleaded, ever the bloody peacemaker.

'I'm not spoiling anything, it's her. It's always her, but you're too blind to see it. She doesn't give a stuff about any of us, never has, never will, and I hope you finally see that before she ruins everything.' Iggy clamped a hand over her mouth before she let her words truly run away with her. She felt like she was teetering on the edge of a knife and if she stepped the wrong way, she'd slice not only herself to ribbons, but Arthur too. 'I'm sorry, this isn't the time. I'd better go back to the dancefloor before I say anything else.'

She rose from her chair and was surprised when their mother stood up to face her. 'You should be thanking me for what I did!' Turning, she pointed from Arthur to Tristan who'd wandered over to join them, the ridiculous hat still perched on the back of his head. 'You should all be thanking me.'

'Christ, what's this?' Tristan said, grabbing a bottle of beer from the table and taking a swig. 'You've had too much champagne, Mother, why don't you go back to your room and have a lie-down?'

'Don't you think you can dismiss me! If it wasn't for me, your future wouldn't be looking so damn rosy.' Helena's face had grown red, her volume increasing to the point she was beginning to draw stares from people around them.

'What the hell is she talking about?' Tristan asked, then turned to her. 'What are you trying to say, Mother?'

'You know! If it hadn't been for me talking to the papers, you'd still be scrabbling around trying to sell tickets for your grand opening.' She rounded on Iggy, that red, shiny nail jabbing in her direction once more. 'And you'd still be fooling yourself that Will wanted you for anything more than a bed-warmer. I showed you what kind of man he is, and saved the family fortunes in the process. So, yes, you should be thanking me!' With a satisfied nod, she flopped down into her chair.

Knees giving out, Iggy found herself dropping down into her own seat. 'I don't bloody believe it.' Will *had* been right all along. Someone in the family had betrayed them.

'But why would you do such a thing?' Arthur leaned across the table towards Helena. 'Why would you sell your own daughter out like that?'

Helena glanced away with a shrug. 'I needed the money. Beaumont left me high and dry, and I was desperate. I kept waiting for you to do the right thing by me, especially once I found out about that damn painting you were keeping hidden from me, but you always were too stupid to catch the hint.'

He reared back, her cold words landing as harsh as a slap. 'I thought you came here because you read about the engagement.'

'And so I did. Like I told you, I assumed you'd bagged yourself an heiress to put the finances to rights, but instead you'd fallen for that little drip without a penny to her name. If she hadn't let it slip on the first night about the Viggliorento, do you honestly think I would've stuck around all this time?'

'Jesus Christ.' Tristan sounded as shocked as she felt, and both he and Iggy knew how poisonous their mother could be. Poor Arthur, though …

Iggy turned to offer him comfort, but instead of the devastation she expected to see, his face was fixed in a firm expression of resolve. 'Get out,' he said to their mother, his voice deadly calm. 'Stand up, turn around and walk out of here or I swear to God I will climb over this table and throw you out.'

'But, Arthur—'

'*Now!*' He sounded so fierce Iggy found herself clamping a hand on his shoulder for fear he really would do as he'd just threatened.

'Hell's bells, I'm too old to rock and roll anymore,' Lancelot said, as he strolled up with one arm around Constance's waist, the other hooked around Lucie's shoulder. 'These two will put me into an early grave.' Sensing the mood, his smile faded. 'Everything all right here?'

'Everything's fine. Mother was just leaving,' Arthur said in that same flat tone.

'Well, about time. Here, let me give you a hand.' Lancelot all but hauled Helena to her feet, hooked his arm through hers and had towed her halfway across the marquee before Helena had so much as a chance to squawk in protest.'

'What was that all about?' Lucie rounded the table to stand at Arthur's side. 'What's going on?'

Her hand on his arm seemed to be all it took to shatter the icy façade, and Arthur raised his face to hers with a tired smile. 'Nothing you need worry yourself about. Not now, not ever. Come on my beautiful bride, dance with me.'

Lucie cast a wary look at Iggy as Arthur led her away but didn't protest. As soon as the pair of the reached the centre of the floor, the DJ switched the music to something slow and the rest of the dancers either settled into couples or drifted from the floor to retake their seats.

Iggy watched Arthur take Lucie's hand and place a kiss on it before he draped it over his shoulder and pulled her close. They swayed together in time to the music, seeming oblivious to everyone else around them. 'Do you think he'll be okay?' she asked Tristan as he claimed the empty seat beside her.

'In time, he will. Lucie will see to that.' He slung an arm across the back of her chair. 'What a bloody mess.'

'Yes.'

'He wasn't wrong.'

'No.'

'What are you going to do about it?'

It was on the tip of her tongue to say there wasn't anything to do about it, but she stopped herself. 'I need some air.'

Tristan didn't protest as she left him sitting at the table and escaped out into the slightly cooler night air beyond the marquee. The fountains had been switched back on, the dancing curtains illuminated in brilliant shades of green, purple and red by the hidden coloured spotlights. Instead of turning away, Iggy strode towards them.

When had she become the kind of person who shied away from the hard things in life? When had she ever given up on anything she truly wanted? She'd chosen to go to the Agricultural University even though it had meant being separated from her brothers for the first time in their lives. She'd locked horns with their tenants and sweated night and day until she'd proven to them she was capable at overseeing the estate lands better than anyone with twice as much experience. She'd overseen all the hard work it had taken to restore the gardens to their former glory. However badly things had ended, if she hadn't sought out Will's assistance, they wouldn't have this remarkable new part of the gardens, either.

Pride filled her as she pressed her toes into the dew-damp grass beneath her bare feet. This land was in her, blood and bone. It was her home, and all she'd ever thought she wanted or needed. But once she was dead and gone, the land would still be here, and other Ludworths would come and go and make their mark upon it before they too became dust upon the wind. She'd done what she needed to do to pay homage to her past, it was time to seize her future.

Determination burning in her veins, Iggy gathered the long skirts of her dress and started to run towards the steps. She was halfway up when a voice she'd feared never to hear again spoke her name.

'Igraine.'

Halting, she stared up at the shadowed figure standing at the top of the steps. 'What are you doing here?'

Hands in his pockets, Will stepped down onto the riser before her. A beam from one of the spotlights caught the side of his face, throwing the scar onto his cheek into harsh illumination. His eyes remained hidden from her in the half-light. 'I came here to talk to you, but it looks like you're in a hurry.'

'I was coming to find you,' she admitted.

That twisty smile she loved so much tugged at the corner of his mouth. 'But you didn't know where I was.'

She shrugged. 'As if I was going to let a little thing like that stop me. I'm very determined when I know what I want.'

Moving down until he was level with her, Will crowded into her space until their bodies were a bare inch apart. 'And what's that?' he said, voice rough with a need that echoed the one deep inside her.

'You. Always, and forever. I thought Bluebell Castle was my home, that I needed to be here to feel whole, but I was wrong.' Raising her hand, she pressed it over his heart. 'This is my home.'

'*Igraine.*' His arms banded around them, trapping her hand between them as he bent his head and claimed her mouth.

It wasn't an easy kiss, like the ones that so often ended a fairy tale. Just like their life together would be, it was hard, and demanding, and a little bit messy as they pulled at each other in their desperate need to be ever closer together. His hands found her hair and tugged her curls free from the complicated chignon they'd been pinned up into, and she managed to wriggle hers out from beneath them and grab at the back of his T-shirt as she sought and found the hot, smooth skin of his back.

No, definitely not a fairy tale kiss. But it was perfect, and it was real, and it was everything she wanted for the rest of her life.

Epilogue

The sounds of children's shrieking laughter filled the air as Iggy wound her way around the packed stalls covering the grass amphitheatre beneath the sparkling fountains of the water garden. A huge splash followed by a roar of laughter and cheers drew her eyes across the showground to where Arthur had once more been plunged into the huge dunk tank by a lucky strike on target. Shoving water from his eyes, Arthur gave a wave to the gathered crowd and gamely clambered back up to resume his position on the mechanised seat.

'Dunk the baronet' was proving one of the most popular draws from the queue of people lined up to take their turn, and every penny spent was going towards a good cause. Rather than just create an area in the garden where children could come and have fun digging and planting, they were looking into setting up a proper charitable trust. The Ector and Kay Ludworth Memorial Foundation was still in the earliest development stages, but Iggy was hopeful she could turn it into a reality from which she could run educational programmes for schools in the local area, and maybe further afield one day.

Warm arms looped around her waist, and Will kiss dropped onto the spot beneath her ear that never failed to make her squirm with pleasure. 'When's it your turn in the tank?' he asked.

Leaning back into his solid chest, she glanced up at him. 'Never mind about me, it's you the crowds have all come to see. If I can get you on that ducking stool, we'll raise a fortune.'

He laughed against her cheek. 'You just want to see me in a wet T-shirt.'

She turned in his arms. 'I'd much rather see you out of it.' As she stretched up to claim a kiss, she spotted a couple of shyly grinning girls over his shoulder. 'Oops, your fan club's found you again.'

'Hold that thought,' he growled, squeezing her hips before he released her and turned with a smile to beckon the girls over. He'd been like that all morning, showing infinite patience from the moment he'd cut the ceremonial ribbon to official open the fete and instead of the crowd pouring onto the showground, most of them had clamoured around him for autographs and selfies. For a man who professed to hate publicity as much as Will, he was putting on a damn good show for the crowd, and she was infinitely grateful to him for it.

Placing a hand on his back, she said. 'I'm going to check on everyone, I'll see you over by the tea tent in a bit, okay?'

'Okay, sweetheart.' He flashed her that smile of his, and it wasn't just the giggling teens ready to swoon over him.

She took her time working her way around towards the refreshment tent, pausing to check with the various vendors that everything was okay, and that none of them had any problems. They seemed to be doing a roaring trade, and there were already huge lines curling around the various food trucks as the public fed their never-ending appetite for junk food. Everywhere she looked, there were smiling faces, and the face-painting stand looked to be a hit from the numbers of tiny tigers, butterflies and glittering fairies she passed in the crowds.

When she reached the tea tent, it was to find that Will had beaten her to it and was squatting down beside a table where her

Aunt Morgana was talking to a woman of a similar age. With her white hair permed into tight curls, and what looked to be a hand-knitted pink cardigan over the bright flowers of her sundress, the woman looked the antithesis of Morgana in her understated navy linen and neat court shoes, but the two of them looked to be getting on like a house on fire, which delighted Iggy no end.

'There you are, my dear.' Mrs Tyler, Will's old next door neighbour beamed at her as though they were old friends and not someone Will had only briefly had time to introduce her to when he'd collected her from the station late the previous evening. 'I was just telling your aunt how proud I am of everything you and my Will have achieved here.'

She reached out to cup Will's cheek with her gnarled fingers. 'And to think that none of this might have happened if I hadn't fallen off that damn ladder all those years ago.'

Will turned his face to press a kiss to her palm. 'I thought I was rescuing you that day, but it was the other way around, wasn't it?'

'Stuff and nonsense,' she said, but Iggy could tell from the colour on her cheeks she was pleased none the same. 'You always had a special talent inside you all along, you just needed someone to spot that potential in you.'

As Will straightened up, Iggy slid into his side, her arm curling around his waist and his about her shoulders in that puzzle-piece perfect fit they'd already found together. 'What about you?' he murmured, nuzzling his lips against her cheek. 'Do you think I've got any special talents?'

Laughing, Iggy stroked his cheek, loving the contrast of rough and smooth on his cheek which said so much of the soul inside the man. 'Let's say you've got *potential.*'

Acknowledgements

Welcome back to *Bluebell Castle*! I can't tell you how much fun I had tormenting poor Iggy and Will on the way to their happy ending. They really gave me the runaround as I tried to write their story, but I'm thrilled with how their story turned out in the end. I hope you will agree they are a perfect match for one another.

I'd like to take a few moments to pay tribute to everyone who continues to support me through book after book, especially all my lovely readers. Every message, every note, every lovely comment I receive about one of my books gives me such an amazing boost – thank you. x

Huge thanks as ever to my wonderful husband. I couldn't do this without you. x

To my fantastic editor, Charlotte Mursell, who is simply the best. x

#TeamHQ. I am beyond lucky to be working with such an incredible publishing team, long may it continue!

My online support network of fellow writers, who prove every day why this is the best job in the world. Thank you, Philippa, Jules, Darcie, Bella and Rachel for getting me through the tough times and making sure I celebrate the good ones. I love you all. x

Finally, to all the book bloggers and reviewers out there who give up their time to support authors and spread their love of reading far and wide. Thank you! x

Turn the page for an exclusive extract from *Sunrise at Butterfly Cove*, the first novel in the enchanting Butterfly Cove series …

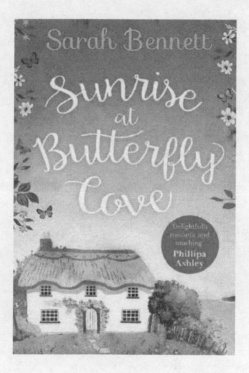

Prologue

October 2014

'And the winner of the 2014 Martindale Prize for Best New Artist is ...'

Daniel Fitzwilliams lounged back in his chair and took another sip from the never-emptying glass of champagne. His bow tie hung loose around his neck, and the first two buttons of his wing-collar shirt had been unfastened since just after the main course had been served. The room temperature hovered somewhere around the fifth circle of hell and he wondered how much longer he would have to endure the fake smiles and shoulder pats from strangers passing his table.

The MC made a big performance of rustling the large silver envelope in his hand. 'Get on with it, mate,' Daniel muttered. His agent, Nigel, gave him a smile and gulped at the contents of his own glass. His nomination had been a huge surprise and no one expected him to win, Daniel least of all.

'Well, well.' The MC adjusted his glasses and peered at the card he'd finally wrestled free. 'I am delighted to announce that the winner of the Martindale Prize is Fitz, for his series "Interactions".'

A roar of noise from the rest of his tablemates covered the choking sounds of Nigel inhaling half a glass of champagne.

Daniel's own glass slipped from his limp fingers and rolled harmlessly under the table. 'Bugger me.'

'Go on, mate. Get up there!' His best friend, Aaron, rounded the table and tugged Daniel to his feet. 'I told you, I bloody told you, but you wouldn't believe me.'

Daniel wove his way through the other tables towards the stage, accepting handshakes and kisses from all sides. Will Spector, the bookies' favourite and the art crowd's latest darling, raised a glass in toast and Daniel nodded to acknowledge his gracious gesture. Flashbulbs popped from all sides as he mounted the stairs to shake hands with the MC. He raised the sinuous glass trophy and blinked out at the clapping, cheering crowd of his peers.

The great and the good were out in force. The Martindale attracted a lot of press coverage and the red-carpet winners and losers would be paraded across the inside pages for people to gawk at over their morning cereal. His mum had always loved to see the celebrities in their posh frocks. He just wished she'd survived long enough to see her boy come good. Daniel swallowed around the lump in his throat. *Fuck cancer.* Dad had at least made it to Daniel's first exhibition, before his heart failed and he'd followed his beloved Nancy to the grave.

Daniel adjusted the microphone in front of him and waited for the cheers to subside. The biggest night of his life, and he'd never felt lonelier.

* * *

Mia Sutherland resisted the urge to check her watch and tried to focus on the flickering television screen. The latest episode of *The Watcher* would normally have no trouble in holding her attention – it was her and Jamie's new favourite show. She glanced at the empty space on the sofa beside her. Even with the filthy weather outside, he should have been home before now. Winter had hit earlier than usual, and she'd found herself turning the lights on mid-afternoon to try and dispel the gloom caused by the raging storm outside.

The ad break flashed upon the screen and she popped into the kitchen to give the pot of stew a quick stir. She'd given up waiting, and eaten her portion at 8.30, but there was plenty left for Jamie. He always said she cooked for an army rather than just the two of them.

A rattle of sleet struck the kitchen window and Mia peered through the Venetian blind covering it; he'd be glad of a hot meal after being stuck in the traffic for so long. A quick tap of the wooden spoon against the side of the pot, and then she slipped the cast-iron lid back on. The pot was part of the *Le Creuset* set Jamie's parents had given them as a wedding gift and the matching pans hung from a wooden rack above the centre of the kitchen worktop. She slid the pot back into the oven and adjusted the temperature down a notch.

Ding-dong.

At last! Mia hurried down the hall to the front door and tugged it open with a laugh. 'Did you forget your keys—' A shiver of fear ran down her back at the sight of the stern-looking policemen standing on the step. Rain dripped from the brims of their caps and darkened the shoulders of their waterproof jackets.

'Mrs Sutherland?'

No, no, no, no. Mia looked away from the sympathetic expressions and into the darkness beyond them for the familiar flash of Jamie's headlights turning onto their small driveway.

'Perhaps we could come in, Mrs Sutherland?' The younger of the pair spoke this time.

Go away. Go away. She'd seen this scene played out enough on the television to know what was coming next. 'Please, come in.' Her voice sounded strange, high-pitched and brittle to her ears. She stepped back to let the two men enter. 'Would you like a cup of tea?'

The younger officer took off his cap and shrugged out of his jacket. 'Why don't you point me in the direction of the kettle and you and Sergeant Stone can make yourselves comfortable in the front room?'

Mia stared at the Sergeant's grim-set features. *What a horrible job he has, poor man.* 'Yes, of course. Come on through.'

She stared at the skin forming on the surface of her now-cold tea. She hadn't dared to lift the cup for fear they would see how badly she was shaking. 'Is there someone you'd like us to call?' PC Taylor asked, startling her. The way he phrased the question made her wonder how many times he'd asked before she'd heard him. *I'd like you to call my husband.*

Mia bit her lip against the pointless words, and ran through a quick inventory in her head. Her parents would be useless; it was too far past cocktail hour for her mother to be coherent and her dad didn't do emotions well at the best of times.

Her middle sister, Kiki, had enough on her hands with the new baby and Matty determined to live up to every horror story ever told about the terrible twos. Had it only been last week she and Jamie had babysat Matty because the baby had been sick? An image of Jamie holding their sleeping nephew in his lap rose unbidden and she shook her head sharply to dispel it. She couldn't think about things like that. Not right then.

The youngest of her siblings, Nee, was neck-deep in her final year at art school in London. Too young and too far away to be shouldering the burden of her eldest sister's grief. The only person she wanted to talk to was Jamie and that would never happen again. Bile burned in her throat and a whooping sob escaped before she could swallow it back.

'S-sorry.' She screwed her eyes tight and stuffed everything down as far as she could. There would be time enough for tears. Opening her stinging eyes, she looked at Sergeant Stone. 'Do Bill and Pat know?'

'Your in-laws? They're next on our list. I'm so very sorry, pet. Would you like us to take you over there?'

Unable to speak past the knot in her throat, Mia nodded.

Chapter 1

February 2016

Daniel rested his head on the dirty train window and stared unseeing at the landscape as it flashed past. He didn't know where he was going. Away. That was the word that rattled around his head. Anywhere, nowhere. Just away from London. Away from the booze, birds and fakery of his so-called celebrity lifestyle. Twenty-nine felt too young to be a has-been.

He'd hit town with a portfolio, a bundle of glowing recommendations and an ill-placed confidence in his own ability to keep his feet on the ground. Within eighteen months, he was *the next big thing* in photography and everyone who was anyone clamoured for an original Fitz image on their wall. Well-received exhibitions had led to private commissions and more money than he knew what to do with. And if it hadn't been for Aaron's investment advice, his bank account would be as drained as his artistic talent.

The parties had been fun at first, and he couldn't put his finger on when the booze had stopped being a buzz and started being a crutch. Girls had come and gone. Pretty, cynical women who liked being seen on his arm in the gossip columns, and didn't seem to mind being in his bed.

Giselle had been one such girl, and without any active consent on his part, she'd installed herself as a permanent fixture. The bitter smell of the French cigarettes she lived on in lieu of a decent meal filled his memory, forcing Daniel to swallow convulsively against the bile in his throat. That smell signified everything he hated about his life, about himself. Curls of rank smoke had hung like fog over the sprawled bodies, spilled bottles and overflowing ashtrays littering his flat when he'd woven a path through them that morning.

The cold glass of the train window eased the worst of his thumping hangover, although no amount of water seemed able to ease the parched feeling in his throat. The carriage had filled, emptied and filled again, the ebb and flow of humanity reaching their individual destinations.

Daniel envied their purpose. He swigged again from the large bottle of water he'd paid a small fortune for at Paddington Station as he'd perused the departures board. The taxi driver he'd flagged down near his flat had told him Paddington would take him west, a part of England that he knew very little about, which suited him perfectly.

His first instinct had been to head for King's Cross, but that would have taken him north. Too many memories, too tempting to visit old haunts his mam and dad had taken him to. It would be sacrilege to their memory to tread on the pebbled beaches of his youth, knowing how far he'd fallen from being the man his father had dreamed he would become.

He'd settled upon Exeter as a first destination. Bristol and Swindon seemed too industrial, too much like the urban sprawl he wanted to escape. And now he was on a local branch line train to Orcombe Sands. Sands meant the sea. The moment he'd seen the name, he knew it was where he needed to be. Air he could breathe, the wind on his face, nothing on the horizon but whitecaps and seagulls.

The train slowed and drew to a stop as it had done numerous

times previously. Daniel didn't stir; the cold window felt too good against his clammy forehead. He was half aware of a small woman rustling an enormous collection of department store carrier bags as she carted her shopping haul past his seat, heading towards the exit. She took a couple of steps past him before she paused and spoke.

'This is the end of the line, you know?' Her voice carried a warm undertone of concern and Daniel roused. The thump in his head increased, making him frown as he regarded the speaker. She was an older lady, around the age his mam would've been had she still been alive.

Her grey hair was styled in a short, modern crop and she was dressed in that effortlessly casual, yet stylish look some women had. A soft camel jumper over dark indigo jeans with funky bright red trainers on her feet. A padded pea jacket and a large handbag worn cross body, keeping her hands free to manage her shopping bags. She smiled brightly at Daniel and tilted her head towards the carriage doors, which were standing stubbornly open.

'This is Orcombe Sands. Pensioner jail. Do not pass go, do not collect two hundred pounds.' She laughed at her own joke and Daniel finally realised what she was telling him. He had to get off the train; this was his destination. She was still watching him expectantly, so he cleared his throat.

'Oh, thanks. Sorry I was miles away.' He rose as he spoke, unfurling his full height as the small woman stepped back to give him room to stand and tug his large duffel bag from the rack above his seat. Seemingly content that Daniel was on the move, the woman gave him a cheery farewell and disappeared off the train.

Adjusting the bag on his shoulder as he looked around, Daniel perused the layout of the station for the first time. The panoramic sweep of his surroundings didn't take long. The tiny waiting room needed a lick of paint, but the platform was clean of the rubbish and detritus that had littered the Central London station he'd started his journey at several hours previously. A hand-painted, slightly lopsided *Exit* sign pointed his way and Daniel moved in the only direction available to him, hoping to find some signs of life and a taxi rank.

He stopped short in what he supposed was the main street and regarded the handful of houses and a pub, which was closed up tight on the other side of the road. He looked to his right and regarded a small area of hardstanding with a handful of cars strewn haphazardly around.

The February wind tugged hard at his coat and he flipped the collar up, hunching slightly to keep his ears warm.

Daniel started to regret his spur-of-the-moment decision to leave town. He'd been feeling stale for a while, completely lacking in inspiration. Every image he framed in his mind's eye seemed either trite or derivative. All he'd ever wanted to do was take photographs. From the moment his parents had given him his first disposable camera to capture his holiday snaps, Daniel had wanted to capture the world he saw through his viewfinder.

An engine grumbled to life and the noise turned Daniel's thoughts outwards again as a dirty estate car crawled out of the car park and stopped in front of him. The side window lowered and the woman from the train leaned across from the driver's side to speak to him.

'You all right there? Is someone coming to pick you up?' Daniel shuffled his feet slightly under the blatantly interested gaze of the older woman.

His face warmed as he realised he would have to confess his predicament to the woman. He had no idea where he was or what his next move should be. He could tell from the way she was regarding him that she would not leave until she knew he was going to be all right.

'My trip was a bit spur-of-the-moment. Do you happen to know if there is a B&B nearby?' he said, trying to keep his voice light, as though heading off into the middle of nowhere on a freezing winter's day was a completely rational, normal thing to do.

The older woman widened her eyes slightly. 'Not much call for that this time of year. Just about everywhere that offers accommodation is seasonal and won't be open until Easter time.'

Daniel started to feel like an even bigger fool as the older woman continued to ponder his problem, her index finger tapping against her lip. The finger paused as a sly smile curled one corner of her lip and Daniel wondered if he should be afraid of whatever thought had occurred to cause that expression.

He took a backwards step as the woman suddenly released her seat belt and climbed out of the car in a determined manner. He was not intimidated by someone a foot shorter than him. *He wasn't.*

'What's your name?' she asked as she flipped open the boot of the car and started transferring her shopping bags onto the back seat.

'Fitz ...' He paused. That name belonged in London, along with everything else he wanted to leave behind. 'Daniel. Daniel Fitzwilliams.'

'Pleased to meet you. I'm Madeline although my friends call me Mads and I have a feeling we will be great friends. Stick your bag in the boot, there's a good lad. I know the perfect place. Run by a friend of mine. I'm sure you'll be very happy there.'

Daniel did as bid, his eyes widening in shock as *unbelievable!* Madeline propelled him in the right direction with a slap on the arse and a loud laugh.

'Bounce a coin on those cheeks, Daniel! I do so like a man who takes care of himself.' With another laugh, Madeline disappeared into the front seat of the car and the engine gave a slightly startled whine as she turned the key.

Gritting his teeth, he placed his bag in the boot before moving around to the front of the car and eyeing the grubby interior of the estate, which appeared to be mainly held together with mud and rust. He folded his frame into the seat, which had been hiked forward almost as far as it could. With his knees up around his ears, Daniel fumbled under the front of the seat until he found the adjuster and carefully edged the seat back until he felt less like a sardine.

'Belt up, there's a good boy,' Madeline trilled as she patted his knee and threw the old car into first. They lurched away from the kerb. Deciding that a death grip was the only way to survive, Daniel quickly snapped his seat belt closed, scrabbled for the aptly named *oh shit!* handle above the window and tried to decide whether the journey would be worse with his eyes open or closed.

Madeline barrelled the car blithely around the narrow country lanes, barely glancing at the road as far as Daniel could tell as she sang along to the latest pop tunes pouring from the car radio. He tried not to whimper at the thought of where he was going to end up. What the hell was this place going to be like if it was run by a friend of Madeline's? If there was a woman in a rocking chair at the window, he'd be in deep shit.

The car abruptly swung off to the left and continued along what appeared to be a footpath rather than any kind of road. A huge building loomed to the left and Daniel caught his breath. Rather than the Bates Motel, it was more of a Grand Lady in her declining years. In its heyday, it must have been a magnificent structure. The peeling paint, filthy windows and rotting porch did their best to hide the beauty, together with the overgrown gardens.

His palms itched and for the first time in forever, Daniel felt excited. He wanted his camera. Head twisting and turning, he tried to take everything in. A group of outbuildings and a large barn lay to the right of where Madeline pulled to a stop on the gravel driveway.

Giving a jaunty toot on the car's horn, she wound down her window to wave and call across the yard to what appeared to be a midget yeti in the most moth-eaten dressing gown Daniel had ever seen. *Not good, not good, oh so not good …*

**Don't miss *Starlight Over Bluebell Castle*,
the next book from Sarah Bennett,
coming later this year!**

Dear Reader,

Thank you so much for taking the time to read this book – we hope you enjoyed it! If you did, we'd be so appreciative if you left a review.

Here at HQ Digital we are dedicated to publishing fiction that will keep you turning the pages into the early hours. We publish a variety of genres, from heartwarming romance, to thrilling crime and sweeping historical fiction.

To find out more about our books, enter competitions and discover exclusive content, please join our community of readers by following us at:

🐦 @HQDigitalUK

f facebook.com/HQDigitalUK

Are you a budding writer?
We're also looking for authors to join the HQ Digital family!
Please submit your manuscript to:

HQDigital@harpercollins.co.uk.

Hope to hear from you soon!

If you enjoyed *Sunshine Over Bluebell Castle*, why not try another gorgeously uplifting read from HQ Digital?